A Funny Olc

Born in 1966 in Margate, Kent, Jonathan Pidduck
is one of four children. He now lives in Ramsgate and
has one daughter, Laura. He practices as a solicitor
in Folkestone. *A Funny Olde Worlde* is his first novel,
though more are planned in a similar vein.

Jonathan Pidduck

A Funny Olde Worlde

Matador
9 De Montfort Mews
Leicester LE1 7FW, UK
Tel: (+44) 116 255 9311 / 9312
Email: books@troubador.co.uk
Web: www.troubador.co.uk/matador

ISBN 1 904744 45 1

Typeset in 10pt Stempel Garamond by Troubador Publishing Ltd, Leicester, UK
Printed by The Cromwell Press, Trowbridge, Wilts, UK

Matador is an imprint of Troubador Publishing

For Laura

Thane stood up to his ankles in water in the cellar of the small deserted farmhouse in Sussex. The Watcher sat cross-legged in front of him, completely naked except for the heavy iron amulet around his neck. Thane noticed, with mild embarrassment, that the water level was a few inches too low to allow the Watcher to preserve his dignity. Although Watchers never wore a stitch of clothing, it was strangely disconcerting to see one of the most powerful beings in the universe exposing himself in a flooded basement near Hastings.

Every planet has its own Watcher. Each is responsible for monitoring the events taking place in his own world, and each can at any time make contact with any other of his kind around the Universe. The theory is that each of them is therefore aware of, or can find out, everything which ever happens, no matter where it takes place, simply by communicating with his counterparts in other worlds. In practice, however, most only ever do this in emergencies, since they are generally an extremely anti-social race who are particularly bad at small talk.

"I sat on the third bar-stool from the left," said Thane.

The Watcher lifted his head for a moment to face him. Thane knew that he did this more out of politeness than curiosity, since he was totally blind. The only images he would ever see were those that shimmered in the stagnant water around him.

"You sat on the second to the left."

"The third," Thane insisted.

Thane was an inter-galactic mercenary. It was not as glamorous a job as it might sound. Most of his time was spent loitering around lifeless planets, waiting for a gateway to open to transport him to his next assassination. When he was not waiting around, he was either terminating petty tyrants, or protecting them from other mercenaries. It was not unknown for him to be protecting them one month, and then being paid to come back to assassinate them the next. He took no pleasure in killing them, any more than he felt remorse for doing it. He had been trained to terminate since the age of four, and it was simply a job to be done. Besides, in order to keep his

1

mercenaries licence he could not accept contracts to kill anyone whose life was considered by the relevant Watcher to be necessary for the well being of the planet concerned. In other words, as far as he was concerned, he only terminated people who were asking for it.

"I know it was the second," announced the Watcher, "because I could see you in the water, here. When that pert young barmaid wasn't waving her legs around in front of me, that is."

"You could see her legs?" Thane asked.

"Yes," the Watcher replied, guardedly. "Not that I was looking, mind you. She just kept getting in the way."

"So it was the second from the left as you look at it *from behind the bar*. Which makes it the third from the left as you look at it from my side of the bar. You sent me to the wrong place,"

"Maybe," the Watcher conceded, grudgingly. His race had a tendency to pick up the characteristics of the dominant life form of the planet under their charge. After observing their every move for tens of thousands of years, it was, perhaps, hardly surprising. Thane had noticed with mild surprise that this one was happy to speak with him, even though it prevented him from fully concentrating on the events unfolding in the pool around him. More unusual still, he would have argued all night given half a chance. All Watchers, of course, were convinced that they were never wrong. It was just that most of them never felt the need to prove it.

"Of course, it was up to you to clarify matters if you were at all uncertain," put in the argumentative old man, as if to underline the point.

"Okay, if it makes you happy, let's just say it was my mistake."

"It does, and it was!"

"The fact remains that this human of yours has gone to Hedral in my place. We both know what that means."

"Yes. It means you'll have to bring him back. We can't have unlicensed people wandering around in the wrong galaxies through no fault of my own, you know. It'll end in tears."

"Where will I find this man?"

"Go back through the tunnel in the public house. Get the right barstool, this time. The other end of the tunnel may have shifted a little since yesterday, but this end is still in the same place."

"Not that pub, again," complained the mercenary. "Why do all the tunnel entrances on Earth have to be in pubs?"

The Watcher looked thoughtful for a second, or gave a look as close to one of thoughtfulness as it was possible for him to give having regard to the confines of the pudgy contours of his face. Looks which were intended to be expressive started off promisingly enough, but were invariably swallowed up by the layers of fat encasing his face before they could make their bid for freedom in the outside world.

"This is a question," explained the Watcher sagely, "that has occupied the finest minds of the Universe for Time Immemorial, yet no-one has ever come up with a better theory than the one which has just this minute occurred to me."

"Yes?" asked Thane, deciding to humour him.

"Tunnels open where there is a tear in the fabric of reality," the Watcher told him. "And nowhere else on Earth is reality quite as thin as it is when you're down the pub!

Yet again, Halfshaft had opened his mouth before his brain was in gear. He was a failed wizard. In a recent survey commissioned by the Magician's Society (East Hedral branch), it had been ascertained that the average wizard had mastered over one thousand spells by the time he reached the age of fifty. Halfshaft had got the hang of two of them. He could create fire, and he could conjure up water from thin air to put it out again. These limited skills, he knew, made him a particularly bad advert for his profession, but he consoled himself with the thought that his was always the first name on the guest-list at barbecues.

In the past, his lack of ability had not really bothered him. Everyone suspected that he had about as much talent as a singles bar for elderly witches, but his foul temper and ready sarcasm had allowed him to bluff his way through countless awkward predicaments without anyone being able to prove it. He had therefore been given the benefit of the doubt, and was treated with the respect due to one of the two most revered wizards at Spartan Castle. This was not much, because there were only two wizards there, and the other – the "Grand Wizard" – got more than enough respect for both of them.

It was Halfshaft's dislike of his colleague which had put him in this unfortunate position. The Grand Wizard was, he had to admit, a quite remarkable magician, with shape changing powers second to none. Six days a week, he would change himself into a dragon, and prowl around the perimeter of the Castle grounds, repelling marauders, devouring bandits, and giving passing tradesmen a nasty shock. On the seventh day, however, he stayed in his private chamber, sitting cross-legged on his bed with an eighteen-inch pipe clenched firmly between his teeth. Halfshaft, without a hint of professional jealousy, made no secret of the fact that he considered the pipe to be an extension of the Grand Wizard's masculinity. It was because he made no secret of it that he was now just minutes away from almost certain death.

The duel was to take place in a locked chamber. King Spartan himself was to supervise it. It was, to all intents and purposes, a fight to the death. Whereas the loser might not actually die – unconditional surrender and desperate grovelling was usually enough to avoid this ignominious fate – he would be expected to do the decent thing and go into voluntary exile. This, Halfshaft decided, was his only chance of salvation. Not going into voluntary exile, of course. That would be suicide. No, instead, while they were giving him the chance to do the decent thing, he could hide in the ladies lavatories, and cry like a girl when they tried to drag him out. It was a tactic that had got him out of numerous scrapes in the past.

There was no way that he would win the duel itself. He was hopelessly outgunned, and he knew it. Worse still, everyone else knew it, too. It was plastered all over the ugly gloating faces of all his "friends" and neighbours, who had crammed into the courtyard outside to witness his disgrace. He had tried to even the odds by attempting to learn new spells, but had discovered that the time-honoured adage about old dogs applied equally to wizards who were getting on a bit. He had even considered hypnotism in the hope that he could convince the Grand Wizard that martyrdom would be a good career move, but had given up on the idea when he found out that it involved swinging a timepiece in front of the eyes of the intended victim. He couldn't even lift a sundial, yet alone swing one.

Everybody who was anybody (and quite a few people who were not) had crowded into the courtyard outside the chamber, peering in at the two opponents on the off chance that they might have a quick warm-up before the doors were closed on them. The duel itself would take place in private, as was the custom ever since King Justice V had accidentally been turned into his own grandfather by a stray spell (to the horror of everyone, not least his proper granddad, who developed an identity crisis and died of confusion not long afterwards). There was nothing in the rules, though, to prevent the combatants from hurling the odd thunderbolt at each other before kick-off to keep the fans amused. But on this occasion, neither did anything but sit in their respective corners, waiting for the signal to do battle.

All of the cynics who had denounced Halfshaft as a talentless fraud had been forced to wait a very long time for this moment. There in the crowd was William Taylor, the soldier who had paid him a small fortune for a "brutal strength" spell, only to beaten up by his own wife for selling their prize pig to raise the funds for it. And Henry Morgan, the blacksmith who had wanted a potion to make him like an animal in bed, but had ended up confined to his chamber with legs as swollen as a hippopotamus. He could see a dozen or two others, all of whom would be equally as keen to scrape his bloodied carcass off the floor at the end of the day, and divide it up between them as souvenirs. They were a sentimental lot, after all.

He looked over to the Grand Wizard to see if there was any sign of anxiety or doubt there. Nothing. Halfshaft noted resentfully that the magician had even brought his sodding pipe with him.

King Spartan raised his right hand regally into the air, signalling the crowd to silence. Although the courtyard was packed solid, none of the gathering ventured any closer than an arm's length to their monarch. They valued their heads too highly for that.

"We all know why we are here. A very serious accusation has been made against the most revered and respected wizard who has ever served under Us. This accusation has been denied, and the Accuser has been challenged to a duel to test the truth of his ridiculous allegations. Let God be with the man who speaks truly."

"God be with him," approved the whole assembly, getting into the swing of things.

"And let the Devil take the man who is not."

"The Devil take Halfshaft!" cried the crowd, in what the wizard concerned felt to be a particularly unfair attempt to pre-judge the issue.

"Before the duel commences," continued the King, "it is my duty to introduce the two opponents. On my right, we have Cyrellius, the Grand Wizard."

Cyrellius, thought Halfshaft. No wonder he calls himself the Grand Wizard. I'd make up a name for myself too if I was called anything as ridiculous as that. Then he realised that he actually had a name about ten times as ridiculous as that, and made a mental note to change it if he ever lived long enough to get the chance.

Spartan spent the next seventeen minutes listing the various titles the Grand Wizard had earned. Guardian of the Gates; Liberator of the People; Holder of the Golden Shield of Zandor. You name it, he was it. Somehow, Halfshaft just knew that he must have been head prefect at school.

"And Protector of the Holy Shrine at Beacon Castle," finished Spartan. "Oh yes, and he was also head prefect at school."

This brought a polite round of applause from the crowd. It wasn't every day you got to see someone who had been to school, after all.

Halfshaft closed his eyes and prayed that Spartan would give him an equally impressive build-up.

"To my left," announced the King, "we have – what's your name again, you?"

"Halfshaft, Sire," mumbled the mortified wizard.

"To my left we have Halfshaft-Sire," Spartan went on. "He's a bit of a conjuror, I'm told."

The assembly sniggered maliciously. Halfshaft vowed silently to get even with each and every one of them if ever he got the chance. But he was cut off in mid vow as the King clicked his fingers and the doors of the duelling chamber slammed shut, leaving the two old wizards alone together to fight to the death.

T he Hedral Watcher sat cross-legged on the floor of the underground cavern, staring sightlessly into the waters of the slow-flowing stream around him. The current circled his broad belly, searching in vain for a short cut around the island of flab in its path. He ignored the trickle of the stream against his skin, having grown accustomed to it over many thousands of years. He just waited silently in the darkness, naked and bloated, his unfocussed eyes constantly scanning the icy water about him for portents which only he could read.

It was then that Rod made his unexpected entrance. Seventeen stone of drunken biker appeared in mid-air, and catapulted across the cavern, his arms flailing wildly about him as he fought in vain to keep his balance. The profound silence of the chamber was shattered by the sound of violent curses, interspersed with unhealthy gurgling noises, as his face skimmed across the water like a bomb seeking a dam to bust. He came to a shuddering halt, his face wedged between the accommodatingly chubby thighs of the Watcher. After several panic stricken seconds of spluttering, thrashing around and prising apart, he finally managed to extricate himself. He stood up, peering about the cave in bewilderment.

"You smell of alcohol," complained the Watcher, who seemed otherwise unperturbed by the dramatic entrance.

"And you're a fat naked bloke sitting in a puddle," Rod retorted.

"You will find the wizard in the castle," the Watcher went on, ignoring his outburst. "Seventeen miles to the north-west. Hurry."

"What's going on? I was in the pub two minutes ago, having a quiet drink with my mates. The next thing I know, some bald old pervert's got his legs wrapped round my ears. Call me old-fashioned, but that's not the way I like to pass my Saturday nights."

He waited for an explanation, but the "old pervert" was no longer paying attention. Instead, he was staring back into the water again, as if transfixed by some secret vision.

Rod laughed.

"Friday nights maybe, but never on a Saturday. And you could at least have bought me dinner first!"

There was still no reply.

Sighing, he looked about him for a way out. Just for a second, he thought he saw the reflection of a forest in the stream, but as soon as he tried to focus upon it the image had vanished.

"Where's the nearest taxi rank, then?"

Without awaiting a reply, he waded to the nearest bank, and hoisted himself out the water on to the slippery rocks above. His wet denim jeans clung stubbornly to his legs, and he reached for the wad of notes in his pocket to check that they were still dry. They were. He envied them.

There were a dozen or so passages leading from the cavern, and he noticed for the first time that one was illuminated by a faint glimmer of light. As he watched it, the light became stronger, playing upon the ripples on the surface of the stream. As it grew brighter, the large naked bald bloke suddenly came into sharp focus. Rod took an involuntary step backwards, and slipped back into the stream. He struggled on to the bank again, and upon checking his pockets discovered that his money had turned into a sodden pulp. It was not going to be his day.

After a few more close calls on the treacherous rocks, he finally made it to the mouth of the tunnel. There were two large slabs of stone on either side, reminding him of the sliding doors of a walk-in wardrobe. With one final look back, and a resigned shake of his head, he stepped between them, entering the passageway. The moment he did so, the stone slabs swung to noisily behind him, cutting off any possibility of retreat. At the same time, the light went out, leaving him in icy darkness.

For the first time since his explosive arrival in the cavern, he felt a surge of panic deep in the pit of his stomach. For some strange reason, he had the sensation that he had just been shut away in a fridge.

H alfshaft squinted in the darkness, trying desperately to see his opponent. "Let's discuss this sensibly," he suggested.

"You mocked my pipe, came the reply. "I don't see you laughing now."

"You don't see me doing anything now," retorted Halfshaft unwisely. "Pitch blackness tends to have that effect."

He heard the Grand Wizard stamp his feet, and the walls of the chamber started to glow a dull orange, illuminating the two wizards in an eerie, pulsating light.

It should be noted that every wizard has his own way of creating magic. The Grand Wizard had to stamp his feet for any but the simplest of spells, whereas Halfshaft clicked his fingers. Another wizard of his acquaintance had to scratch a part of his anatomy which shall here remain nameless. Suffice it to say that he got struck off after performing conjuring tricks at a children's party.

The Grand Wizard was standing just a few feet away, a confident grin on his wizened face. He held his ridiculously long pipe in his left hand.

"Do you find my pipe amusing now?" he enquired, prodding Halfshaft in the chest with it.

"No," he replied. "I stopped laughing at phallic symbols when I was about twelve."

8

Idiot, he thought to himself. You're digging your own grave. And you've even supplied the shovel!

"No more talk!" bellowed the Grand Wizard, stamping his foot furiously on the ground. Halfshaft was not sure whether he had done this in a fit of temper or as the cue for a spell, but had the feeling he was in for a rough ride either way.

"Look, it's only a pipe," he reasoned. "There's no need for us to fall out over a pipe, is there?"

When he started speaking, he had been looking at the Grand Wizard. Before he had finished his sentence, he was looking at a huge, scaly, fire-breathing dragon. The breath from its nostrils singed his beard, until the smell of burning hair made him feel nauseous. The expression of malice on the beast's face left him with little doubt of its intentions. All in all, the transformation was not an encouraging one from his point of view.

As Halfshaft tried to cover his face with his hands, the dragon knocked him off his feet with a powerful sweep of its tail, sending him sprawling to the stone floor. Resting one giant reptilian claw on his chest to pin him down, it brought its snout to within inches of his unguarded, vulnerable face. He closed his eyes, waiting for the inevitable stream of all consuming flame to turn him to ash.

"Boo."

The pressure on his chest had gone. He opened his eyes. The Grand Wizard was standing before him, smiling smugly down at him.

"I thought you were going to kill me," gasped Halfshaft in relief.

"Oh, but I am. But not straightaway. It's not every day I get to duel with a wizard, especially one of your abilities! Let's see what you can do before I finish you off."

Halfshaft climbed unsteadily to his feet, dusting himself down as he did so. He pointed a finger at his fellow wizard as he bent down to retrieve his pipe.

"Leave it there!" he ordered, in a tone which he considered to be authoritative and commanding.

"Sod off," replied the Grand Wizard, who considered it to be neither.

Halfshaft finally lost his temper. All the fear and degradation of the days leading up to the duel now found an outlet. With a shriek of indignant rage, he clicked his fingers to unleash a stream of all-consuming fire at his opponent. Unfortunately, it did not quite turn out that way. The tiny flame which sprung from his finger was, he realised astutely, hardly what the occasion demanded. He never performed well under stress, as many of the less reputable women at Spartan Castle could testify. Insult was added to injury as the Grand Wizard approached him, guided his finger to the bowl of his pipe, and used it to ignite the tobacco inside.

"Thank you," he smirked. "Very considerate of you. Now it's my turn again."

He stamped his foot, turning himself into an enormous crab. Its leathery shell and viciously snapping claws temporarily sent Halfshaft into bewildered paralysis. He had never seen a crab before, but some ancestral memory deep inside him stirred him to action. Somehow, he had a feeling that it could only move sideways. The room was fairly narrow, and if he could just keep in front of it, then maybe it would be boxed in. By keeping still, as far in front of those spiteful pincers as he could, he might just stay alive. And who was to say that the Grand Wizard might not be so impressed by his problem-solving abilities, that he would forgive and forget, call a halt to the proceedings, and invite him down the tavern for a tankard of ale and a nice game of dominoes?

All of these thoughts flew through his brain in an instant. Unfortunately, in the next instant he dismissed them all as total rubbish, and decided to rely upon another tactic entirely.

Gathering his robes up around his legs, he proceeded to run like buggery.

Rod had finally grasped the idea that he was no longer in Kent. He had been wandering around for hours since finding his way out of the underground caves, without seeing anything even faintly resembling home. No pubs, no kebab-houses, no signs of civilisation at all. And now it was starting to get dark, he noticed there were two moons. He had no idea where he was, or how he had come to be there, but felt that he had to make it to the castle which the fat naked bald bloke had mentioned, if he was to have any hope of getting to the Club that night. And he was determined to get there if he could. He was on a promise.

His hopes took a blow when he emerged from thick, shoulder-height grass to find his path blocked by a river. He wondered whether this was the same one he had seen in the cave. If it was, he had been wandering around in circles all this time. In any case, it now looked much rougher and deeper than before, and – swimming not being his strong point – he decided his best bet was to follow it along the bank until he found a shallow place to cross.

After just a few minutes, he noticed a black figure standing by a badly collapsed bridge ahead of him. He hurried onwards, and found an old hag on the riverbank, peering out across the water to the far side. She had a fat body, with thin straggly limbs protruding from it, like some grotesque parody of a spider. He was surprised he had not caught sight of her earlier, because the spot would have been within his view from the moment he had reached the river. She was dressed in dark rags, which fluttered pitifully in the breeze about her, as if trying to escape her wrinkled, unwashed body. If they were, then he could not say he blamed them.

"Young man," she called to him. "Young man. I need to get to the other side of the river, but although this is the shallowest point, the current is still too strong for my old legs."

"You want to get yourself a dinghy," Rod joked. "Row yourself across. Unless you've got old arms as well!"

"But my arms are weak. And I would not know a "dinky" if I saw one. Will you carry me, across?"

"How deep is it?" Rod enquired, dubiously.

"Up to your waist," the hag told him. "But don't worry about me. I could stay dry if I cling to your back."

Something stirred in the back of his brain. Some childhood story he had once heard. Man gives lost old biddy a piggy-back across a raging river; lost old biddy turns out to be more than meets the eye; lost old biddy later saves man out of gratitude. Besides, he could hardly leave her here.

"Do you know the way to the Castle?" he asked.

"Yes," she replied. "If you help me over the river, I'll take you part of the way."

"Okay, then" invited Rod, with a sigh. "Hop on board, Grandma."

With a surprisingly energetic leap, she mounted his back, and clung on to him as he waded into the water. The shock of the icy waves battering his legs nearly drove him back out again, but she spurred him on, squeezing him with her spindly old legs as if he were a carthorse.

By the time he reached the middle of the stream, the water had reached his chest. Once or twice, he thought he had lost her as the current tried to rip her from his back, but each time she clung on ever tighter, cajoling him onwards. Slipping on the mud beneath his feet, he finally struggled out on to the far bank, cold and uncomfortable, his clothes sticking wetly to him like a badly designed second skin.

The old woman dismounted, and squeezed his arm in gratitude. "Thank you," she said with feeling. "Thank you very much."

"That's okay," he told her gallantly. "My pleasure. Now, where's this castle, then?"

She pointed back to the other side of the river.

"It's over there."

Rod frowned, puzzled.

"So what are we doing over here, if you're taking me over there?" he asked. "It was some sort of test, wasn't it?"

"No," she responded. "I'm afraid it wasn't. It's just the only way I get to straddle young men nowadays!"

Halfshaft dodged as the crab reached out a claw for him, in a vain attempt to run around it. It scrabbled across the floor towards him, knocking him over. Once again, he found himself lying helplessly prostrate beneath a wild and untamed beast of monstrous proportions. It was the first time this had happened twice in one day since he had dated Big Bertha at college.

Halfshaft clamped his eyes shut as the creature extended its hideous claws towards him. One claw closed around his face, and he felt a strange tugging at the top of his head. It occurred to him that the thing must have been ripping off the top of his skull, but that the shock was acting as an anaesthetic, preventing him from feeling any pain.

The crab stamped one of its legs against the floor, and the pressure on Halfshaft's head disappeared. He opened his eyes. The Grand Wizard stood nearby, smirking and clasping some sort of material in one hand.

Halfshaft's hand went up to his head. His skull was still there, and in one piece. The top half of his wizard's hat, however, was missing. His badge of office had been desecrated.

"My hat!" he screeched. "What have you done to it?"

"I've trimmed it down to size. You're head shouldn't be quite so big after all this, so you've no need for such a big hat, have you?"

The moment called for a witty remark, a viciously satirical observation to unsettle the Grand Wizard, to show him that Halfshaft remained in control and unrattled.

"Your mum's an old dog!" he shouted. Oh well, he thought, what it lacks in satire, it more than makes up for in vitriol.

The Grand Wizard spoke slowly and deliberately. "This is now a fight to the death. I will no longer be satisfied with your snivelling, unconditional, humiliating surrender. Your next spell will be your last."

"I have no more spells," replied Halfshaft. "I've already tried roasting you without success. And you know full well that my only other spell is to conjure up a jet of water. I could soak you and give you a nasty cold, but it's not really the stuff that duels to the death are made of, is it?"

"Then prepare to meet your Maker."

The Grand Wizard lifted his foot, but before he could bring it back down again to set his spell in motion Halfshaft had snapped his finger and sent a jet of water spurting into his face. Halfshaft hoped desperately that this might at least put his adversary off so that the spell would go wrong. Perhaps his revered opponent would turn himself into a jumbo sausage roll, and he could pick him up and eat him. Unfortunately, he was to be sadly disappointed. Before his eyes, the Grand Wizard transformed himself into a twelve-foot cobra.

"Oh dear," mumbled Halfshaft, temporarily at a loss for a more appropriate expletive. "Oh dear, oh dear, oh dear."

The snake reared up above him, its tight scales rubbing against the ceiling. Eye met eye. Halfshaft, like a frightened rabbit, was totally unable to move. Instead, he stood transfixed, staring up at the swaying reptile, wondering whether he might have been able to turn himself into a mongoose if he had paid more attention in shape-changing classes as a boy. But of course he hadn't paid attention. Big Bertha had seen to that.

13

"Oh dear."

The cobra struck at him. Its gum sank into his arm. Its gums, but not its fangs.

"You've got no teeth!" exclaimed Halfshaft. "Your spell went wrong!"

The snake retreated, puzzled. The walls lost some of their luminosity as the Grand Wizard began to lose concentration.

"Pathetic! Rubbish! Worst spell I've even seen."

The snake slapped its midriff against the floor. Nothing happened. It tried again, without success. Starting to panic, it banged its scaly belly against the floor faster and faster, but to no avail.

"You've got no feet!" crowed Halfshaft, his triumph complete. "You can't change yourself back again without stamping your feet, and you've got no feet to stamp. You're helpless. At my mercy!"

The light oozed out of the walls and disappeared altogether, leaving the chamber in darkness once again.

Halfshaft dropped to the ground, groping around for a weapon. His fingers closed around the stem of the pipe. Standing up, he swung it experimentally through the air a few times. He nodded to himself, satisfied. It was just about heavy enough. Poetic justice, here I come.

The Grand Wizard heard his pipe swishing through the air. By the second or third swish, it had dawned on him the use to which Halfshaft intended to put it. He tried to talk to him, to reason with him. Let's forget all this nonsense, he wanted to say. Call it a tie. We'll have a god laugh about this tomorrow. But all he could do was hiss.

"So there you are!" exclaimed Halfshaft. He swung the pipe in the direction of the noise, the bowl thwacking against the floor inches from the snake's frail skull.

The cobra started to panic. It slithered wildly around the perimeter of the room, circuit after circuit, as Halfshaft rushed around behind it, lashing out about him with the pipe, trusting in the Law of Averages to ensure a direct hit sooner or later.

There was a heavy knock on the door. The King's voice rang out from outside.

"Has the duel finished? I wish to enter."

"Not yet, not yet!" cried out Halfshaft. But his concentration was broken, and he ran into the flint wall. He fell to the floor, half dazed.

He made a conscious effort to pull himself together. He knew that Cyrellius would find a way to turn himself back into his natural form as soon as he had time enough to collect his thoughts. There was no time to waste sitting on the ground counting the stars in front of his eyes. He had to find the reptile quickly, grab it, and bash the thing over the head. Otherwise, it might turn into a survival-of-the-fittest type duel, and then he'd really be in trouble.

It was then he had a stroke of luck. The cobra slithered right into him as he lay sprawling on the ground. With one arm, he hugged its neck to his chest. He raised the other high in the air, gripping the pipe tightly in his hand. He hesitated for a second. He had never killed before. But the snake started thrashing around, frantically trying to loosen his grip, and the instinct of self-preservation took over. He brought the bowl of the pipe down towards the snake's head with as much force as his cramped position would allow.

The pipe struck Halfshaft in the leg. At that moment, the door of the chamber flew open and the King burst in. Halfshaft squinted at the light, and clasped his injured knee, only to discover it was bleeding. There was no sign of the snake anywhere.

"Where's the Grand Wizard? What have you done with him?"

"Where's the snake?" asked Halfshaft, in response. "I had him right here. Where is he?"

"I asked first," roared Spartan. "Stand up when I'm talking to you."

He tried to stand, but failed miserably and ended up in a pain-wracked heap on the floor.

"Do not defy me! Stand up!"

"What do you think I'm trying to do?" snapped Halfshaft. "Sit-ups?"

He knew immediately, of course, that he had made a mistake. A big one.

"You shouldn't have said that," warned King Spartan.

"I know."

"You remember the last person who dared to be sarcastic to me."

"Yes."

"My mother."

"Hanging was too good for her," added Halfshaft, hoping desperately to get back into Spartan's good books.

"That's why I had her tarred and feathered first. She knew she deserved it. I told her, so what if I'm only seven? I'm the King. I'll decide what time I go to bed!"

The King tired of the conversation. He turned to the guards standing outside the chamber and motioned for them to seize the wizard.

"Throw him in the dungeons. I don't want to see him again until he tells me what he has done with Cyrellius."

"I beat him in mortal combat," cried out Halfshaft, shaking off the grip of the nearest guard. "I vanquished the Grand Wizard. That makes me his successor. The new Grand Wizard. You can't arrest me."

Spartan stared at him disdainfully. "He has defended this castle for forty years against all manner of foes. Could you do that?"

"Well I – "

"He has provided us with water during the drought season and food during the famines. He has ensured that we are all properly clothed and provided for. He has taught our children and trained our warriors. Could you do these things?"

"Sort of."

"Without him, we will fall to the next band of trolls that pass by. You are responsible for this. You could not have defeated him without some sort of treachery. I want to know what you have done with him. Unless he returns from wherever you have sent him, I vow before all those assembled here that you will spend the rest of your days rotting in the deepest dungeon in this castle."

"But I don't know where he is! I was just about to bash his head in with his pipe when he disappeared. Vanished into thin air."

"Then you'd better hope he will re-appear. Otherwise, you'll never see the light of day again. Take him away."

Four guards seized Halfshaft, and dragged him out of the chamber to the dungeons below.

Rod sat in the old lady's hut, peering through the gloom at the mug of steaming liquid on the table in front of him. Despite her invitation for him to drink up, he was not too keen on touching the stuff. For one thing, she had ladled it out of a large bubbling pot which looked suspiciously like a witches' cauldron. For a second, she kept cackling as she handed it to him. And for a third, he wasn't too keen on the way she kept calling him "my Pretty".

"Come on," she coaxed him. "Just a sip or two, before you go off to this castle of yours."

"No, that's all right, Darlin'," he assured her. "I'll have something when I get there. Always travel to castles on an empty stomach, that's what my old mum used to say."

"No," she insisted. "What sort of hostess would I be letting you go off without so much as a drink, after all you've done for me."

She did have a point. He had earned a drink. Quite apart from carrying her back and forth across the river, she had told him that her legs were getting tired as they came into view of her cottage, and he had had to carry her the last half mile or so. Her legs weren't so tired, though, to stop her from trying to wrap them around his waist at every available opportunity.

"Come on, then," she chided. "What are you waiting for? Halloween?"

"I'm really not that thirsty," he explained. "I'm more hungry than anything."

"I'll get you some bread," she volunteered. "We can dip it in your drink. Make it go down easier."

He shook his head.

"It'll give you the strength of ten men," she promised.

He remained unmoved.

"It'll put hairs on your chest," she prompted, in desperation.

He shrugged.

"What is it you want?" she asked.

"Spurs to win the Cup Final."

"Yes," she exclaimed, with as much conviction as she could muster. "It goes without saying that it will do that."

"Hang on," Rod protested. " You don't even know who..."

"Just drink the bloody stuff, will you!"

Despite his misgivings, he decided to take a swig of it. After all, what was the worst that could happen? He raised it to his mouth. Just as his lips touched the rim, another old lady burst into the room, waving an accusing finger at his host.

"You were going to keep this quiet, weren't you, Martha Catwort? After all I've done for you. You catch a young man for drugging and riding, and you don't breathe a word of it to me. You know I've got arthritis."

"He can't carry both of us, can he?" Martha protested. "And I found him first. Go and find your own."

"I wouldn't find another one like this. Look at the size of him. Plenty of room on that back for two, especially if you lost a stone or two. Anyway, we could always take turns."

"Now hang on," Rod interrupted. "No-ones getting on my back. Not unless you've got a granddaughter in her twenties, anyway. One without warts and facial hair. No offence."

"Shut up and drink your potion," they both told him in unison.

"Remember that time," the newcomer said, resuming her conversation with Martha, "that you were desperate for those toads' eyes for that anti-ageing spell you were working on. You didn't mind sharing then, did you, my girl?"

"That's true," Martha conceded reluctantly. "And it worked a treat," she added, running a gnarled old hand across the wrinkles on her face.

"And that time you wanted to borrow some sugar," her friend went on, conscious of the fact that she was losing some of her impetus.

Martha said nothing in reply. Instead, she cast a surprised look around the room. As one, the two witches rushed outside, just in time to see Rod disappearing over the horizon.

Martha shook her head in disappointment.

"That's the problem with the young people of today," she told her friend. "It's all self, self, self."

There must have been ten thousand of the creatures assembled in ranks in the vast underground cavern. Before them stood their leader. Their King. Their Creator. He had been called many things in his time: Demon, Warlock, Fiend. He preferred Chameleon. Not that this was his real name. He just thought it had a rather pleasant ring to it.

The creatures at his command were vile and hideously misshapen parodies of the troll race he despised so much. Their skin was black and shrivelled, as if they had each had the same unpleasant encounter with a blow torch in their not too distant past. They were impossibly thin, with the ribs of many actually piercing the skin of their chests for lack of room inside. This appearance of frailty was reinforced by the unnatural angles at which their arms and legs were connected with the rest of their bodies. But this appearance was deceptive. As long as they had hands to hold their swords they would fight for him. No army in Hedral could stand against that degree of determination.

The Warlock himself defied description. This was because he did not have one particular shape to describe. One moment he could be an eagle: the next, a troll. It was not that he changed his shape into these things. It was more that he had no shape of his own to begin with, and had to become some other being to give him a visible form. He was an ethereal spirit, and as such he adopted whichever form would best serve his purpose at any given time. He was presently a disturbingly large gargoyle. He found it suited his image.

He surveyed the legions before him with satisfaction. The time had not yet arrived when he could unleash them on the unsuspecting world above. But he knew that the man from Earth was on his way. He would not have long to wait.

L ate that evening, Rod arrived at the Castle gates. He had had all sorts of problems finding the place. That fat old bugger in the cave hadn't given him any directions, and he had been wandering around in circles for hours before finding a signpost. Worse still, he was convinced that he had heard the cackling old hag from time to time, demanding a ride, but whenever he looked behind him he saw nothing.

He crossed the drawbridge and rapped heavily against the postcullis, noting with satisfaction the dramatically eerie noise it made as it rang out in the night. A sentry appeared on the far side of the heavy iron grid and waved a sword in his general direction.

"I'm armed and dangerous" the sentry called out nervously. "What do you want?"

"I'm unarmed and harmless" came the reply. "Open the door or I'll clout you one."

The sentry disappeared, but came back seconds later with two others. They hung around behind him, presumably for moral support.

"I'm in charge here," said the sentry, rather unconvincingly. "You can't come in. Go away."

"You don't look like you've had much practice at this" observed Rod. "Your first night is it?" he asked, conversationally.

"Well yes, it is a matter of fact," confided the sentry. "We're usually guarded by GW, you know, but he's vanished. We're all a bit jumpy, because we're practically defenceless without him."

"Sssshhhh!" the other guards cautioned in unison.

"It's none of your damn business anyway," said the sentry. He rattled his sword against the portcullis in a sudden attack of bravado. "I'm armed and dangerous. Go away."

Rod ignored the command. "I've come to see the Wizard." He felt vaguely ridiculous. He half expected the scarecrow, tin-man and lion to come bounding into view at any moment.

"The wizard?" Suddenly, he had the sentry's full attention. "Which wizard?"

"There's only one wizard isn't there?"

"Oh, you know about that, then." The sentry looked perplexed. He disappeared again, and came back with two more soldiers. For the first time, Rod felt uneasy. These ones actually looked as if they knew what they were doing. One of them approached the portcullis.

"You have business with the wizard here?"

"Yes," Rod confirmed. "Who are you?"

"My name's Rufford. I've come to take you to see him."

The portcullis was raised, as if by some invisible signal. The two professional soldiers hemmed him in as soon as he was inside, and guided him away from the gates.

"If you would like to come this way."

The other guards closed in around him. Rod pointed to the first sentry and told him to get back to his post. Before the sentry knew what he was doing, he had obediently scurried back to the gateway, saluting furiously as he did so.

"Armed and dangerous!" laughed Rod. "He cracks me up he does. Why are we going down here?"

"It's the scenic route to your quarters," replied one of the guards, as he escorted Rod down the staircase leading to the dungeons.

"That's okay, then. I thought you were taking me off to the dungeons for a minute."

The toothless cobra which materialised on Thane's lap caused quite a stir in the "Rising Sun". Only the drunk by the pool table had taken it into his stride, remarking to no-one in particular that you didn't get many of those in there nowadays.

Even Thane – who had weathered all manner of crises in the past – was taken aback. He had chosen the correct barstool. He had felt the air being sucked from his lungs as the tunnel opened about him. So far, so good. But then the huge reptile had materialised in his lap, and started to coil itself around him. He leapt to his feet, sending the cobra crashing to the ground. As it hit the floor, it transformed into a 70 year old wizard with a severe attitude problem.

"He nearly killed me! Imagine the shame of it! Defeated in mortal combat by a seventh rate wizard with a brain the size of a eunuch's cod-piece!"

He suddenly became aware of the other people in the bar, all but one of whom were sidling nervously towards the door. Only Thane stood his ground.

Cyrellius jabbed a temperamental finger at the barmaid, stopping her in her tracks as she tried to inch her way to the safety of the street outside.

"You! Wench! Was it you who opened the tunnel for me?"

She squirmed, and looked round for support. Unable to find any of her regulars who were willing to make eye contact, she looked back at the seething wizard, and shook her head quickly to reassure him that she was not in the habit of opening her tunnel to total strangers.

"Then it was you!" he declared, arresting the progress of a rake-thin brunette as she tried to squeeze through the crowd by the door.

"Who me?" she enquired meekly, playing for time.

"Don't you have a go at her, you freak," said her boyfriend, planting himself between the girl and the wizard with as much defiance as he could muster at such short notice.

The wizard raised his hand above his head, ready to send a bolt of lightning crashing down on to the insolent mortal before him. It was then that Thane struck, jerking his arm behind his back and placing his favourite blade to his throat in one smooth, well-practised motion. The bar emptied in seconds.

"I'm Thane. I think we should have a little chat."

"Thane? The mercenary? It was you whom I'm supposed to meet!"

"You're the Grand Wizard?"

"The very same. And I'll show you just how grand my wizardry can be if you don't release me in the next three seconds."

Thane relaxed his grip.

"What are you doing here? I was supposed to meet you on Hedral."

"I was in mortal combat with this vile little toad, who flustered me in mid-spell. Just temporarily, of course. I would have sorted myself out in no time. But then I felt the tunnel open, and I slithered in to it. It seemed like a good idea at the time. Anyway, we need your help. Something I could have done alone if I was three or four years younger. There's this Warlock..."

"Not now," interrupted Thane. "The police will be here any minute and you've drawn enough attention to us already. We've got to get back to Hedral before that Earthling does any serious damage. Come on."

Thane strode off towards the door. Cyrellius hurried after him, grabbing a handful of bottles of extra strong cider from behind the bar as he went. If he was going to be stuck on this foul planet for a while, then he was determined to sample as much of this alien culture as possible before returning to his own world. Six pints of it, to be precise.

Rod could not help but feel that his position had gone from bad to worse. Getting mounted by some wrinkled old witch was hardly the highlight of his life (although he could think of a few of his drunken sexual encounters which were in the same ball-park), but even that had to be better than being knocked unconscious and banged up in a damp cell with a camp wizard.

"This is my cell," Halfshaft shrieked at him. "One to each room, I know my rights. Get out!"

"Course I will. I'll just use my magic invisible key, shall I?"

"You've got a magic invisible key?" exclaimed Halfshaft in astonishment.

"Too right," Rod assured him. "I keep it up my magic invisible bottom."

"Bastard," screamed the wizard. "Bastard, bastard, bastard!"

"So I've been told," Rod conceded. "By my Dad, and he should know. Do you mind if I ask you a question?"

"Yes."

"What happened to your hat? It looks like someone's cut the end off it!"

Halfshaft attacked without warning, attempting for some bizarre reason to shove the remnants of his desecrated hat down Rod's throat. The fury of the assault sent the biker back a few steps, but he quickly recovered himself, and fended off the furious wizard with one arm as he used the back of his free hand to try to wipe his tongue free of the taste of damp cloth and hair grease.

"What's your problem? Calm down, Mate. It's only a hat!"

"It's not just a hat. It's a wizard's hat. My wizard's hat! Can you understand that?"

"Yeah. It's a hat for wizards. And that's what you are, is it? A wizard?"

"No," replied Halfshaft. "I'm the sodding tooth-fairy."

"Then you must be the one I'm here to see. He didn't tell me you were the tooth fairy as well, though. I wouldn't fancy having a dodgy old geezer like you sneaking into my room and leaving a bag of sixpences under my pillow when I'm having a kip."

This insult enraged the wizard still further. He berated him with all the abusive remarks he knew, which took a very long time.

Whilst Rod was waiting patiently for his over-excited cellmate to wear himself out, he took the opportunity to check out his prison. It was a fairly large granite chamber, lit only by the torchlight shining through the bars from the corridor outside. The reflected rays from these torches faltered halfway across the room, leaving the far side of the dungeon in complete darkness. There were no windows, no furnishings, and no means of escape.

It was already cold, but he felt the skin crawl on his arms as the temperature suddenly dropped lower still. He sensed rather than saw a flicker of movement in the darkest corner of the cell, a black shadow moving across a midnight background.

"And anyone who thought your mother was the ugliest woman in the world could never have met your father," Halfshaft ranted on. "He was so such an ugly man, that he was fourteen before they realised they'd been feeding the wrong end!"

"Hang on a minute," whispered Rod, attempting to motion him to silence.

"And it's nice to see you've taken after him. You've got all the looks and charisma of a collapsed wart."

"Will you shut up?"

Rod grabbed the wizard's arm and pulled him closer.

"There's something else in here with us. Over there."

Halfshaft obligingly shut up. He squinted into the darkest corner of the cell, but could see nothing. He felt afraid. In the cold light of day, he did not believe in ghosts or evil spirits, but it was much harder being sceptical when you were floundering around in a dimly lit dungeon. Centuries before, these cells had been used as torture chambers, with suspected spies chained to the walls with their innards spewing out of their stomachs like badly stuffed scarecrows. Rumour had it that Spartan still did a spot of torturing even now, when the mood took him, which it no doubt did on a regular basis. What if there was something skulking in the gloom, ready to lurch out and pull him screaming back into its Underworld lair? Waiting to tear him limb from limb, so that it could throw his mangled torso into a pit of rats, to be bitten and pulled to pieces, one agonised strip of flesh at a time. What if...?

"Are you thinking what I'm thinking?" Rod asked.

Halfshaft shuffled behind Rod, and pushed him gently but firmly towards the part of the cell that the Thing occupied.

"Yes," said Halfshaft. "I was just thinking that the first person to speak should volunteer to have a look round to check that we're alone. And damn my slow reactions, you got in first!"

"Me? Go in there?"

Halfshaft nodded frantically.

"One of us has got to do it. And it was your idea."

"Okay. What's the worst that could happen? Besides, if I find anything in there, I know you'll be there to back me up."

"Yes. I'll be backing up all right."

Rod stepped forwards, and was immediately swallowed up by the shadows. The wizard was left alone, trying to stop his imagination from filling his mind with quite such horrific images. Rats, he told himself. Just normal, everyday rats. Maybe even just mice. Giant mice with rabies, that craved shredded wizard flesh to feed their young. Mice with the faces of human babies, with talons that sank into your flesh like fish-hooks, pulling you into their den in a feeding frenzy lasting until your shuddering body could take no more, pared of every muscle and sinew so that only your eyes remained, eyes which watched the terrifying orgy of blood and gore until they too fell prey to the razor sharp teeth that plucked at the butchered carcass that had once been you.

"Have you found anything in there?" Halfshaft squeaked, his throat dry with terror. No reply. Why was it so dark in that part of the dungeon? It should not be that dark, not with the torchlight shining through the door. Not so dark that Rod disappeared completely the moment he stepped into the shadow.

"Hello? Anyone there?"

Still no answer. Had they got him? Were they feeding on him even now?

He took a cautious step forwards, unwilling to enter the shadows but more reluctant still to remain alone – so open and vulnerable- in the torchlight.

"What's happening?" he whispered. "Come out. Answer me. Please."

From the corner of his eye, he saw something leaping out at him from the void. He spun away in terror, fleeing to the door and hammering on it for dear life. No guards appeared to save him. No one could help him now. He felt a malicious presence swooping down upon him from behind, and knew that he was going to die.

King Spartan ordered Trog to sit down. Trog had replaced Leofric as Captain of the Guard nearly two years ago. He was malicious, bad-tempered and ignorant. The perfect commanding officer, in fact. No chance of a military coup whilst he was in charge. He couldn't even spell it, yet alone arrange one.

Unlike ninety nine per cent of his colleagues he was actually a very capable soldier. He was half-troll and half-human, although no one really knew which half was which. His troll ancestry gave him the strength of three men and the freedom from conscience which allowed him to make good use of it. His human side gave him the sense to leave his troll family (who did nothing but stand on cliff tops throwing rocks at passers-by and biting the heads off any who made it to the top) and come to work at the Castle. That way, he could get paid 3 guineas a day for throwing rocks at people and biting their heads off.

Trog was unusually ill at ease in Spartan's presence, and when an eight foot tall troll cross-breed in full chain-mail refuses to relax then most people find it difficult to relax themselves. Spartan was no exception.

Trog sat on the bench set out for him in the King's private chamber. A chair would have been neither large enough nor sturdy enough for him. The bench creaked, but held firm. He continued to fidget as Spartan spoke to him.

"I want you to torture the stranger, find out if he knows anything about the Grand Wizard, then kill him. Do you understand that, Trog?"

Trog's mind was on other things. The Grand Wizard had disappeared. The defence of the Castle now rested entirely on his shoulders. Half the guards under his command could not tell the difference between a sword and a crossbow, and the other half could tell the difference but thought that both were types of gardening implement. That might explain why they had taken so long to dig up the potatoes at the last harvest. They had not needed weapons in the past to protect them from the outside world. They had had wizardry. Until now.

"Trog? Are you listening to me?"

Then the stranger had appeared, the fourth this year. Strange clothes, strange accent, strange everything. All the others had been executed on the King's orders. This one would be, too. But this was the first who had actually come to the Castle. The others had been hunted down, and captured by the Grand Wizard. Why had this one just walked up to the Castle gates, and demanded entry? None of it made sense.

"I hope for your sake you're paying attention!"

Worse still, Doon had been sighted within hours of the stranger's arrival. Doon! But that was impossible. He had to deal with it before it came to the King's attention that someone – whether it was Doon or not – had entered the Castle unchallenged.

"Trog! If you ignore me for one more second, I will have you hanged, drawn, and eighthed! Quartering would be too good for you!"

Trog leapt up from the bench to stand to attention, banging his head on the stone ceiling as he did so. The collision between skull and rock made more of an impression on the ceiling than on the troll.

"What is the matter with you?"

"Nothing."

"Nothing?"

"Nothing I can't deal with."

"Then there is a problem."

"No. Nothing I can't deal..."

"Tell me about this problem."

Trog gave up. Verbal sparring was beyond him. And it was unwise to provoke the King.

"Doon has been seen in the servants' quarters."

"You know as well as I do that Doon can not have been seen anywhere."

Spartan hesitated for a moment before continuing.

"Was anyone with this...man?"

"No."

"Good. Listen, Trog. I do not want this apparition to speak with the stranger. There's too much at stake here to take any chances. Come to the dungeons with me. I'll question the stranger now. And then you will kill him."

A heavy hand fell on Halfshaft's shoulder, pulling him away from the dungeon door. "Now I have you!" The wizard stifled a scream. Something in that voice was familiar. He had heard it before; recently. Very recently, in fact. It wasn't some avenging demon from the depths of Hell. It wasn't even an unusually large mouse with a hungry family to support. It sounded like...

"Only me!" beamed Rod.

"You...you..." Halfshaft protested, for once lost for words.

"You were very brave? Yeah, I know. But there's nothing back there but spiders and cobwebs. You must be seeing things."

"You saw me."

Rod and Halfshaft exchanged glances.

"Did you say that?" they asked each other in unison.

"I did."

A man stepped out from the shadows Rod had just searched. He was deathly white, and his clothes were in tatters, large shreds of soiled cloth hanging off him like peeling skin.

Rod recovered first. "Nice suit you've got there, Mate. You'll have to give me the name of your tailor some time."

"He must have been watching us all this time," whispered Halfshaft. "Skulking in the darkness. Spying."

"Don't you know me?" the man asked.

Halfshaft stared at him for a while. If it wasn't for that beard, those dirty clothes, the chronic loss of weight, it could be...

"Doon?"

"Yes. Doon."

"But it can't be. I thought you were..."

"Dead? Yes, I know. So did everyone else. That's why they buried me."

Thane and the Grand Wizard stood in the Watcher's cellar, water lapping at their ankles. They had had a hard time getting there. It was too far to walk, and public transport didn't seem a viable option in the particular circumstances. In the end, they had taken a taxi. The taxi driver had not been too pleased with this. He had not been in it at the time.

The Police had chased them. Thane had had to drive with one hand, using the other to prevent his over-excitable companion from hurling lightning bolts at their pursuers. He had previously prided himself on his ability to blend in with the natives of the planet he was visiting. This made it even more galling that he had been chased by the Police whilst in possession of a stolen taxicab and a psychopathic magician.

The Wizard had become addicted to alcohol. Since taking the cider from the public house in Kent, he had been producing bottle after bottle from thin air at such an alarming rate that Thane had considered collecting the deposits from the empties and using the money to pay his bail if the Police ever caught up with him.

The Wizard was now standing in the cellar with his robes pulled up around his knees, singing "Show me the way to go home" in a flat baritone. It is one of the curiosities of the Universe that this song is known in every inhabited galaxy in existence, and is sung in each of them only when the singer is totally and utterly plastered. As Cyrellius explained in tune that he had had a little drink about an hour ago which had gone straight to his head, the mercenary knew that it was going to be a very long day indeed.

"What do you mean, it'll cost me?" Thane asked the Watcher, trying to blank out the plaintive warbling in his left ear.

"Just that," replied the Watcher. "The entrance to the tunnel has moved. I can tell you where to find it but it will cost you."

Thane frowned.

"What will it cost me?"

"I need your help to move to another location. Tonight. This place is going to be viewed tomorrow by a couple from the City. I think they'll buy it. They're desperate for more space, you know. Especially now the little one's on its way. I must be out before they come here. I mustn't be seen."

The Grand Wizard stopped singing. "I have a very important question!"

"Yes?"

"Why's that man got no trousers on?"

"He's a Watcher," Thane reminded him.

"He's a flasher," the wizard retorted.

"You remember Watchers. You know the one on your planet. They can see everything."

"So can I," Cyrellius protested, swaying from side to side. "And it's not a pretty sight. Make him put his trousers on immediately!"

"You'll have to take the water, too, of course. Thirty or forty gallons should be enough until I get settled in. By seven o'clock tomorrow morning. They're filming a new Kylie video at eight, and I want to be tuned in for that."

"I have a second important question," exclaimed the Grand Wizard theatrically. Everyone ignored him.

"How far are you going?" asked Thane.

"Only half a mile or so. There's another deserted farmhouse just down the road. It has it's own flooded basement, of course, but the consistency of the water looks all wrong. Best to top it up with some of mine."

"My question," continued Cyrellius, "is this. On my planet, a Kylie is a little fishy."

"That's not a question," the Watcher interjected, sensing the opportunity for an argument. And then aside, to Thane:

"There's nothing sadder than a pickled wizard, I always think."

"It's a pickled fishy!" Cyrellius enthused, clapping his hands in delight. "No wonder you find this Kylie so appealing. I wouldn't mind a bite of one myself!"

"Can we get back to the point, here?" Thane protested, quickly losing the will to live.

"I don't know," said the Watcher. "I haven't got the least idea what it was, now."

"Where is the entrance to the tunnel?"

"Don't know," replied the Grand Wizard petulantly. "What's that got to do with little fishies?"

Thane pinched the Wizard's shoulder, and he collapsed senseless to the floor. "Where is it?" he asked again.

"I'll tell you as soon as we've moved."

"You do realise that this delay may mean I don't get to Hedral in time to save that Earthling of yours?"

A genuine sadness passed over the Watcher's face for an instant. He had grown quite attached to the species peopling his planet. Even the ones without bosoms.

"From what I have discovered from the Hedral Watcher, I do not think you would be in time to save him even if you entered the tunnel here and now. His fate, it seems, is sealed."

Spartan and Trog stormed past the guardhouse towards the dungeons. Around them, guards who had moments before been sleeping or daydreaming leapt to their feet, desperately trying to look alert and efficient. All failed dismally on both counts.

Spartan seized the nearest by the arm.

"Which are they in?"

"Who?"

"The prisoners, damn you! Quick. Which cell?"

"That one, your Majesty."

"Open it. Now!"

The guard started hurrying along the corridor towards the cell in which Rod and Halfshaft had been detained.

"Run!"

He sprinted down the passageway, coming to an abrupt halt at the door. He hesitated for a second before dashing back to the King, standing to attention in front of him.

"Well?"

"The door, your Majesty. It's locked."

"Of course it's bloody locked!" Spartan exploded. "This is a dungeon! Why must I be surrounded by imbeciles all my life!"

"I haven't got the key," stuttered the imbecile, miserably.

"Who has?"

"Captain Sykes has. Sire!"

"And he is – where exactly?"

"He's gone to bed, your Majesty. With..."

"...with a nasty head cold," another guard interrupted hastily, glaring at his colleague. He wilted as he realised that he now had the King's attention. "Very nasty cold, it is. His nose is running and everything. Wouldn't be surprised if he had the flu."

"Oh dear," the first guard exclaimed. "I didn't know he was poorly. Otherwise I would never have agreed to him slipping off guard duty to sleep with my sister."

Spartan exploded.

"Hang him!" he ordered Trog, pointing at the first guard. "Hang him, too!" he added, pointing at the second. "Find me Captain Sykes and hang him twice!"

"What about the sister?" Trog asked, happy to have some interesting work to do at last.

"Send her to my quarters," Spartan whispered to him. "I'll punish her myself!"

"Anything else?" Trog enquired.

"Yes. Get that damn door open now!"

Trog trotted down to the cell door. He was enjoying himself. Three hangings later on and he could rip the stranger's arms from their sockets as soon as he got to him. If Doon was inside, so much the better. The man was obviously hard to kill, so he could string it out a little. Maybe even beat his record.

He planted his feet firmly on the ground, gripped the bars of the door, and braced himself. He pulled with all his might, striving to rip them from their setting. Instead, he managed to tear the whole door from its hinges, propelling himself backward at speed into the hard stone wall of the passage. Spartan rushed past him into the cell, anxious to see if the prisoner had Doon with him.

"Do you know what?" said the first guard. "I'm not sure that door was locked, now I come to think of it. I hope the buggers haven't escaped!"

The cry of regal anguish that emanated from the dungeon confirmed their worst suspicions.

"Oh dear," sighed the first guard. "My sister's going to be in for a real hammering tonight!"

In fact, Rod, Halfshaft and Doon had not escaped through the unlocked door, but along one of the secret passageways which riddled the Castle. Doon led them into the old deserted kitchens, and from there down a maze of stairways and corridors into a dark and draughty room that had clearly not been used for many years.

Halfshaft had mixed feelings. Though grateful for being rescued from the wrath of the King, he was rather perplexed at being trapped in an empty room with a man whom he knew to be dead and buried, and a stranger whom he wished to be dead and buried. He had heard talk of vampires stalking the Castle after dark, and had even seen one late one night whilst out on a drinking binge. The creature had been cunning, though, turning into Mrs Jenkins from the Crusty Cob bakery when he belted it around the head with a sack of garlic in a fit of drink-induced bravado. Mr Jenkins had later confided in him that he had often made the same mistake, and had battered the poor woman about the skull with a bag of the stuff on many an occasion. You could never be too sure, and in any case it had done her no harm at all as far as he could tell.

The more Halfshaft pressed him for an explanation, the less inclined the corpse appeared to give him one. Corpses tended to be like that, though: very secretive.

"Would you want to talk about it if you had been buried six foot beneath the ground?" he asked.

"I would," Rod announced.

"And you, Wizard? Would you want to talk if you had felt the coffin tight against your body?"

Halfshaft grudgingly shook his head.

"If it had been you who dared not breathe for fear of gulping in your last breath of oxygen? You, who wanted to raise your hands to your mouth and scream, but could not do so because your arms were pinned cruelly to your sides by the narrow grave?"

"No," said Halfshaft uneasily. "No, I wouldn't"

"If it had been you who'd felt the worms boring into your body, making a meal of your flesh until they exposed you to the very bone?"

"Shut up!" screeched Halfshaft, leaping to his feet. It was too much; it was just too much.

They sat in silence for a few minutes, save for the sound of Halfshaft pacing around the room as he tried to come to terms with what he had heard. Burial alive was a particular nightmare of his, and had been ever since that time Bertha had rolled over on to his face one restless night. She had suffocated him for a full and frantic minute before he managed to free himself by whacking her repeatedly about the bottom with the bedpan. She had not been at all happy about this, he recalled, especially as he had been using the pan not ten minutes beforehand, and she had punished him by forcing him to wear her sodden night-gown for the rest of the night. Now, Doon's over-graphic description of his ordeal had brought it all flooding back to him, if flooding wasn't too evocative a word. He felt the clothes sticking to his body, but was uncertain whether it was sweat, or a warm and sticky flashback to the night in question.

"It could have been worse," remarked Rod casually, urinating against the wall as if in approval of Bertha's terrible revenge.

Doon flinched. Halfshaft stared at the biker as if he were mad, but then hurriedly averted his gaze as Rod turned to face him.

"How?" asked the wizard incredulously. "How could it possibly have been worse than him being buried alive?"

Rod shrugged.

"He could have been cremated!"

There was a full moon, bathing the Sussex countryside in soft, silvery light. Archie Watkins sat on the hillside by the road, his back resting against the very tree-trunk against which he had first consummated his lust for the delectable young waitress from McDonalds. There had been a little less foliage on the bark then, of course. She had only been sixteen at the time, after all. But tonight was her eighteenth birthday, and he would choose a different tree if Jade could make it to their secret rendezvous. Let no-one say that he was a creature of habit.

He heard a sound from the far side of the hill. Could it be his Jade? Had she given Wayne, her new husband, the slip to resume their affair back here where it had all started? Was she wearing those saucy knickers he had given her for Christmas the night before her parents caught them sharing a Big Mac and large fries, and gave him the beating of his life? Question after question piled into his mind, adding to the uncertainty, adding to the excitement of their illicit liaison. He stood up, leaning casually against the tree-trunk to give him that roguish air which he knew she loved so much.

Over the brow of the hill came two men, one of them wearing a pointy hat and a frock. They held a blanket taut between them, on which a naked bald man was reclining. He was staring fixedly into a bucket of water which he held in his arms, resting it upon his ample belly. The two men carrying him were in some distress, finding it difficult to bear his weight. The one in the frock stumbled, splashing the blanket with water from the fat man's bucket.

"Idiot!" shouted the fat man. "How can I see Kylie now!"

The other man caught sight of Archie for the first time. He gave him a friendly smile and a nod of acknowledgement as he staggered past.

"Good evening," he said.

"Good evening," Archie replied.

He watched them in silence as they disappeared down the road together, stumbling and cursing as they went. After a quarter of a mile or so, the road curved round to the right, and they disappeared from view. As they did so, an H-reg. car bearing L-plates mounted the brow of the hill, and pulled up on the grass verge nearby. A girl got out. She stood silently in front of him, waiting for lust, passion, affection even. He looked at her thoughtfully for a minute or two.

"It's a funny old world," he reflected.

Jade nodded in apparent agreement, as she started to unbutton her blouse.

"So what now?" asked Halfshaft. "We can't stay here forever."

"I know this old lady who lives nearby," Rod volunteered. "We could probably hang around with her for a few days. There is one snag, though."

"Which is?"

"You'd have to let her ride you like a pony quite a lot."

"No," ruled Doon hastily. "We stay here and wait. They'll send out a search party to track you down. They can travel faster than us, so..."

"So we let them go first," said Rod. "And then we follow after them."

"Precisely."

Halfshaft was not satisfied.

"And what if they give up the chase, double back, and meet us on the way home?"

"Would you return home empty-handed" Doon reasoned, "if you had Spartan waiting for you when you got there?"

Halfshaft snorted. He was not keen on losing an argument to a dead body.

"They'll get suspicious when they can't find our tracks."

"No they won't. You're a wizard. The wizard who defeated the Grand Wizard in mortal combat. They'd get suspicious if someone like you didn't cover his tracks."

"That's true," Halfshaft conceded. "I was very brave, you know. You wouldn't believe the horrors I had to face in there. I even had crabs at one point!"

"That's nothing," Rod put in. "I've had those loads of times, and they're not so bad once you get used to them."

As the sun struggled above the tops of the trees on the horizon, Trog set off from the Castle gates, dragging the reluctant horse behind him. The horse's eyes and nostrils flared in fear. It had dim memories of being ridden by the troll-cross some months before, and of the crippling pain it had felt as its legs buckled under his weight. It need not have worried. Trog had learnt his lesson. The horse was simply there to carry his baggage as far as the Forest. Then he would eat it.

His orders were to track down the stranger and kill him. He could kill Halfshaft as well if he could find him, but the stranger was his main target. If he failed, it would be back to throwing boulders with his uncles and aunts. That might sound fun, he conceded, but there was no future in it. Sooner or later, they would run out of boulders, and chucking small pebbles at passers-by would not have had the same effect. Besides, he would not fail. He never did.

Spartan stood watching him from the ramparts as he disappeared into the distance. He winced, as the portcullis was lowered heavily – too heavily – to the ground. He bit his lip, doubt taking hold of him for the first time. If anyone could track down the stranger it was Trog. But what if he failed? The stakes were so high, so very, very high. Everything depended on the stranger's death.

He turned away, and stalked towards the nearest stairway, a gaggle of guards flocking behind him like goslings seeking the safety of their mother's plump breast. Had they known that Rod, Halfshaft and Doon were sitting in a room not 100 yards away, then they would have been more nervous still.

After hours of listening to the wizard whinging, and the stranger telling incomprehensible tales about women from a land called Essex, Doon was desperate for a change of subject.

"All right," he relented. "I'll tell you everything. I'll tell you how I came to be here. But first of all, I must re-write history for you. Centuries ago, a warlock called Chameleon appeared in the Black Mountains to the north of the Great Forest. He raised trolls from the dead, and used them to conquer the North. Even the Lord of the Trolls paid homage to him, to save battling his own dead ancestors.

That was when Harold the Invincible appeared, half dead, near Spartan Castle. He spoke of battles in alien worlds. He'd got struck in the eye with an arrow in his world, passed out, and woke up here. He was nursed back to health, save that he lost the sight of one eye. He had with him a sword. An ordinary sword in his own world, but one which developed magical properties here. It made the wielder invincible."

"I know all this from my history lessons," Halfshaft interrupted.

"I know some of it myself," Rod said. "The bit about Harold anyway. I turned up for history once, an' all. 1981, I think it was."

"Then you are from Earth!" exclaimed Doon.

"Yes," Rod told him. "I know where I come from. I've just got no bastard idea where I am now!"

"Let me explain. This Harold of yours is a great hero here. Word reached the Castle that the Warlock was marching on it. Harold rallied an army, formed an alliance with the Amazons and the wood dwarfs (a miracle in itself), and met the Warlock's forces at the battle of Crow Hill.

Halfshaft grunted impatiently.

"...And the Warlock's army was defeated, Harold killed the Warlock with his sword, and the grave can still be seen to this day by anyone stupid enough to risk wandering through the Forest on a site-seeing trip. Tell me something I don't know!"

"Okay," said Doon. "The historical version is all lies. The Warlock's army was defeated, but he escaped and fled back to the Black Mountains, where he made a last stand with the remnants of his army. The second battle took place in a giant cavern beneath the mountains, and his troll army was cut to pieces. He was imprisoned there with their corpses in eternal punishment for his wicked deeds. Ostosis sealed the tunnel leading down into the cavern with a spell to prevent anyone getting in or out and Harold's sword was left there in the entrance as a memorial to the allied dead."

"That's not what Mrs Hoskins told us in Class 3d," argued Halfshaft.

"It was kept secret to prevent anyone trying to rescue him. All gave their oath to Harold on this. Only the King of the Wood Dwarfs and King Spartan were told what had happened. But the secret died with them. Until, that is, I found a manuscript, written by the old King himself, sealed up in the wall in my chamber. It told of the second battle, right down to the exact location of the cavern in which the Warlock was imprisoned. I showed it to the Grand Wizard, who showed it to the King. And he sent us off to the Black Mountains to bring back the sword.

We took Leofric with us. He was Captain of the Guard here before Trog. A fine soldier. We would never have made it through the Great Forest without him. But we got there, and sure enough, there was the sword, just where the manuscript said it would be. But none of us could pull it out. The manuscript said that only one of Harold's kind would be able to free it, but we thought that the Grand Wizard with all his powers would be able to do it. Even he failed."

"Clever trick this sword-in-the-stone stuff," said Rod. "Bet I know where he got the idea from."

"When the Grand Wizard finally gave up trying to prise the sword from its setting, he set off into the tunnel. We tried to follow, but Ostosis spell was too strong for us, and we could get no further than the sword. We waited for him for hours, and when the sun finally set, we were ready to give him up for dead and return home. Just as we were leaving, he came back.

He told us that the Warlock was still in the cavern, and had offered him power beyond our wildest dreams if we freed him from his prison. He had brought his troll army back from the dead, along with the allied soldiers who had been slain in the cavern. The Grand Wizard had only to lift Ostosis' spell to allow them to leave the cavern, and the World would be his for the taking.

We asked the Grand Wizard how he had managed to escape after refusing to help the Warlock. He told us he had not refused. The spell was a powerful one, but he had put it into reverse. Within a hundred weeks, it would be weak enough to allow the Warlock to break free, bringing his legions of corpses with him. Within a hundred weeks, all hell would break lose. And you, Rod, are the only man who can stand in his way.

I t would soon be dawn, and Leofric knew he could wait no longer. He would have to ask her, and pray that she agreed to help him. If she refused, their mission would fail before it had even started.

He had been the first man to set foot in the Amazon village for centuries, possibly the first since Harold himself had been here. Others had, of course, made the journey without actually setting foot in it, having been carried in on poles to which they had been tied by their wrists and ankles. The Amazons knew how to bring their guests back in style.

He was still uncertain why they had accepted him into their community. Had he still been Captain of the Guard when he had been captured, he would probably have been executed on the spot. But they had taken him in when they found out that he had been banished from the Castle by Spartan himself. More important still, their chieftain, Rana, had taken a fancy to him when he played shamelessly on her vanity, convincing her that she was of royal stock. Since then, she had called herself "Queen", renamed her Chieftain's hut "the Winter Palace" and adopted him as her "consort".

It was strange being the boyfriend of an Amazon queen, but he could live with it when the alternative was not to live at all. So what if she was seven feet tall? So what if her only attire consisted of two or three strategically placed squirrel skins? If anything, her attire (or lack of it) made her the ideal girlfriend, and the squirrel fur gave him somewhere to bury his nuts in the winter.

They sat together, side by side, in the doorway of the large mud hut which they knew simply as "home", waiting for the sun to rise over her realm. He watched as Takina, her handmaiden, tended the fire nearby, waiting for her to leave so he could speak with her queen in confidence. But Rana would not allow him this luxury.

"What is troubling you, Leofric?"

"There's something I must ask you. If we could speak in private."

"We are in private. She's just a servant. Ignore her."

All her fellow Amazons treated Takina in this way. She was considered inferior for a number of reasons. Inferior in appearance, having the misfortune to have been born blonde rather than having the black hair so valued by the rest of her tribe. Inferior in size, being a mere five foot seven. And even inferior in style and dress-sense, wearing one too many squirrel skins than was considered fashionable at the time. And it was best not to even get the others started on the occasion she had suggested that they stop eating meat, and stick to a diet of corn cake instead.

Two years ago, he would have argued the point, insisting that the girl should leave. As Captain of the Guard at Spartan Castle, he had been used to people respecting his views. But he knew better than that now. Rana had made her decision, and her intense pride would not allow her to change it for him. He would have to explain himself in Takina's presence.

"I have a friend. A man named Doon. He'll be passing through your territory soon. He'll have another man with him. They must travel through the Great Forest together. It would mean a lot to me if you could grant them safe passage, and lead them to the dwarf twins."

"The dwarf twins? What use will they be?"

"They'll guide them through the Forest."

"They will lead them to their deaths."

"But if I reason with them, tell..."

She held up her hand, motioning him to silence. Not one of her most endearing habits, he had to admit.

"You are not thinking of going with them?"

"Not if it displeases your Majesty."

"It does."

"Then I'll remain here with you. But help them, please. For me."

Rana was quiet for awhile as she thought over his request. He gazed ahead, trying not to get distracted when Takina crossed his field of vision, bent over the fire, and tossed more logs on the blaze.

The Queen of the Amazons was reaching a decision which would determine whether he would go down in history as one of the greatest men who had ever lived. Now was not the time to get caught sneaking a quick peak at her servant's knickers.

"You ask a lot. It is within my power. Shamen knows where the dwarfs can be found. But Amazons don't give safe conduct. We can't have outsiders wandering through our territory, yet alone giving them help on the way. Spartan would think me weak, and we would risk war."

"It is Spartan who is weak. I know; I was there. He would never challenge the might of a great warrior queen such as you. And this really is very important to me. I would not risk your displeasure in asking this of you if it did not mean a great deal to me."

As he spoke, the sun struggled over the horizon, desperately fighting its way into the skies, hoping to claim a permanent place in the heavens. It struck Leofric that the sun was blissfully unaware that its fate was already sealed, and that it would end the day – as all others – plunging to its death on the far side of the world, sad and spent. He put the thought from his mind. He was not a pessimist by nature.

Rana stared into the sun for a few minutes, charting its progress across the sky above her. Leofric sat patiently beside her, awaiting her answer. He knew how much he was asking of her. The fate of his mission hung in the balance.

After a while, she turned to him, her eyes fixing his. He noticed a change in her manner which he had not seen before. She was somehow softer than before. For the first time since he had known her, she seemed more woman than monarch.

"You were once a great soldier. You have sacrificed all of that to live here with me. That can't have been easy for you. I would rather have died than do that, but you have given up everything for me. How can I deny you this one wish?"

He touched her cheek tenderly.

"Thank you," he said.

In his gratitude he suddenly felt that he really did love her, and that she loved him. Together, they could live forever.

But then Takina sneezed, Rana became Queen again, and the moment was lost for all time.

"That's ridiculous!" protested Halfshaft. "He couldn't stand in the way of a troll army," he reasoned, pointing dismissively at Rod. "He can barely stand at all, without his knuckles scraping the ground."

But Doon ignored him,

"We were horrified, of course. If the Warlock had been able to conquer everything north of the Great Forest before, how much more could he do now? Spartan Castle is nothing like the force it was then, and the power of the wood dwarfs has been on the decline for centuries. The fact that the three of us had made it through the forest alive is proof enough of that. The Amazons are still a force to be reckoned with, but they hate us even more than they did in Harold's time, so an alliance would be out of the question. The Warlock would be able to conquer our whole world, virtually unopposed.

"So you want me to come over here with a few of my mates, and give him a good hiding?" asked Rod, dubiously. "I know some pretty hard blokes, but I don't think they've ever done this sort of thing before."

"No, that's not really what I had in mind," Doon reassured him. "If we could get some of your friends over, so much the better. But I don't believe that would be possible."

"What did you do about the Grand Wizard?" Halfshaft interrupted. He was hoping that it involved something painful, and was irritated that the story was being spoilt by all this talk of Rod being some sort of saviour. He was not a saviour. If anyone was a saviour, it was Halfshaft. He had only recently defeated the Grand Wizard in single combat, and now he was being upstaged by a hairy alien who had only recently escaped from gaol. The same gaol as he had just escaped from himself, granted, but his was a miscarriage of justice. In Rod's case, he felt sure that he had got everything that was coming to him.

"Leofric struck him on the head with a rock."

Halfshaft stifled a giggle.

"And he died," Doon went on. "I swear that he died. Then we fled. Back through Troll Country, across the desert, through the Forest and back to Spartan Castle. But who did we find when we got there?"

"The Grand Wizard?" ventured Rod.

"Yes" Doon affirmed. "It seems he had taken some sort of healing potion, which enabled him to recover from any physical injury he sustained, save from those inflicted by magical means. The potion had even been able to revive him from death. When we met him again, he offered us another chance to join him. He told us the Warlock wanted the three of us to act as his governors while he went on to conquer other lands. If we would not help him, then he would turn to Spartan and Trog. Trog had been standing in as Captain of the Guard when Leofric was away. I refused but Leofric agreed to assist him. As proof of his loyalty to the Grand Wizard, he had to execute me himself, that very evening. I don't think the wizard was convinced of his loyalty even then, but Leofric can be very persuasive when he wants to be.

I was devastated at Leofric's betrayal. If there was one person I would have trusted in all the world, it would have been him. But still I refused to join them. Even if I had wanted to govern the Warlock's kingdom, I would not have trusted him. He is not the type to share power. As soon as he is free, he'll turn on those who release him and he will destroy them. Better to be executed honourably, I thought, than to die at the hands of a demon. Leofric gave me a last drink, and then killed me with his sword."

"Do you want to run that by me again?" Rod asked, feeling as if he had missed something somewhere along the line.

"He killed me. Then I was buried. But that night Leofric dug me up and..."

"Now I'm with you. He's one of those necro-whatsits. I don't see the attraction in it myself; it's dead boring. And while he was...you know, working out his frustrations, he realised you weren't dead, and..."

"No!" cried Doon, in horror. "What kind of world do you live in? He knew I would be alive. He told me that he had stolen some of the Grand Wizard's healing potion, and put it in the drink he had given to me. He couldn't tell me in advance, because he needed my reaction to be genuine when I was put to death. I don't think he gave me enough, though. I've been feeling really ill ever since.

Shortly afterwards, the Grand Wizard must have told Spartan everything. Leofric was exiled. The King wasn't keen on sharing power with a mere soldier. They don't know about my resurrection, of course. And I mean to keep it that way."

"Trog doesn't know about all this, then?" asked Halfshaft.

Doon shook his head. "I doubt it. Do you think that Spartan would ever allow a troll-cross to be on equal terms with him? The King will not be content to be one of three governors. He will want to rule everything himself. He will probably try to do away with the Grand Wizard at some stage. But not yet. He still needs him at the moment. To track down Harold's kind. Like our friend Rod, here."

Rod looked confused.

"Sorry. You've lost me again."

"Leofric and I have been on the look-out for another of Harold's race so that we can return to the Black Mountains, and kill the Warlock. With his army around him, only someone wielding the sword -someone invincible – can defeat him. Only one of Harold's kind can remove it. This has to be done by someone from your world.

You are not the first of your race to come here. Indeed, one of them was from the tribe of Essex which you mentioned, although if your stories of their womenfolk are true, then it is hardly surprising that he could not help us. Spartan can not allow any harm to come to the Warlock, so he has had all of them killed. My task is to prevent the same thing happening to you.

You must come with me and defeat the Warlock before he escapes. You have nothing to lose. If you stay here, you will die, like all the others. But with the sword, you are invincible. You can come to no harm. Furthermore, it is written in the manuscript that the only way back to Harold's world is to be found in the Cavern. If you are ever to return home, then you must get past the Warlock first."

"What about me?" asked Halfshaft, feeling left out.

"You can help us with your magical powers. You defeated the Grand Wizard, so you've earned a place on our quest. You could enter the history books as the man who saved his generation from slavery."

"That would get me a lot of women, wouldn't it?" nodded Halfshaft, thoughtfully.

"As many as you could handle," Doon assured him.

"I've handled quite a lot in my time. Not all of them were conscious, of course."

"Hang on a sec," interrupted Rod. "I just need to get this straight. You're saying that I should leave here with you, because if I stay, the

King'll murder me? And even if I survive that, I'll be stuck here for all eternity. They sound like pretty good reasons to me to get out of here pretty damn sharpish."

"And the women," prompted Halfshaft. "Don't forget the women."

"You can keep them, Mate. I've seen the state of the women here – one of them was riding around on my back for half an hour – and if she was anything to go by, I think I'd rather be a eunuch."

"Just say the word," Halfshaft told him. "Just say the word."

The entrance to the tunnel had moved. For the past two evenings, it had hovered over the barstool (the third from the left) in the Rising Sun, sucking up bikers and spewing out cobras. Today, it was in the ladies toilets in a McDonalds restaurant in Hastings. Someone up there had a sense of humour, thought Thane, as he considered his options.

The Grand Wizard sat facing him across the plastic-coated table, washing down his quarter-pounder-with-cheese with yet another bottle of cider. His eyes had long since glazed over, and he alternated bites and swigs on automatic pilot, totally oblivious of his surroundings. The only time he had registered anything since his arrival had been when he had bitten into his burger, and got a mouth full of gherkin. His face creased in outraged disgust for a few seconds, but several gulps of alcohol later, he was back on the path to oblivion, the whole distasteful episode forgotten.

Thane looked at his watch. Eight minutes to go before the tunnel opened. If he could keep the wizard quiet for a while longer then he might just...

He was stopped in mid-thought as the wizard lurched to his feet. Three men had just walked past, their heads shaven and their clothes smelling of glue. One had tattoos all over his face – never a good sign – and blood on his jacket. He was limping badly. Not men to cross when you're trying not to make a scene.

"Don't say anything," Thane cautioned his companion.

"Hey, you," called Cyrellius, bringing the limping man to a halt.

"You talking to me, Mate?"

"Don't say anything," Thane repeated. "Just sit down."

"You're worried I'm going to offend him," said the wizard. "Well I wasn't. I was just going to compliment him."

44

"You're not gonna compliment me, you poof," the man told him.

"You're right," the wizard replied. "I was going to, but I've forgotten what I wanted to say now."

He sat back down. The men moved on. Thane consulted his watch again. Cyrellius watched the men approach the counter, and his face brightened, no doubt illuminated by the little light bulb which had appeared in the cloud bubble above his head, as his memory came back to him.

"That's a nice dance you got there, Darling," exclaimed the Grand Wizard, a big grin on his face. "That's what I wanted to tell you!"

The man hobbled back towards him, and leant across the table, his face just inches away from that of Cyrellius. Thane got to his feet, positioning himself between the man and his friends, cutting off the reinforcements, ready to strike at whoever moved first.

"Are you taking the piss out of me, Freak?"

The Grand Wizard nodded his head vigorously. "Yes."

The skinhead threw a punch at him. Thane grabbed his arm, and jerked it backwards, forcing it up behind his back. As the others closed in on him, he swung their friend at them, bowling them over like skittles. They leapt to their feet again, and closed in warily, waiting for an opportunity to strike.

Help came from a surprising quarter. One of the waitresses – just a teenager by the look of her – planted herself in their path.

"No fighting," she told them. "It's not allowed in here. Not on a weekday."

"Can we come back on Saturday, then, Love?" asked the Limper.

"It's my day off," she told them. "Saturday will be fine."

The three of them backed off a few feet to compare their diaries. Saturday looked good. Until one of them pointed out that the hard bloke and the old man in the Merlin outfit could be miles away by then. There was a job to do, and they would have to do it now. They squared up again.

The waitress looked around for help. None of her colleagues were anywhere to be seen. It was then that she caught sight of the man who had just walked in through the door.

"Archie!"

He looked up, startled. He stared at her for a second, and then, pretending not to notice her, began to retrace his steps towards the automatic door.

"Archie, it's me! Over here. I need your help."

He stopped in his tracks, still evading her gaze. His brain struggled with some dilemma as if in an agony of indecision over whether to supersize his fries. She called his name again, a note of irritation creeping into her voice.

Thane checked his watch again. Three minutes left. If he was to time it right, they would have to go soon. Maybe they could slip away now, whilst everyone was staring at the man in the doorway?

Archie dragged himself reluctantly to her side.

"Hello, Jade. I thought you were on mornings this week."

"Are you avoiding me?" she asked.

"Your husband," he explained. "My wife," he added hopelessly. "My God!" he finished, as he noticed Thane and the Grand Wizard for the first time.

Thane took hold of Cyrellius' arm, and started to steer him away.

"You two!" Archie exclaimed "The ones with the fat naked bloke and the bucket!"

"Told you he was a poof," said the Limper, nodding wisely. "And look. They're going off to the bogs together, now!"

"This is going well," giggled Cyrellius, as Thane hauled him towards the ladies' toilets. "We'll be home by teatime."

Things went from bad to worse. An indignant taxi-driver burst into the restaurant, nearly knocking himself senseless as the automatic doors opened a little too slowly for his liking. He was followed by half a dozen police officers, and a police dog named "George".

Thane disappeared into the toilets, dragging the Grand Wizard with him.

"That was them, guys!" shouted the taxi-driver. "Get me back my taxi! Get them!"

"Excuse me, Sir," cautioned one of the policemen. "This is a police matter. I'm trained to deal with situations like these, so leave the decisions to me."

"And?" the taxi-driver enquired.

"Okay, guys," the officer commanded. "Get him back his taxi. Get them!"

As one, they rushed at the door to the lavatories. The first there tried to shoulder it open. It shook, but held firm. Someone was holding it closed from the inside. A colleague joined him, then another, and inch by inch they started to force the door open.

Thane stood on the other side, straining with all his might to keep the door closed. His feet slipped on the floor tiles as he struggled to gain a firm purchase. Slowly, he was being pushed backwards. The Grand Wizard huddled in a cubicle behind him, slumped over the ceramic basin in the position favoured by repentant drunks ever since toilets were first invented.

Another police officer added his weight to the scrum outside, and Thane opted for a strategic retreat. He released the door, and leapt backwards into the wizard's cubicle, sliding the flimsy bolt in place just as the policemen came piling into the room.

"Give it a kick," urged Archie, who had bravely followed them in. He was a good man to have around in an emergency.

One of the policemen duly obliged, despite the disapproving looks from his commanding officer, who was getting fed up with everyone giving orders to his men without asking him first.

The door shot open, cannoning off the wall of the interior with such force that it swung shut again. The officer came forwards, determined not to let anyone steal his thunder a second time, and gave the door a prod with his truncheon. It creaked open, and everyone crowded around him to peer inside.

The cubicle was empty. The wizard and his companion had gone.

Had it all been in vain, Halfshaft wondered, as they gazed up at the Castle wall above them. The day spent engaged in small-talk with a corpse and an alien; the evening spent scurrying from room to room, waiting sometimes for hours at a time for a passageway to clear before creeping down it like common criminals. And only to be thwarted by a dead end just as they had seemed destined to escape.

Doon gave no explanation for leading them into a courtyard from which there was no exit. Instead, he just stood by the wall, touching it as a man would caress his wife: impatiently, and with a dissatisfied shake of his head.

Halfshaft grew impatient.

"When you've finished groping the walls, do you think we might move on? I think there's a particularly attractive fence just round the corner which might take your fancy."

"Sssshhh," cautioned Doon. But it was too late. There was the sound of footsteps on the battlements above them, and they made out the silhouette of a sentry above them.

"Halt! Who goes there?"

"Who goes where?" Rod enquired, hoping to confuse him.

"There," came the somewhat lame reply. "Who goes THERE. Down there. Where you are."

"It's me," Rod told him.

"State your name now, or I'll raise the alarm."

"Leave this to me," said Halfshaft. "I'll frighten him with my magic."

"No!" shouted Doon, but it was too late. Halfshaft had conjured up a two-inch flame on his fingers, which gave off enough light to enable the sentry to identify the three escaped prisoners below.

"Impressive, huh?" Halfshaft enquired. "I don't think we'll have any more trouble from him, now."

A bolt from a crossbow shot past him. He grimaced as he realised that his nose would have been pierced had it been just a little longer.

The wizard started to frantically wave the small flame in the air, in a desperate attempt to intimidate the sentry into fleeing. At the same time, he noticed Doon grab Rod by the wrist, and run full-speed into the wall. As he turned towards them, he saw Doon disappear through it, dragging Rod behind him. All of a sudden, he was alone in the courtyard.

Well, not quite alone, he reminded himself, as another bolt shot through the air towards him. He ducked instinctively, and felt rather than saw the arrow shoot through the air over his left shoulder. Another near miss. And maybe third time unlucky. There was only one thing for it. If the others had gone through the wall, then he would have to do it, too.

Closing his eyes, and saying his prayers, he rushed headlong into the wall. Pain exploded inside his head, his legs crumpled beneath him, and he collapsed pitifully to the ground.

"I don't want to die," he mumbled, half-concussed.

An arrow struck the ground between his thighs.

"I'm not too keen on that, either," he added

He glanced upwards, catching sight of a second archer above. His bow was drawn and aimed, ready to succeed where the first bowman had failed. Death or castration, depending on the sentry's aim. Maybe he should have stayed in the dungeon with the giant rats after all.

He froze, waiting for the arrow to skewer him to the spot. But then an arm emerged from the wall, encircled his waist, and hauled him through the bricks to the grass outside, just as he heard the hiss of bolt leaving bow.

He had emerged on the far side of the wall. Rod released his robes, and made a token effort to dust him down.

"What kept you?" the biker asked.

"How did you do that?"

"It's a magician's doorway. You can walk through it, even though it looks solid."

"How do you know that?" enquired Halfshaft, in bewilderment.

Rod laughed, and gestured towards Doon.

"Your mate told me."

Doon stood nearby, impatient to be off. Rod moved closer to Halfshaft, and whispered to him:

"Better keep an eye on him, though. He wasn't too keen to hang around for you."

"Let's go now," Doon cut in, nervous at the whispering. "They dare not follow us at night, not without Trog here. But if we are still anywhere near the Castle by day-break, then I will not be the only dead man amongst us."

Yesterday, he had been sitting in McDonalds munching on a quarter pounder with cheese. Now, less than 24 hours later, Thane was sitting in a rowing boat in an unfamiliar ocean, keeping a wary eye on the grey fin which cut through the water just a stone's throw away. The Grand Wizard slept at his feet, his beard flecked with vomit. Why had he ever become a mercenary? Maybe he would have been better off as a newsagent.

They had materialised on an island which contained only a deserted shrine, a tangle of dead trees and bushes, and the rowing boat. The Grand Wizard had told him that they were on the island of Bickos, home of the infamous Hedral suicide sect. Several generations ago, a handful of deranged soldiers had deserted Spartan Castle, and fled to the island. Disillusioned with life, they preached that death was the ultimate release from pain, and was to be sought at all costs. The sect proved to be surprisingly popular at first, attracting converts from all over the country. Less surprisingly, it did not last very long, because all its followers killed themselves.

The wizard had tried to tell him more, but had succumbed to a violent bout of retching, and slipped into a drink-sodden slumber. Thane had bundled him into the rowing boat, and struck out for the mainland some seven or eight miles away. He had covered less than half the distance when the shark appeared.

The shark closed in on the rowing boat. From the distance between its dorsal fin and tail, Thane judged it to be a twenty-footer. Seagulls wheeled overhead, crying out to one another in anticipation of a meal with a difference. They were fed up with fish. A little shark-shredded meat would make a welcome change.

The shark glided smoothly beneath the waves, passing dangerously close to the hull of the boat. Thane slipped his hand into his jacket, checking that his knives were still in place. They would not be a great deal of use in a fight with a shark, but they made him feel better.

A puddle of water appeared from beneath the sprawled wizard, trickling gradually across the bottom of the boat. Thane groaned aloud. If there was one thing worse than a pickled wizard, it was an incontinent pickled wizard. Mindful of the fact that he was going to have to travel all the way to Spartan Castle with him, he hauled Cyrellius away from the puddle of liquid before he had soaked too much of it up. As he moved him, water started to pour into the vessel, lapping at his feet within seconds. He could now see that a hole had been bored into the hull. With a sigh, he realised what the wizard had wanted to tell him before passing out. The suicide sect at Bickos had put holes in their boats, to prevent anyone on the island having a change of heart and trying to escape. Escape in a leaky boat was suicide, which was – according to the group's dogma – a bloody good thing. But for the pressure of the wizard's body over the hole, they would have sunk ages ago.

He looked towards the shore. It was still a good few miles away, and he had an unconscious wizard to think about. As the water lapped about his ankles, he saw the shark ahead, ploughing back through the water towards the rowing boat, its hard grey dorsal fin cutting through the waves like a chain saw through polystyrene. There was no time to bail out the boat; it was starting to sink already. His only hope was to awaken the wizard, and to keep the creature occupied whilst Cyrellius struck out for shore.

It was then that the second shark cannoned into the boat from behind him. The thirty-foot Great White smashed through the flimsy wood, oblivious to the splinters which tore into its hard leathery hide. Its head thrashed around on the boat, its jaws snapping together inches away from the wizard's unprotected face. The boat sagged under the shark's weight, and Cyrellius started to slip towards the slashing jaws.

Thane grabbed him by the waist, and flipped him over the side of the capsizing boat into the sea. He stepped forwards, driving a long thin knife as deep into the shark's lifeless eye as he could manage. The creature wriggled away from him, and slid back into the waves, taking his knife with it.

"Damn," he cursed. "I've had that knife since I was six."

He dived into the water, and searched desperately around him for the Grand Wizard. There was no sign of him. As he trod water, the first shark closed in on him, but then dived under the water when it was just twenty feet away. He realised that it must have gone down in search of the wizard, looking for easier prey.

For a second, he considered diving down to help the wizard, but dismissed the idea. He could be a long way down by now. He might already be dead. And if he was still alive, there was no way that he would manage to get the unconscious wizard ashore with two gigantic sharks circling in the sea around them.

He produced a second knife from its sheath inside his jacket, and clamped it between his teeth. With a sigh, he set out for the beach on the horizon. Below him, the two huge sharks closed in on the Grand Wizard as he sunk slowly and obliviously into the depths of the sea.

As they sat in the long grass, Halfshaft noticed that Doon looked even worse than he had at the Castle. The radiant light of the ascending sun washed out any last remnants of colour from his skin, and it seemed unlikely that he could have looked any less healthy even if he had still been dead.

Everything around them was a blaze of colour, a brilliant mosaic of green, gold and yellow in celebration of Nature at her most glorious. Birds sang overhead, revelling in the warmth of a balmy summer's day. But Doon was untouched by this, as brooding and sickly as an oozing pimple on the forehead of a beauty queen.

Rod was in a clump of bushes nearby, having inexplicably explained that he was going to see a man about a dog. The only dogs for miles around were the wolves in the Great Forest, and what reason could anyone have had for wanting to see them? Besides, why would he have gone looking for them in a bush?

Halfshaft forced his mind away from these intriguing questions, and turned his attention back to Doon. The corpse was nervous. That was understandable. They were in Amazon country, and just being there was under normal circumstances about as close as you could get to a death sentence without challenging Trog to a playful game of Murder In The Dark.

"What do you reckon our chances are of getting out of this alive?"

"Virtually nil."

"Ever the optimist."

Doon stared at him.

"What do you expect me to say? No one crosses Amazon Country and lives. If we manage it somehow, we have to get through the Forest without getting ripped to pieces by the dwarfs, the wolves or the trees. Then there's troll country to cross. And after all that, we've got the Warlock waiting for us."

"Good job you've got me here, then," Halfshaft told him. "I defeated the Grand Wizard. If I could only work out what I did to him, we'd have it made!"

Doon glanced around at the nearby clump of trees to check that Rod was still out of earshot.

"It's not too late for you to go, you know. I'm stuck with this quest, whether I like it or not, and we need Rod. But what's to stop you slipping off? Why die with the rest of us?"

Halfshaft pondered the question for a moment or two. He had his reasons. Firstly, he needed to prove to himself that there was a point to his life. He was tired of being a second class magician. He finally had a chance to do something, to make it all worthwhile.

And secondly, though he would never admit it, he felt he owed it to Rod to hang around. They had not got off to the best of starts, but the alien had just saved his life (all be it in an oafish, over the top type way, but that had to count for something).

Besides, he had a third reason as well.

"I quite fancy the idea of seeing some of these Amazons before I go anywhere. I hear they only wear squirrel skins, and there are some pretty tiny squirrels round here from what I've seen."

"Stop!"

"And what with them being so tall, and the squirrels so short. Now if they wore buffalo, I might not be so keen to hang around."

"Enough! Are you mad? They could be hiding in the grass this minute. They're so proud. If they heard you talk of them like that, they'd kill us in seconds!"

"The squirrels?"

"The Amazons!" Doon exploded.

As he shouted, a ring of Amazons rose from the ground around them. Halfshaft stared at them incredulously. The grass was barely a foot high. The women were all at least seven feet tall, yet he had seen none of them until they had stood up. How could they have been so close without him noticing them?

In the distance, he saw Rod emerge from the bushes, and head back in their direction at a saunter. At the same time, one of the Amazons left the circle, and stalked towards them, like a lioness towards her prey. She stood several inches taller than the others, and had jet-black hair, which lay about her shoulders and breast like a slipped black halo. She had no need to introduce herself. She exuded the authority of a queen.

Doon pulled Halfshaft close to him, and whispered quietly in his ear before she got too near.

"Say nothing to offend her. One wrong word, and we are all dead."

"This is wise advice indeed," Rana told them. "Maybe you will live yet."

She turned to watch Rod as he wandered idly through her ring of warriors. With all eyes upon him, he passed her by and came to a halt at Halfshaft's side. His companions tried to catch his eye, silently pleading with him to say nothing which would cost them their lives.

"Okay guys," he addressed his companions. "Who's the tart?"

When Takina entered the hut, she was upset to see the wizard dangling on a spit above a roaring fire. She put it out straightaway. Fires were her job, and

53

no one else should have been lighting them without telling her first.

"Are you my guard?" Halfshaft enquired, as he hung by his wrists and ankles above the smoking remains of the blaze.

"No," Takina told him. "The others are being guarded, but Queen Rana didn't feel that you needed one."

"What will happen to us?" he asked vaguely annoyed that they had not felt him worthy of guarding.

"Whenever we take prisoners, the others get to mate with them before they're killed."

Halfshaft shuddered. Out of the frying pan, into the fire.

"They're going to kill me after they mate with me?"

"No."

He breathed a sigh of relief. He must have misunderstood her. Things were never as bad as they seemed when you were a magician of his powers.

"No. They're just going to kill you. No one wanted to mate with you. They even offered you to me, which is saying something, I can tell you. I always get last choice of everything."

"What do you mean, no-one wanted to mate with me? What's wrong with me?"

"Too beardy, I'm afraid. Amazons are very fussy about facial hair. They're afraid it might run in the family. And too scrawny. And they reckon your personality's pretty damn bad as well. Oh, and some of them think..."

"See, you can't think of one good reason," Halfshaft interrupted, before she had time to add to the list. "Not one. I'm not having this, do you hear me? I'm a top class wizard, you know. I've defeated the Grand Wizard in single combat. I demand that someone shags me before I die!"

Takina started making up the fire again. It was all she ever seemed to be entrusted with, and it came so naturally now, that she did it without even thinking. It was her form of stress release. Halfshaft's tirade had struck a chord. He was a great wizard, it seemed, yet they could not even take him seriously enough to post a guard in the hut. And she had the potential to be a warrior, she was certain of it. But just because she was a little different from the others, they treated her like dirt. No, worse still, they treated her like they would treat a man. She had had enough.

"Don't you hate it," she asked, "when no-one cares about you enough to ask what you want to do with your life?"

"Yes," Halfshaft replied.

She lit the fire, and started tending the flames.

"And when they all assume that there's nothing you can do, when you know that you could be as good as any of them if they only gave you the chance?"

"Yes," the wizard agreed again, a little anxiously this time, as the fire reached greedily up towards him.

"And how they all laugh at you, because your bra size is smaller than theirs?" Takina went on, as she fed more branches into the flames.

"No. You're on your own on that one, I'm afraid."

She grabbed another armful of branches, but his howl of fright came just in time to prevent her from hurling them on to the pyre.

"Sorry," she apologized. "I was getting carried away."

She squatted near to him, and looked searchingly into his eyes.

"I feel I can talk to you," she told him. "I've never had any one I could talk to before. Maybe I should have mated with you after all."

"If you could just let me down from here, we could talk or mate until your heart's content. I won't run away. It's just that it's hard to mate when you're tied up."

"Rana and Leofric manage it. I've seen them."

"Rana and Leofric aren't knackered old wizards with rheumatic knees. Are you going to let me down, or what?"

She shook her head sadly.

"I want to believe you, but I can't. You'll escape, and then they'll never trust me. One day I'm going to prove myself to all of them, you just see if I don't."

She got to her feet, and left. Halfshaft watched her go, stifling the urge to call her back. What would be the point? He was doomed. It seemed a very high price to pay for being beardy.

Trog grinned as he spotted the wooden sign nearby. He could not actually read what it said – trolls not being renowned for their literacy – but its shape and style had been described to him by Spartan. He had found Horace and Hubert, the dwarf guardians of the Forest.

It was the first piece of good luck he had had since leaving the Castle the morning before. He had been unable to find any trace of the tracks of his prey – much to his surprise – and had spent much longer than he would have wished skirting Amazon Country. Although he would have been confident taking on a couple of them in hand to hand combat, he knew that it would only take one carefully aimed arrow to kill him. He could not risk that. How would he ever be able to explain that to the King?

Then there had been that incident with the bandits. None of them had survived, of course, but they had injured his horse, and he had needed to make it into sandwiches there and then. Without the horse, he had to carry all his own provisions, and this had slowed him down. And all the while, the stranger had been getting further and further ahead of him.

Spartan had told him the way they would go. Through the Great Forest, across Troll Country, and then into the Black Mountains. He was to follow their track, and somewhere along it he would overtake the stranger and his companions. Or their bodies, if someone else found them first. He had to catch them before they reached the trolls, and it had never occurred to him that they would make it even as far as the Forest. Maybe the wizard, Halfshaft, was better than everybody seemed to think.

But now to the matter in hand. There were two paths through the woods. One led to almost certain death, and that was the safe path! The other was worse still. Only the dwarfs could tell him which of the paths he should take. But Horace always told the truth, and Hubert always lied. Everyone seemed to think this was a problem, but he could not see why. Maybe it was his animal cunning, but he had a foolproof way of finding the safe path.

Two dwarfs sat atop a mound where the track split in two. One had a grey beard; the other had a beard of white. Trog strode towards them, drawing his sword as he went. It was best to show them from the start that he meant business.

"Which one of you two is Horace?" he demanded, jabbing his sword at the nearest of them.

"I am," lied Hubert.

"Which is the safest path through the Forest?" he enquired, placated. He returned his sword to its sheath

"The left," Hubert assured him, gesturing towards it in a trustworthy fashion.

"And you're the one who always tells the truth?"

Hubert nodded vigorously.

"Absolutely."

Trog grinned triumphantly, and strode off towards the left hand fork.

"Amateurs," he scoffed as he disappeared into the woods.

Hubert and Horace exchanged knowing glances.

"You're such a liar," Horace told him.

"No harm done," responded Hubert. "It's not as if he's going to die a horrible death in there, is it?"

They laughed so much that Horace fell off the mound.

"I've done all I can," Leofric told Doon. "He insulted Rana. What did you expect her to do? You're just lucky you're not out there with them."

Rod and Halfshaft were tied to a stake outside the hut. It was raining heavily, and their clothes were soaked through and through. They both peered miserably into the dry hut, straining to hear what Doon and Leofric were saying about them, over the sound of the falling rain.

"We need the alien alive," Doon retorted. "Everything depends on him. He can't free the sword if he'd dead, can he? Rana is supposed to be your woman, isn't she? So sort her out!"

"Rana's nobody's "woman"! And if you speak to me like that again, I'll finish you off properly this time. You'd be dead if it wasn't for me. Dead and buried at the Castle, or lying in the queue for the morgue with those two outside."

Doon backed off. He knew Leofric could rip him to pieces, and it was only their friendship which was holding him back now. He needed his help. It was just a shame that they all had to depend on the whims of the Bitch Queen from Hell as well.

"Okay, I'm sorry. I'm just saying. Your girlfriend can do what she likes with the wizard, but we've got to keep the alien alive. And it doesn't look like we're making a very good job of it at the moment."

"They'd be dead already if it wasn't for me. He called her a tart! Have you any idea how hard it was for me to talk her into at least giving them a chance?"

"Chance! What chance has he got?"

Leofric sighed. He glanced out of the hut at the two men outside. "Not a lot. But you never know. They have to face the Amazon ordeal. Halfshaft has to defeat the Shamen in a duel of raw magic. If he's defeated the Grand Wizard, he can beat her, I'm sure. Her magic's failed her completely of late."

"I'm not interested in him. What about Rod? Can he win his ordeal? Can he win his freedom?"

"I don't know. He must fight Trugga. She's unbeaten at bare knuckle fighting. She's built like a boulder, with a chin to match. He'll have to kill her before she takes a step backwards."

"And he must fight her? And be executed, if she doesn't kill him first?"

"Unless he wins."

"Unless he wins!" Doon made a visible effort to stem a rising tide of exasperation. "We must make sure that he wins. Think of the consequences if he fails."

"Oi, you two," Rod called out to them from his stake. "Can't you chuck us out a blanket or something? I'm freezing my nuts off out here!"

"See what I mean?" Doon persisted. "That's our warrior out there. We can't let him take on this Trugga of yours."

"Rana won't call off the ordeal."

"Then Rod must fight Shamen instead. You said yourself that she's lost her magic. She can't hurt him. He'll survive the magic contest, and we can all go off to the Black Mountains and live happily ever after."

"But what about Halfshaft?"

"The wizard can wrestle Trugga."

"She's twice his size. She'll rip him to pieces. At least Rod would have a chance against her."

"I'm sorry Leofric. He's not my problem. I only brought him along because I didn't want to leave any witnesses in the dungeon. If he's such a great wizard, he'll find a way to beat her. If he's not, then he'll be no great loss, will he?"

Thane cursed as the sea gull swooped down towards him yet again. For the last few miles, it had been circling above him as he swam, shrieking unintelligible curses at him as he headed for the shore. On a couple of occasions, he had needed to duck below the waves to dodge out of the flight-path of the frenzied bird as it had dived towards him.

What an inhospitable planet, he thought, as he waded on to the beach. Suicide sects, giant sharks, and now crazed seagulls with attitude. No wonder the Grand Wizard had taken to drink.

He ducked yet again as the large bird buzzed him from above, missing him by inches. It landed further down the beach, and waddled round to face him, still squawking in frustration.

He picked up a sea-smooth pebble from his feet, and sent it skimming through the air, low and hard, towards the bad-tempered creature. It struck it square between its beady yellow eyes. It staggered theatrically from side to side, like a drunk trying to line himself up with the urinal after a heavy night on the town, before collapsing into a heap of beak and feathers, its spindly legs pointing pathetically to different parts of the sky.

"That'll teach it," Thane said, as he made his way off the beach. "There's nothing worse than a stroppy seagull"

Doon and Leofric watched in trepidation as Rana gave the command for Rod and Halfshaft to enter their respective huts to start the "ordeal". Their attention was focused on Rod. It was his fate that would decide the future of their planet.

The Shamen had entered Rod's hut an hour earlier to allow her time to prepare her spells. She was the human equivalent of a preying mantis: tall, rake-thin, and constantly ready to pounce. No one knew how old she was, but her grey hair and toothless mouth were proof that she was no spring chicken. Because of this, she got very little practice in actually getting to pounce on anybody, because all the men she met tended to put up a very good struggle (for the weaker sex).

Although ancient, Time had dimmed neither her mind nor her memory. Her knowledge, Leofric knew, could help them get through the Great Forest alive, as she knew the whereabouts of the legendary dwarf twins. But first Rod would have to try to survive against her in a battle of spells. This should not, he believed, be all that difficult, since her magical abilities had inexplicably deserted her some months previously, after she had disappeared in the company of a couple of large women. Since then, her powers seemed to have burnt themselves out.

As he considered these things, a scream shattered the silence. It came from the hut. Next, he heard a banging noise, followed by curses and the sound of splintering wood. A foot shot through an earthen wall of the hut, then withdrew hastily, only to be followed by an arthritic old elbow. Someone shouted with rage from within.

"What magic is this?" whispered Rana, in awe.

An unpleasant thought crossed Doon's mind. He drew Leofric close to him.

"There is something I've been meaning to ask you, my friend."

"Yes," Leofric enquired loudly, speaking over the screams and howls which were now erupting from the hut with ever increasing frequency.

"You did tell Rod that his ordeal has changed? Tell me he knows that he is no longer brawling with Trugga, but is exchanging spells with the Shamen?"

Leofric opened his mouth to answer. Before he could do so, there was one final piercing shriek from the hut, and Rod sauntered out, smiling in satisfaction at a job well done.

"All right, lads," he greeted them. "I've duffed up the old biddy. Who fancies coming out for a pint and a kebab?"

Halfshaft stood in the hut, squinting in the darkness, conscious of the fact that this was the second time in three days that he'd been involved in a magical duel to the death. This time, however, he was a little more confident. His self-respect had increased considerably. If he could defeat the Grand Wizard in combat, and get the others out of the Castle almost single-handedly, then he should be able to defeat some old witch. And then he'd be free. Or the other Amazons would be mating with him at the very least.

She stood several yards away from him, grinning smugly. Built like a boulder, in fact, which was unusual for an Amazon. Rolls of fat spilled over her over-stretched fur loincloth, sagging down almost to her knees. Her thighs protruded either side of her barrel-like stomach, each of them not far short of the thickness of his waist.

It was a good job this was only a battle of spells, he thought to himself, as he watched her cracking her knuckles in the corner. If this had been hand to hand combat, she would have killed him!

She took a step nearer, and he put his plan into effect.

Doon had told him that he was to be pitted against the Shamen, and had tried to teach him a few of the Grand Wizard's spells so that he could protect himself. A few incantations, learnt off by heart should scare the life out of the old girl. He hadn't had a chance to try them out yet, but who knows? If they were good enough for the Grand Wizard, they had to be worth a try.

He drew himself up to his full five feet ten, raised his arms above his head, and chanted:

"Woc yllis uoy ffo reggub!"

A strong enchantment indeed, but the woman kept on coming. Obviously an even more awe-inspiring incantation was necessary. Without knowing quite what it meant, Halfshaft pointed an imposing finger at the Amazon, and hissed:

"Ecnob elknirw, ffo dos!"

She didn't so much as flinch. By now, she was just a couple of feet away. Halfshaft waited for her first spell. Instead, she grabbed him by both ears, and sent him cartwheeling across the hut. By the time he regained his feet she was upon him again, kneeing him viciously in the groin. As he doubled over, she seized him, lifted him over her head, and hurled him against the wall with all her might.

He picked himself up, and fought to regain his breath. This was not the type of magic he had expected her to use, he had to admit, and he was in two minds whether to accuse her of cheating. As she closed in on him, he thought better of it, and prepared to deliver the ultimate spell, which Doon had told him to use in emergencies only. If this did not stop her, then nothing would.

She hesitated for a second, somehow sensing that he was on the verge of doing something spectacular. Maybe she felt the build-up of wild magic coursing through the hut. In any event, this was his chance. This was his moment of glory.

"Yawa og!" he commanded in a tone which impressed even him. "Uoy etah I!"

Although he could see no obvious effects of the spell, she appeared to be stunned. Maybe her legs had been pinned to the ground? Not wishing to lose the initiative, he followed straight up with the second part of the spell:

"Niaga uoy ot kaeps reven lli ro, yawa og!"

Her face creased up, as if she was struggling to come to terms with some gigantic mental exercise.

"I've got you, Shamen! Admit it! You're beaten!"

She took another step forwards.

"My name's not Shamen," she grunted.

He raised an enquiring eyebrow.

"It's Trugga."

He raised the other enquiring eyebrow.

"And I'm going to kill you, little man."

He ran like buggery.

As she chased him about the hut, he flung the occasional spell over his shoulder at her, desperately hoping that one of them might at least slow her down. It as not until he had told her to "ffo reggub" for the sixth time that he realised that all of the so-called spells Doon had so obligingly taught him were actually just swear words backwards. What a dratsab he thought.

She leapt forwards, grabbing his ankles and sending him sprawling to the ground. She got to her feet, still holding his ankles, and bounced him up and down for a while, toying with him whilst she pondered the best way to finish him off. With all her concentration bent upon him, she failed to notice Rod as he rushed in through the door, and he had leapt upon her back before she had a chance to avoid him.

"Leofric's just told me what happened," Rod called out to Halfshaft, as he tried to wrestle Trugga to the floor. "I've come to even the odds a bit."

Trugga fell backwards, deliberately crushing Rod beneath her. Halfshaft leapt on top of her to drag her off, only realising the drawback of this course of action when Rod squealed in pain beneath their combined weight. Trugga rolled off Rod and on to the wizard, hoping to crush him quickly so that she could concentrate on the newcomer.

Rod climbed breathlessly to his feet. The mountainous Amazon followed suit, satisfied that she had put Halfshaft out of action.

"I am Trugga," she told him. "And I am going to destroy you."

"I am Rod," he replied. " And you can come and have a go, if you think you're hard enough!"

She seized him, and pulled him towards him in a bone-crunching bear hug. Halfshaft tried to struggle up to come to his aid, but was frustrated to find that his legs no longer worked. Rod grabbed her by the shoulders, trying to push himself away from her, but without success. She was just too strong for him.

She grinned at him in triumph.

"Come on, then," she taunted. "I'm right in front of you. Aren't you going to try to hit me or something?"

"I don't hit women," he gasped, as the breath was slowly squeezed from his body.

"No?" she replied, mockingly.

"No."

He headbutted her. She sank slowly to the floor.

"I don't mind nutting an old cow like you, though."

It was dark, and no one noticed the creature as it flew over the castle battlements. It made its way straight to the King's chamber, gaining access through an open window. Spartan was not there. It's keen sense of hearing distinguished voices in the corridor outside. One was apologetic; the other, indignant and aggressive. The latter could only belong to the King. It lay in wait for him by the door.

The voices got louder. A guard stammered excuses, but was shouted down. The door to the chamber burst open, and Spartan erupted through it, slamming it closed behind him. He was on his own.

"Must I always be surrounded by idiots?" he bellowed. He then caught sight of the hideous giant bat nearby. He pulled away from it in horror, drawing his arms across his face to protect himself from attack. As he did so, the creature changed shape, taking another form entirely.

The King's hands gradually dropped away from his face, and he stared at the being before him for several seconds before sufficiently overcoming his shock to be able to speak.

"Can it really be you?"

It could. And it was.

Being bound hand and foot, there was not much else for Rod to do pass the time but talk to his guard Gerasa. She had heard of Harold, and he wondered whether any other famous historical figures had found their way here before him.

Columbus, Nelson, Napoleon, Gary Lineker: all were names which meant nothing to her. He asked if Quasimodo rang a bell, but the joke was wasted on her. Strangely enough, she thought "Shergar" sounded familiar, but couldn't swear to it.

She kicked him when he asked where they were keeping Halfshaft, and told him to put all thoughts of escape out of his mind. He persisted, asking whether his friend was guarded. She laughed at this. They had heard about the wizard. He did not need a guard. Takina was looking after him.

After a while, she tired of his questions, and gave him a bash with the blunt end of her javelin to keep him quiet. When this failed to do the trick, she gave him a poke with the sharp end instead. This had the desired effect.

She was the first to hear the scratching noise outside. It sounded like some small animal clawing on the wall of the hut. She ignored it for a few minutes, but the scratching became louder, and more persistent. Eventually, she sprang to her feet, and stalked out of the door, giving him a "don't-even-THINK-about escaping" look as she did so.

The sound stopped the moment she stepped out of the hut. She was back within moments, testing the bonds around his wrists and ankles upon her return. She sat on the ground beside him, her long bare legs stretching out beside his rather less well-proportioned ones. She left the javelin across her knees, in case she had need of it.

As soon as she had settled, the scratching started again. She jumped straight up, and slid silently out of the hut, glaring at him as she did so as if holding him personally responsible.

"Don't worry about me," he called after her. "I think I'll turn in for the night. Could you set the alarm for 9ish when you get back?"

She was gone a little longer than before, having made two full circuits of the hut this time. When she returned, it was clear from her perplexed expression that she had found nothing to account for the noise outside.

Too fretful to bother checking his bonds again, she dropped back to the ground by his side. Moodily, she ground the javelin into the crumbling earth, digging out a small crater. She was up on her feet again, and out the door almost before the scratching restarted. All vestiges of caution were abandoned in her haste to discover the source of the commotion and deal with it once and for all. After a while, Rod heard a clanging noise followed by a dull thud, a muffled groan, and what sounded like dancing feet.

Before he could give any further thought to this strange sequence of unconnected noises, Halfshaft entered the room, dancing a jig of delight, a dented saucepan clenched in his right hand. He was followed by Takina, who set to work on untying Rod, as the wizard leapt and pirouetted around the hut with unrestrained joy.

"Is he okay?" asked Rod, still not entirely sure what was going on, but assuming that it had something to do with escape.

She nodded, without slowing her pace. The knots were tight, and time was short.

"I got her!" Halfshaft cried jubilantly, illustrating the point with a full-blooded swipe of the saucepan. "I thought I was just a wizard, but bugger me if I'm not a warrior as well!"

The knots fell apart at Rod's wrists, and he shook the rope to the ground. As he set to work on his ankles himself, Halfshaft came to a halt before him, and gestured grandly to his Amazon companion.

"Rod, I would like you to meet Takina. I had to bring her along with me. It's her saucepan."

Thane arrived at Spartan Castle at dawn. His journey had been gruelling but uneventful. Some weird old hag had tried to give him drugged tea, but apart from that it had passed without incident.

He was further behind schedule than ever, but had no choice but to seek out the King. He needed inconspicuous clothes, directions, and an update on what was going on. In particular, he had to find out whether anyone had seen the biker from Earth.

Four soldiers met him at the gates. One of them introduced himself as Rufford, acting Captain of the Guard. He was, he was told, being taken for an audience with the King.

Rufford chatted away to him, trying to put him at his ease. But if there was one thing Thane had learnt from that unpleasant incident in Alpha Centauri, it was that the more someone tries to make you relax, the more likely it is that they are secretly planning to chop you into cubes with a double-handed axe, and leave you scattered around the Black Orchard as a feast for the bone-crunchers. Or, if you were on Earth, that they were going to sell you over-priced double-glazing.

Several passageways, a handful of staircases, and a dozen ingratiating smiles later, they stopped outside an imposing oak door. Two more soldiers stood outside it. Thane was now acutely aware that he was outnumbered six to one. Not his favourite odds.

"I'm afraid you'll have to hand over your weapons," Rufford told him, apologetically. "This is the King's chamber. No-one can enter here armed."

"No," the mercenary replied. "I don't even sleep without my knives on me."

"Then I'll show you out. You'll need to go on your way without seeing the King. He won't allow anyone in there if they're armed. I'm sorry. There can be no exceptions."

Thane weighed up the situation. He had three options. He could give up his knives; he could keep them and go ahead on his quest without seeing the King, even though he did not have much idea where he was supposed to be going; or he could stick a blade in the nearest soldier, force his way into the King's rooms, and demand the information he needed. The last option seemed pretty appealing, but there was one thing which militated against it. Spartan had hired him, and it was the King who would be paying his bill at the end of the day. People tended to begrudge handing over their money if you start slaughtering their underlings (or even if you just knock them about a bit). He did not really seem to have much choice but to disarm.

Rufford waited patiently as Thane produced knife after knife from various parts of his clothing. He handed them, one at a time, to the nearest soldier, who winced every time the mercenary tossed another blade into his outstretched arms. Bowie knives, throwing knives, pocket knives all materialised from nowhere and joined the pile.

"Careful, now" Thane cautioned, as he balanced a 12 inch hunting blade on top of his other weapons. "That may be sharp."

"Thirteen," counted Rufford. "They'll be returned to you once you've seen the King."

"Fourteen," the mercenary corrected. "And they'd better be."

He watched uneasily as the soldier disappeared down the corridor, gingerly clutching the weapons to his chest. No more blades, but at least the man's departure meant the odds had been shortened to five to one. And besides, he still had three phials of acid in his pocket that should make a pretty interesting fight of it if the worst came to the worst.

Rufford knocked at Spartan's door.

"What is it?" snapped an irritated voice from inside.

"He's here."

As if at some unspoken command, the door swung open. Rufford stood aside to make room for Thane to pass. To the mercenary's surprise, none of the soldiers followed him into the room. One of them closed the door behind him.

He was even more surprised when he recognised the man sitting at the King's side, though he determined straight away that he must not show it.

"We meet again," he said simply.

"We do indeed," the Grand Wizard replied.

Rana was livid. Leofric had vanished overnight. Doon and the other strangers had left as well. Gerasa had been found in an unconscious heap in the village that morning. And to add insult to injury, Takina had run off with a saucepan.

Within minutes of waking, she had summoned three of her best Amazons to the meeting place in the village centre, and given them their orders. These were concise and to the point. Go to the Great Forest. Find the men. Kill them all, except Leofric, who should be brought back alive. And keep a lookout on the way for a lazy blonde Amazon with a cooking implement.

They left immediately. Rana stayed behind to seek out the Shamen. She was disturbed to discover that she had disappeared as well. Leofric had wanted the woman to find the dwarf twins for him. He must have taken her as a guide. She had given him everything a man could want: a roof over his head, a little pocket money, regular mating sessions, and exemption from being skinned alive and beheaded (which was the usual sentence for being caught on Amazon land in possession of male genitalia). And he had repaid her by stealing her witch! Such was the ingratitude of the male species.

She summoned Trugga, and the two of them set off together after the runaways. It made her uneasy that they had taken the Shamen with them. What if they managed somehow to use her magic for their own ends? It was best that she supervised their execution herself, just to make sure that nothing went wrong.

It did not take them long to find the men's tracks, but it did take her awhile to puzzle out why Takina's tracks were intermingled with those of the runaways, and why there was no sign of the Shamen's tracks at all.

"Takina must be following the prisoners!" surmised Rana, incredulously.

"Yes," agreed Trugga wisely. "And they must have cut the Shamen's feet off!"

"No stump marks," Rana explained, pointing to the tracks as she jogged easily beside her puffing friend. "And the footprints are deeper than you would expect. They must be carrying her."

"You are SO clever," Trugga panted, genuinely impressed at her Queen's deductive abilities.

"I know," Rana replied. "And very pretty as well."

Rod and Takina sat beneath the shade of a giant oak tree, watching Halfshaft as he wandered across the plain outside in search of provisions. It was a relief to be rid of him for half an hour or so. Every time they had tried to make plans, he had interrupted with tales of how he had single-handedly fought the Amazon guard using nothing but a saucepan. Each time his version of events had become a little more heroic, and a little less closer to the truth. He was now bursting with pride at the idea that he was a great warrior as well as an incredible wizard, and their only concern was that he did not chance upon any stray bears in his search for food. He was so convinced of his own prowess at the moment that he might just attempt to wrestle them to the ground, and drag them back to camp for elevenses.

It soon became apparent that Halfshaft's part in the great escape had not been quite as prominent as he believed. Takina explained that Halfshaft had discreetly told her everything she could possibly have wanted to know about their mission, but had added that he was only telling her because she had a trustworthy face and he knew she wouldn't go and blab to anyone else like a girl. She had retorted that it was men who blabbed, and they had spent the next quarter of an hour debating the point.

His story had intrigued her, though. They were on a quest to save the world. She could help them. She could make a difference. No, he had told her. Girls could not make a difference. But she could come along with them if she was happy to do the cooking, and maybe darn some socks from time to time. This had led to another quarter of an hour of debate, interspersed with her kicking him in the side to illustrate her points. This line of argument seemed to do the trick, as he had eventually confessed that girls could make a difference, that he had just been teasing her, and that out of all the people in the whole world she was the person whom he felt they most needed to help them fulfil their mission. She had then given him one last kick (she was not used to violence, but found it surprisingly therapeutic), told him to stop patronising her, and had released him from his bonds.

They had then set out to free Rod. Being a servant, she had no weapons as such, but improvised by tucking a fish knife into the waistband of her pelt, and arming Halfshaft with a well-weighted saucepan.

With their limited armoury, they would have been no match for Gerasa. She was one of the most capable Amazons in the village. Halfshaft was all for the two of them rushing into the hut to overpower her, but she had eventually persuaded him that they would have ended up kebabed on her javelin. Eventually, he had agreed with her idea. He would scratch around outside the hut, lead Gerasa off on a diversion, and Takina would then sneak into free Rod whilst she was away.

Unfortunately, things had not quite worked out that way. On the first two attempts, they had been unable to lure Gerasa far enough from the hut for Takina to slip in. On the third occasion, Halfshaft had dropped his saucepan whilst trying to make his escape. In the time it took him to stop and pick it up, Gerasa was upon him. Takina had appeared from the darkness and dealt her a right hook of which Rana herself would have been proud (had it not been delivered to knock out one of her own tribeswomen). The Amazon collapsed, just as Halfshaft had recovered himself and taken a swing at her with his saucepan. His blow ricocheted off her shoulder and struck her head with the resounding clang which Rod had heard inside.

"Didn't you tell him you'd already knocked her out?" Rod asked.

"Why? Why not let him have his moment of glory? There's an Amazon proverb that confidence makes lions of us all. If we're going to go on this quest, it's better that he's a lion."

Rod watched Halfshaft as he ran manically around the plain in his role as hunter-gatherer. He smiled.

"I don't know about lion. He looks more like a guinea pig on drugs to me!"

"He's heart's in the right place," Takina replied.

"I know," agreed Rod. "He might be a grumpy old sod, but he's OUR grumpy old sod. And a least you know where you stand with him. If he doesn't like you, he tells you. For quite a long time, sometimes! Not like Doon. There's something about him I don't trust. But maybe that's just me being prejudiced. I've never hung around with a corpse before."

Takina stood up and stretched. She scanned the horizon for some sign that Doon and Leofric were on their way. Halfshaft – upset that Doon had given him a worthless spell for use in his duel with the Shamen, and doubly upset that he had then been given the task of fighting Trugga instead – had been in favour of pressing on without them, but his companions had overruled him. They were all concerned that the Amazons would be out looking for them by now, but they needed Leofric to help them find the dwarf twins. They had no choice but to wait, and to hope that Doon and Leofric arrived before the Amazon search party.

Rod watched her as she stretched. She was a good-looking woman, and she had a brain on her, too. She said that she wanted to help them, so that she could prove herself to the other Amazons, but he felt it was more than that. It wasn't the Amazons she needed to convince of her value; she needed to prove it to herself. She was just as much in need of confidence as the funny wizard he could see tugging up toadstools in the distance, in the mistaken belief that they were mushrooms.

When you read books about this stuff, people were always assisted in their quests by people with amazing superhuman abilities. People who could fly, or fight, or see into the future. He had ended up with an insecure Amazon and a mad magician with a saucepan.

And being the person he was, he would not have had it any other way.

"You're hurting me!" grizzled the Shamen yet again. Doon had one of her bony knees clasped under each arm, whilst Leofric – running backwards – supported her body. They had tried to carry her by her wrists and ankles but she was so tall that her body kept dragging along the ground. Even now, they occasionally dashed her head against the odd rock as they tried to cross the bumpy terrain at speed, both of them hoping that a bit of concussion might make her whinge a bit less. So far, it had had the opposite effect.

"You're hurting us!" Leofric retorted as they scuttled onwards. "How can a scrawny old crow like you weigh so much?"

"It's the magic in me," she replied, proudly. "A spell is taking shape. And you will be at the sharp end of it if you don't release me this instant."

"And you'll be at the sharp end of my boot if you don't stop making stupid threats that you can't back up. You've got no more magic in you than I have, woman. Now stop your prattling and tell us where we can find the dwarfs."

Doon had woken him in the middle of the night with the news that Rod and Halfshaft had escaped. Leofric was all for going straight after them before the alarm was raised, but Doon, rational as ever, had pointed out that there was no point leaving unless they took the Shamen with them. Without her, they would find neither the dwarf twins nor the pathway into the Forest. Had he known how heavy the old crone would weigh, though, he might not have conceded the point so quickly.

They finally saw the Great Forest at the bottom of the slope they were approaching. It sprawled out for mile upon mile in front of them, a sticky black mass of gnarled old trees and withered branches. Leofric shivered. They had been this way once before, and nearly perished in the process. And that was on the "safe" path. They needed to find the dwarfs again, and find out which of the pathways was now the more dangerous of the two. And they had to find Rod before he wandered into the Forest without them.

"Where are they?" he asked her.

"Who?" replied their captive, just to be awkward.

Doon dropped her.

"Don't play games with us, witch. Where are the twins?"

"Don't know," she pouted.

Leofric drew his sword.

"But I think that might be a good place to start looking," she added hurriedly, pointing a spindly finger at a stretch of trees on the outskirts of the Forest several miles distant.

"All right," said Doon, grabbing her knees again. "Shall we go?"

Leofric slid his sword back into his sheath, and picked up his end of the burden again.

"Can't she walk, now?" he asked. "She's a dead weight."

"That'll be the magic in me," she reminded him. "Ready to strike at you when you're least expecting it. I doubt you'll make it to the bottom of this hill."

She broke wind violently, to underline the threat. Doon dropped her ankles in disgust. At the same time, Leofric released her body, and she tumbled to the ground.

"That's no way to treat a lady," she scolded them. "All men are pigs."

But the pigs were not listening. Instead, Doon followed Leofric's gaze. On the horizon behind them, he saw three Amazons travelling rapidly in their direction.

"What are our chances?" he asked.

"None," crowed the Shamen loudly from their feet.

"Not good," Leofric admitted. "And there may be more on the way. But who knows? Even Amazons have off days."

The Shamen had risen to her feet, and was trying to slink away unnoticed as the two of them conversed. It was quite difficult for a seven-foot tall old biddy with creaking knees to achieve this, though, and they seized a wrist each and pulled her back again before she had managed three yards.

An idea occurred to Doon. He pressed his knife to the leathery skin of her wrinkled belly.

"We do, of course, have a hostage."

Leofric grinned.

"Let's just hope they don't make us keep her!"

It was painfully obvious that the Grand Wizard had neither forgiven nor forgotten Thane's decision to abandon him to the sharks. Throughout their long conversation, he appeared to have great difficulty suppressing the indignation and umbrage which bubbled away under the surface. He was not a happy bunny.

He was still very weak, that much was clear. The long pipe which was propped against the wall by his side looked more like a walking stick than a smoking implement. He was frail and haggard, but whether this was as a result of the sharks or the cider, it was hard for the mercenary to judge.

Once Thane and Spartan had been formally introduced to one another, the Grand Wizard explained how he had escaped.

"After you deserted me, I was almost eaten by sharks. I turned myself into one of the creatures to pacify them, but it just seemed to make them worse, so I became an even larger shark and ate them both. That was a mistake. Fish always gives me wind.

I knew that I had to make it ashore before I lost consciousness again. I came to the surface, and tried to turn myself into a bird. It required a long and complicated spell, because sharks don't have legs."

Thane was mystified by this last remark, but resolved against stopping the wizard. He did not look as if he would take too kindly to any interruptions.

"I turned into a gull, and flew ashore. I was understandably upset that you had left me to die, so I amused myself by swooping down at you a few times. Then I landed on the beach to wait for you. And when you arrived, you tried to kill me with a pebble!"

Both the wizard and Spartan turned to stare at Thane, awaiting an explanation. The Grand Wizard was on the point of exploding, he could tell. His eyes were narrowed, and his breathing had quickened. Thane was struck by the contrast between the wizard's moods. On Earth, he had been genuinely friendly, albeit whilst under the influence of an incredible quantity of cider. But now he came across as being thoroughly poisonous and objectionable. Thane had met wizards before, and each and every one of them had been insufferably proud men. He wondered whether the drastic change in Cyrellius' attitude towards him might have been triggered not so much by the incident with the sharks, as by the fact that the wizard had humiliated himself on Earth and despised Thane for knowing this. Was he acting this way because he feared that Thane might expose him as a drunkard? And if he was so worried about it, to what lengths might he go to keep his secret safe?

Maybe it was not such a good idea surrendering his knives to the guards, after all.

Halfshaft had strayed into the Forest itself in his search for food and water. Although the lower branches of the trees were thickly intertwined, the Forest was not totally inaccessible and he was able to battle quite a way into it before being forced to a halt.

He was more concerned about food than water. It had been many hours since they had last had anything to drink, but if the worst came to the worst he could conjure up a spurt of water or two. No one would be too keen on drinking his bodily fluids, he knew, but beggars couldn't be choosers. His main objective, as far as he was concerned, was to find something he could cook in his saucepan.

He had heard many stories about the Forest – most concerning wolves, spirits and vicious wood dwarfs – but felt relatively secure wandering around its boundary. Besides, he had his trusty saucepan with him. He swang it through the air, reassured at the pleasing swishing noise it made. For the first time in his life, he felt as if he was really in control. He had defeated the Grand Wizard in a magical duel, beaten the Shamen in combat, and knocked an Amazon warrior unconscious. It was a pretty impressive list of achievements for a failed magician.

By the time he had finished congratulating himself on his skill and prowess, he realised that he was lost. The density of the trees and shrubs at the Forest edge had cut off his view of the outside world. A little light filtered through the branches above him, but he still had to squint to see anything. He tried retracing his steps, but if anything the light got worse, and his surroundings less familiar.

He tried to overcome a mounting sense of panic by reminding himself that he had not travelled far into the Forest, and that he could only be a stone's throw away from his friends. Unfortunately, he didn't have a clue which way to throw the stone. Every time he took a step forward, he managed to convince himself that it was one step deeper into the woods, and he finally resolved that it would be better not to move at all.

He considered his options. Shouting for help was a possibility, but he would be mortified if it turned out that he was only a few steps away from the edge of the Forest. After the saucepan incident, he had his reputation to think of. On the other hand, wandering around in the darkness until he was eaten had little to commend it either.

An idea struck him. If it was lighter, he might just see enough to allow him to retrace his tracks. A crushed twig, or a scuffed patch of earth was all he would need to send him off in the right direction. He conjured up a small flame on his fingers. For a second, the trees which were huddling in on him seemed to shrink away from it, but he always had had an overactive imagination.

He swept the light about in an arc in front of him, trying to find some clue as to the right way out. As he did so, the flame touched an overhanging branch, setting it alight. In his mind, he heard a sound midway between a creak and a scream, and the limb pulled sharply away from him. In his panic, the flame went out. The tree, regrettably, did not.

Just as the trees had previously appeared to be leaning away from him, they now crowded towards him. A branch caught him spitefully across the face, cutting him above his left eye. Another rapped him heavily on his shin, nearly knocking his legs out from beneath him. He fought to keep his balance, fearing that if he fell to the ground he would never get up again.

From afar, he heard a woman's voice call out the word "none", and without pausing to consider who had said it, or why, he battled his way towards it. He struggled wildly onwards as tree limbs bore down upon him, pressing him towards the treacherous ground. Creepers stealthily reached out for him, wrapping themselves around his ankles as he battled past them. On the verge of hysteria, he lashed out with his saucepan in all directions, beating back the branches and kicking wildly at the vines as they coiled snake-like around his legs. All the while, the scream inside his head grew louder and shriller, as the bough of the ignited tree thrashed around in agony in his wake.

Inch by painful inch, he forced his way through the malignant undergrowth. A vine wrapped itself around his face, dragging him backwards, but in his desperation to escape he bit clean through it and fought his way on.

The screeching stopped suddenly. It was replaced by voices, tiny beguiling voices which told him something he would really rather have not known. They said he was heading in the wrong direction. If the voices were telling the truth, he was heading deeper and deeper into the Forest.

It was too late to change direction. Cursing and praying in equal measure, he put his head down and battled on. Towards death or salvation, he knew not which.

"What has the Watcher told you?" the Grand Wizard asked.

"You want me to kill a Warlock," Thane replied. "That's about it. You were going to tell me more on Earth, but you were in no fit state to..."

"Then let me tell you now," Cyrellius interrupted. "And let us see how brave you really are.

Many centuries ago, our land was invaded by a warlock named Chameleon. His army consisted mainly of corpses. After each battle he fought, he brought to life the dead of both sides to serve under him. The more he fought, the stronger he became.

A man from Earth – Harold the Invincible – came here, and led our armies against him. There were men, Amazons, even wood dwarfs, all joining in the common cause, one last stand against evil. The two forces met at Crow Hill, in the Great Forest. Against all the odds, the Warlock's army was defeated. Much of the credit for this must go to Harold, who fought like a demon with his magic sword.

The Warlock retreated to his lair in the Black Mountains, but Harold gave chase. An ancestor of mine – Ostosis – was one of those who accompanied him.

Harold and Chameleon fought again, this time in the Mountain itself, and the Warlock was defeated a second time. Ostosis sealed the Warlock into the mountain by magic, and placed Harold's sword in the entrance to keep the spell in place. If it is ever removed, the spell will be broken, and the Warlock will march again. But no one from our world can touch the sword, so Harold died believing that the Warlock would be imprisoned there forever.

Not long ago, a stranger was found near the Castle. It is our usual practice to execute all strangers on sight as part of our immigration policy. But this one was so oddly dressed that I decided to torture him first."

The Grand Wizard paused. His injuries made it difficult for him to breathe and the effort of speaking was temporarily too much for him. Spartan – who had been looking for an excuse to take over the tale- seized the opportunity to take centre stage, and carried on where his friend had left off.

"Cyrellius and I questioned the stranger. Incredibly, he came from the same world as Harold. At first, we were pleased, thinking this man might be a great warrior who could lead us to glory against the Amazons and dwarfs, but it was not to be. We locked him in a room with three swordsmen, and he was cut to pieces in seconds. He was no hero after all!"

The Grand Wizard jumped in, stealing the initiative back from his monarch.

"Then more Earthlings started to appear. Our concern must be obvious, even to a thug like you. For centuries, the Warlock had been imprisoned beneath the mountains, without hope of release. But any one of these men could have set him free, and doomed our whole planet in the process. There is no one strong enough to stand against him, now."

"I can't lead an army," Thane intervened. "I'm an assassin, not a general."

"That was not what we had in mind," replied the Grand Wizard, icily. "May I finish?"

"Of course."

"We killed all the earth men who came here, but it would only take one of them to get through, and we'd be lost. The only solution was to kill the Warlock before any of them could free him."

"Which is where I come in," Thane said quietly to himself. It was not said quietly enough, though. Both the King and the Wizard glared at him like enraged librarians, seething at this further interruption. Thane shrugged his shoulders and allowed them to continue.

"Which is where I came in," Cyrellius corrected. "Although this Kingdom is not the power it once was, I am the equal of any of my predecessors"

"As am I," added the King, hurriedly.

"I can change shape, throw lightning bolts, do anything Ostosis could have done, so I set out to destroy the Warlock once and for all.

I chose two men to accompany me. One was Leofric, Captain of the Guard. The other was my apprentice, Doon. I chose badly.

We travelled together to the Black Mountains, not without incident. Only my genius kept us alive. When we arrived, the three of us entered the Warlock's chamber."

"But the sword?" Thane questioned.

"The sword keeps the Warlock in. It does not keep anyone out. When we entered we discovered a vast army of troll corpses. Most

77

were still lifeless, but several were patrolling the chamber. Whilst Leofric and Doon did their best to hold them off, I did battle with the Warlock. It was a fierce contest, but although I tried everything I knew, I could not win. Just as I thought I was gaining the upper hand, he vanished. This vile stench appeared, and the three of us lost consciousness."

"Gas," nodded Thane.

"I don't need to guess," snapped the wizard. "I know raw magic when I see it. What chance did I have against that? A cobra can do nothing when there is no target to strike. I left the chamber as soon as I could, and awaited my companions outside.

When they eventually came out, I questioned them, fearful that they may have given away details of the Castle's defences under torture. They told me I had nothing to fear. Then they hit me with a rock, and left me for dead."

Cyrellius caught Thane's eye.

"I do so hate being left for dead.

Fortunately, I had taken a potion of mine which heals any physical injury. I have taken some of that potion again today, and now – as then – my injuries will heal in time.

As if to contradict him, a spasm of pain wracked the wizard's chest. He clutched at his tunic, waiting for the pain to pass. The King placed a comforting hand on his shoulder, but then realised that he was missing the opportunity to seize control of the conversation again, and dived in quickly before Cyrellius could compose himself.

"Despite his injuries," Spartan explained, " Cyrellius arrived back here before the traitors. Both were sentenced to death upon their return. However, I could ill afford to lose Leofric – he was a fine Captain of the Guard – and when he blamed everything on Doon, volunteering to execute him himself as a sign of his loyalty, I pardoned him. I can be very generous like that."

"So I lost my servant, and you kept yours," sniped the Grand Wizard. "That seems fair, doesn't it? Besides, Leofric's protestations of loyalty were lies. Another stranger was found near the Castle, and Leofric insisted on questioning him personally. Suspicious, I shape-shifted and listened in on the interrogation. I heard him tell the prisoner – another Earthling- that I was a traitor, and that I was the one who had sold myself to the Warlock. He tried to persuade him to agree to remove the sword from the entrance to the Warlock's prison, telling him that he could kill Chameleon with it. But the real plan, of course, was that the Earthling would simply release the Warlock, and die in the process. The sword makes the wielder invincible, but Chameleon would simply have plucked it from his grasp, and slaughtered him. There is no way that an untrained swordsman can defeat this creature, whatever weapon he may have at his disposal.

It is this story which I believe to have been given to this latest alien. I thought Doon to be dead, but he has been spotted within the Castle walls shortly before the earthling escaped. He has no doubt filled his head with lies. I have no doubt that they are now on their way to the Black Mountains. The alien will believe that he is on a mission to save our world. But he has been misled by traitors. I have already given orders for him to be tracked down and killed. Hopefully, they would have been carried out by now. I want you to kill the Warlock before any more of these strangers appear. And if Trog fails to carry out his mission for whatever reason, then I want you to execute the Earthling on your way."

The three Amazons were just outside striking distance. As long as Doon held the knife to the Shamen's stomach, they remained motionless. But each time he or Leofric took a step backwards, they closed in, allowing them no hope of escape. Sooner or later, more Amazons would arrive, maybe even Rana herself, and it would then only be a matter of time before they were captured or killed.

They stood in stalemate for several minutes, before they heard the sound of rustling from the Forest nearby. All of a sudden, a man wearing the robes of a wizard broke free from the trees. His garments had been badly torn in many places, and his face and hands were scratched and bloodied. The branches of the closest trees seemed to clutch at him as he burst from their grasp, but he beat them off with some metallic implement he had in his hand.

They watched in astonishment as he dashed frantically towards them. As he approached they were able to distinguish the object in his grasp. It was a saucepan.

He did not appear to notice the group until he was almost upon them. Just as it looked as if he would pass them by, though, he gave a startled yelp, changed direction violently, and headed straight towards them. Without warning, he swung his saucepan at the nearest Amazon, knocking her unconscious with a resounding bash to the head. Without stopping to see if his aim had been true, he shot off into the distance, his sawn-off wizard's hat flapping in the wind behind him.

By the time the two remaining Amazons had recovered themselves, he was thirty feet away, galloping wildly towards a clump of trees in the distance. They set off in pursuit. Leofric followed, shrugging off Doon when he tried to hold him back. No one noticed the figures that peeled away from the Forest and came rushing towards them.

The Amazons caught the wizard in seconds, bringing him crashing to the ground like two lionesses downing a frightened zebra. Leofric leapt upon the nearest, pulling her aside, and riding her bare stomach as she twisted and bucked beneath him. Her companion reached for the knife tucked into her waistband at her hip, but just as her hand clasped the hilt, she was rugby-tackled by a feisty blonde Amazon who had charged from the trees to the wizard's rescue.

Rod followed closely on Takina's heels. He surveyed the scene before him in amusement. Leofric sat astride one woman, as she spat and struggled beneath him. Takina and the second Amazon rolled around on the grass, their fur-clad bodies rubbing against each other in a way which reminded him very much of a dream he had enjoyed a week ago last Tuesday. If it wasn't for Halfshaft – who was lying on his back, shouting curses and waving his saucepan ineffectually in the air above his head- the scene could easily have been an x-rated sequel to One Million Years BC. It would have gone straight to video, sure, but he would certainly have got his money's worth from it.

Doon had kept his distance from the fracas, shouting encouragement to Leofric from the sidelines. When Rod went to Takina's assistance, however, he moved in, trying to pull the biker away.

"You can't get involved. It's too dangerous."

"I'll get dangerous, too, if you keep tugging on my bloody arm like that. Now sod off, while I have a go with that saucepan over there."

Doon reluctantly released him. Rod went over to Halfshaft, and gently prised the saucepan from his grasp. Impressed by its weight, he crossed over to the two Amazons, dispatching both of them in turn. Leofric tried to talk him out of it, telling him that he was quite happy for his one to buck around beneath him for another minute or two, but they had a job to do. He then returned the saucepan to Halfshaft's fist. The wizard – who did not appear to have noticed that it was missing in the first place – continued to swat the air with it vigorously.

"Well," Rod addressed the group cheerfully. "We're all back together again. Let's go and play in the woods!"

There were too many unanswered questions for Thane's liking.

"What happened to Leofric?"

"I ordered his execution. My guards, fools that they are, had some difficulty in subduing him, but once Trog came to their assistance the result was never in doubt. He was brought to the block for beheading, but just as the executioner was about to swing the axe, my sister intervened, pleading for his life. She had a soft spot for him, for some reason."

"It might," said Cyrellius, "have had something to do with the fact that she was his mother."

"I can't see that that would make any difference," argued the King. "My mother didn't show much affection for me when I was having her beheaded. Anyway, being a merciful man, I agreed to give my nephew a chance. The executioner was blindfolded and pointed in the right direction. He was allowed just one swing of the axe. If the blow struck, so much the better. If not, Leofric would just be tied up and given to the Amazons, whilst the executioner would be beheaded in his place for gross incompetence.

The executioner brought his axe down straight and true, to give him his credit. Leofric screamed out in agony. There was blood all over the place; the crowd was drenched. It took my servants days to scrub up the cobblestones."

"Did the blow strike him cleanly?" asked Thane, taking a professional interest.

"Unfortunately, it struck his mother. The silly fool had bent down to mop his brow at just the wrong moment. Her head was chopped clean off her shoulders. It really was horrific at the time. It took me ages to see the funny side.

I did, of course, honour my side of the bargain. Leofric was beaten with clubs, tied up, and tossed over the Amazon border, never to be seen since."

The Grand Wizard tired of waiting for a gap in the conversation, and jumped in.

"Will you accompany me to the Black Mountains, and help me kill the Warlock?"

"Yes. That's what I'm being paid to do."

"And will you execute the Earthling on the way, if Trog doesn't reach him first?"

"No. I'm taking him back to his own planet. I'm not licensed to kill him."

"Don't get squeamish on us now, mercenary. This stranger of yours could unleash the Warlock if we let him go. We need him dead."

"I said "no". I'm licensed to do what I do. I don't kill anyone unless it's necessary. Just because you've sent out someone to murder him, it doesn't mean..."

"Murder!" exploded Spartan, leaping furiously to his feet. "How dare you refer to my orders in such terms? He is to be executed, not murdered. Do you reduce my commands to the rantings of a common criminal? I will have an apology, or see you hanged!"

"I am not killing that man," Thane persisted. "I've told the Watcher I'll bring him back, if there's anything left of him to bring."

"Guards!" raged Spartan. "Guards! What's keeping the idiots!"

The door flew open, and Rufford led four armed soldiers into the room. Thane jumped to his feet, and waited for them to attack, preparing to use their momentum against them. He was acutely aware that the Grand Wizard was still in the room, and resolved to seize a weapon from the first soldier to approach him, turning it on Cyrellius before he could formulate a spell.

This did not prove necessary.

"Get out!" the Grand Wizard commanded the guards, in a tone which they thought it wise to obey.

Spartan stared at the wizard in astonishment.

"They're acting under my orders," he protested. "Didn't you hear me give them my command?"

He gestured the soldiers back inside, as they were on the point of filing sheepishly from the chamber.

"Get back in here. Throw this man in the dungeons. He has insulted me. Kill him if he resists."

"Get out!" the Grand Wizard repeated. "I won't tell you again!"

The guards, confused, looked to Rufford for help. Since he was every bit as confused as them, he had no help to give, and desperately avoided making eye contact with any of them. To disobey the King would mean certain execution; to provoke the Grand Wizard would be to risk being fried on the spot. Neither option held much appeal. And then there was the mercenary to consider as well. Best to keep his head down and blame everything on one of his subordinates later. He was a quick learner like that.

Spartan turned furiously on the Grand Wizard, his face almost purple with rage.

"How dare you countermand my orders? You have no right!"

"I have no choice! You know what has to be done. I can't do this on my own. How can he accompany me to the Black Mountains if you have him killed?"

"We'll get another one. He insulted me, for goodness sake! He called me a murderer! A base criminal! Me, of all people! I will not tolerate such an affront."

"And he has left me to die in the sea, without so much as an apology. Which of us has the more serious grievance?"

"You have, but..."

"But you are the King. It's entirely your decision whether he should live or die. But bear this in mind. If you kill him, I will leave Spartan Castle, and will never return. And when your actions have led to the release of the Warlock, as they surely will, you'll be entirely at his mercy. Unless you're relying on these fools to save you?"

He waved his hand towards the guards, who were whispering frantically amongst themselves. Two of them even appeared to be playing the scissors-paper-rock game in a desperate bid to decide which of the orders they should obey. Rufford stood slightly apart from them, looking embarrassed, but no nearer to resolving the dilemma than his men. He gave an awkward shrug when he saw the two men staring in his direction.

"It's their training," he apologized. "I blame it on the last administration."

The King gazed despairingly back at him for a few seconds. He then looked back towards the Grand Wizard, willing him to throw him a lifeline to save him from loss of face. But none came. Instead, Cyrellius pressed home his advantage.

"And what would happen if these fine fighting men here fail to defeat this mercenary?" he continued. "He may be unarmed, but I would still back him against these idiots any day of the week. He's the best assassin around, the Watcher has assured me of that. If he kills them, what chance would you have against him?"

"You would protect me."

The Grand Wizard shrugged non-committedly.

"Who's to say I'd be quick enough. If you don't trust my judgment any more, why trust my reflexes?"

Spartan squirmed uncomfortably. He had never had to back down before in his life. Now, step by step, his so-called friend was backing him into a corner from which his only escape would be a humiliating climb-down in front of witnesses. It was unthinkable.

"Cyrellius!" he cried, reproachfully. "You can not expect me to lose face before my subjects in this way. Especially such mean, pathetic subjects as these."

The mean pathetic subjects nodded vigorously at this, hoping against hope that this act of submission might go some way towards getting them back into the good books of their monarch.

"He's right," one muttered. "I'm mean, and make no mistake."

"And pathetic," added his comrade. "Me, too. Both of those things."

The Grand Wizard made no reply. The King tried a different approach.

"We have been friends for a very long time."

"And will continue to be so, once you have sent these men away."

The King glared at Cyrellius for a full half minute, his face going redder and redder as he willed him to back down. The wizard remained impassive.

"Don't do this to me," Spartan warned.

Still the Grand Wizard said nothing.

Finally, the King lost his nerve.

"Get out!" he screamed at the guards. "How dare you barge into my chamber uninvited? Get out this instant!"

The guards fled, falling over each other to be the first one out. Spartan wheeled on the Grand Wizard for an instant, as if expecting him to add insult to injury by ordering them all back in again. Once satisfied that the wizard was going to say nothing, he flew after the guards, pushing and shoving them, and snapping at their heels like a rabid sheepdog turning on its flock. He slammed the door shut behind them, but then thought better of it, flinging it back open again.

"You're all banished!" he shouted hysterically. "I want you all out of here within the hour or I'll execute you myself."

"That wasn't so bad, was it?" Cyrellius goaded, relentlessly pressing home his victory.

"Get out," Spartan screamed at him. "I want to be alone."

"Certainly," the wizard agreed, amicably. "I'll be talking to the mercenary in my chambers if you need me"

The Grand Wizard walked past the King, with Thane a pace or two behind him.

"I won't forget this," warned Spartan, as they passed him by.

Cyrellius stopped, and looked his sovereign squarely in the face. "Neither," he replied, "will I."

It did not take them long to find the dwarf twins. Whereas the Shamen's original indication of their likely whereabouts proved to be wildly inaccurate, Doon discovered that her memory and sense of direction improved proportionately with the number of times he jabbed her in the buttocks with Leofric's sword.

Once they had located the dwarfs, he released the bony witch. They had no further need of her, and her continual insistence that she had a spell coming ("I've got another one brewing, I can feel it in my bones,") was getting on his nerves. Besides, she was demanding first-aid treatment to the wounds on her bottom, and none of them much fancied the task.

The two twins sat side by side atop the mound, watching the party curiously as they approached. They exchanged knowing looks, as Leofric stepped forwards.

"Which is the safe path through the forest?" he asked.

"The right," Horace told him.

"The left," corrected Hubert, with eyebrows raised in exasperation.

"Are you lying to me?" Leofric enquired, of no one in particular.

"No," they replied in unison.

Leofric thought this answer over for a while, but decided that it didn't help him much. He addressed the white-bearded dwarf.

"Is your friend lying to me?"

"Of course he is," Horace told him. "He always does. He's never told the truth in his life."

"Well, that's it, isn't it?" Leofric asked Doon. "Greybeard's the liar, so we take the right path."

"I am not a liar!" protested Hubert.

"He's right," Doon agreed. "Or at least, he might be. The other one could have been lying when he said he was a liar."

Leofric shook his head in confusion.

"I'm a soldier, not a bloody genius. You sort it out. I've had enough."

Doon stepped forwards. He had had an idea.

"What colour is the grass?" he enquired, cunningly.

The dwarf twins stared at him in pity, but made no answer. Doon tried again.

"I said, what colour is the grass?"

Still no reply.

"Maybe they won't answer obvious questions," Takina suggested. "It would make it too easy. Try asking them something else."

"Is that right?" Doon asked them. "Is that why you refuse to answer me?"

One nodded, the other shook his head.

Halfshaft stood a few feet behind the others. He had sufficiently recovered from shock to be able to stand on his own two feet, but his eyes still looked slightly glazed following his ordeal. He spoke for the first time since leaving the Forest.

"A spell," he murmured.

Nobody quite heard him.

"What was that?" snapped Doon, irritated at the distraction.

"A spell," he repeated. "A truth spell."

Doon snorted derisively. "Excellent idea. Now all we have to do is to find a wizard to perform it!"

"I am a wizard," he snapped back, suddenly animated. "A bloody good one. I am also a warrior. You, on the other hand, are a corpse. A corpse with a nasty habit of turning his back on his friends when they most need you."

Doon regarded him coldly. He was on the verge of replying when Rod intervened.

"Not now, lads. Not when me and Takina have worked out how to get the truth of these awkward little buggers."

"You have?" asked Doon, dubiously.

"We have?" enquired Takina at the same time, more dubiously still.

"We have," Rod replied firmly. He took her by the arm, and led her gently away from the others. They conversed for a minute or two in whispers. Takina's face gradually creased into a frown, and at one point she drew away from the biker, a look of horror on her face.

"No way!" she exclaimed, stepping away from him. "No way am I going to be his bitch!"

He pulled her back towards him, and they spoke in whispers again. Eventually, she stalked from his side, and approached the dwarfs. She bent down by the nearest, put an arm round his shoulders, and put her mouth close to his pudgy little ear. His face lit up as she breathed a sentence or two into it, and within seconds he began to dance an excited jig around the mound, nearly knocking her over in the process. When he finally came to a halt, he beckoned for her to bend back down again, and, after sneaking a quick look down her top, whispered earnestly in her ear. She thanked him, and made her way back to the group.

"It's the left path," she announced, with a hint of a shudder.

Doon was unconvinced.

"Can we be sure of that?"

"After what he made me offer that dirty little dwarf for the truth," she shuddered, "I would be very, very surprised if he's lying!"

They moved off together along the left hand path as directed. Leofric walked alongside Rod and Takina. The narrow path left Halfshaft no choice but to tag moodily along behind them with Doon.

"What did you offer to do to him?" asked Leofric, genuinely intrigued.

"I'm not saying," she told him, blushing furiously. "All you need to know is that I was lying."

Unfortunately, Hubert had been lying, too. The five of them continued along the pathway, unaware of the lethal danger lurking in the trees ahead.

Thane and the Grand Wizard sat in Cyrellius' personal quarters, facing one another across a broad table. A variety of objects were strewn across it, ranging from well-thumbed spell books to phials of steaming potions. Everything there seemed to have some magical use or other. Thane's attention was drawn to a wooden dish nearby, upon which an unsightly gelatinous mound of sickly grey mucus throbbed and pulsated like a melting mutant brain.

"That must be the ingredient for a particularly powerful spell," said Thane, conversationally.

"I'm afraid not," replied the wizard. "It's a boil-in-the-bag dinner."

Thane suppressed a laugh. He had started to relax a little. His weapons had still not been returned, but he had at least been given an opportunity to eat and sleep since his meeting with the King. Thankfully, the food had been nothing like the vile organism which expanded and deflated on the platter before him. He was also starting to trust the Grand Wizard again. If Cyrellius had wanted him dead, he would not have defied the King by keeping the guards at bay. Maybe they could work together after all.

"Shall we return to the business in hand?" Cyrellius enquired.

Thane nodded his assent.

"All right. Can I start by asking you about your parentage?"

"No," Thane declared firmly.

"Your father was a mercenary from your home planet, I understand. Taught you everything you know."

"I don't discuss my family with anyone."

"I am also advised by the Watcher that your mother came from the same planet as Harold. From Earth. That your father was supposed to kill her, but refused. Instead, they ran away together, and you were the result."

"How is this relevant? "

"But they caught up with him in the end, didn't they? And left him with no option but to fulfil his contract. He killed her when you were just eleven."

"And I killed him when I was twelve," Thane retorted grimly. "What's your point?"

"I'm not judging anyone here," Cyrellius reassured him, with a smile that contradicted this. "Their indiscretions, follies and crimes mean nothing to me."

He reached out for his pipe, lit it, and settled back into his chair, deliberately leaving his sentence hanging in the air.

"All I wish to establish," he continued, "is that you are half Earthling."

Thane struggled to keep his temper in check. Controlling your emotions was part of basic training back home. It was just that some people made that training more necessary than others. Emotion is a weakness, he told himself. It is an impediment to carrying out a swift, efficient job. He had succumbed to it once, when he had punished his father, but had promised himself that he would not let it interfere with his profession again. So why did the wizard's gloating reference to his past make him want to seize his pipe and shove it so far down the old man's throat that it would burn his tonsils? Instead, he took a deep breath, and answered the question.

"I am half human, yes."

"Human as in Earthling?"

"Yes."

"Excellent. Then we still have a chance. I need someone to accompany me back to the Black Mountains. I would have liked to go with another wizard, but that's no longer possible. Doon has betrayed me, and never managed to tap into his magical powers anyway. The only other wizard within hundreds of miles of here is Halfshaft, and the least said of his magical abilities, the better. So a mercenary will have to do.

We will travel to the Black Mountains together, and do battle with Chameleon. I will rely on my magic. You will use Harold's sword. As an Earthling, you should be able to wield it."

"I thought the whole point of this was to prevent anyone moving it? Once it's freed, the Warlock gets out."

"There is no choice. Sooner or later, one of your Earthlings will get through. We have to kill the Warlock before that happens. I can't do it on my own. I need your help. You'd be no use without the sword. But with it! The others would have been no assistance; he'd have plucked the sword from their grasp like a toy. But you're a warrior, whatever your other faults may be. Between the two of us, we'll kill him, I know we will."

"I have a price."

"You'll be paid as agreed."

"I have a further price" Thane persisted. "The Earthling who was being held here. If he's still alive, I want him sent back. I'll not see him die. I have my orders from the Watcher."

"He's probably dead already, but if he's survived Trog, you can do what you like with him."

"I'll need a letter from the King, cancelling Trog's orders."

"Trog can't read."

"He doesn't need to. He'll recognise the King's seal."

"True." Cyrellius reflected for a few seconds. "All right the Earthling will be spared if you can reach him in time. I'll get Spartan to give you the letter you want. We'll even leave tomorrow to give you more chance of catching them. That just leaves one matter outstanding. Your apology."

"For what?" asked Thane, temporarily mystified.

"For leaving me to the sharks," the Grand Wizard responded, astonished that the question should even need asking.

Thane sighed. Since the incident with Spartan, he had assumed that this was past history, but Cyrellius was obviously finding it difficult to let it go. He felt that he had more cause to be irritated than the wizard after his family background had been raked up, and was not in the mood to apologise.

"Do we have to go through this again?"

"Yes, we do."

"Look, I'm sorry I had to leave you, but I had no choice. It was you or me, and I wasn't the one who had drunk himself into a coma."

The wizard shifted in his chair, his agitation increasing by the second.

"That was not the apology I was looking for."

Thane shrugged.

"Sorry. That's about as good as I can give. I say it as I see it."

The Grand Wizard stared back at him, his brow creased as he mulled over some moral dilemma. Eventually, he came to a decision.

"I can't accept that as an apology. My honour is at stake here. Apologise properly, or I must challenge you to a duel."

"Not a good idea. If we duel, then one of us dies, and if that happens, who's going to stop your Warlock from escaping? And what was the point of calling off the King's guards, if you're going to try to finish me off instead?"

"I don't want to fight. I have more important things to do. But you've left me with no choice. I won't kill you, just teach you a little humility. And the fact that I called off the King means nothing. It

90

was only his honour at stake, then. This is my reputation we're talking about, now. There's no comparison. I will ask you one more time. Are you prepared to apologise for what you have done?"

"I have nothing to apologise for."

"Then we must duel. And we'll find out just how good you really are, before I make you grovel."

T rog was tired. Very tired. He had entered the Forest the day before, but had come across hazard after hazard. Eventually, it had dawned on him that he fact that he was being attacked on such a regular basis meant that this was very unlikely to be the "Safe" path, and he had started making his way back to give the dwarf twins a piece of his mind and an even bigger piece of his knuckles.

He now faced four or five huge wolves (he was not sure which, since it is difficult to count on your fingers when you're swinging a sword). A fifth (or ninth?) lay dead at his feet, as he tried frantically to free his sword from the carcass before the others attacked. It refused to budge.

The largest of the remaining wolves was now just yards away. Snarling, it crouched on its haunches, ready to leap. Anticipating this, Trog hauled the dead wolf into the air on the point of his sword, and thrust it forwards. The advancing wolf faltered, suddenly finding its path of trajectory blocked by its deceased second cousin, once removed. Whilst it pondered its next move, Trog took the opportunity to smite it on the head with its dead relative using sufficient force to knock it off its feet (or paws, as the case may be).

Another member of the pack saw its chance, and darted forwards, jaws agape. They knew he couldn't last much longer. They had been fighting him for three hours, and though he had killed several of their number, they knew that more were on their way. But more wolves meant less troll meat to go round, and they meant to finish him off quickly if they could.

With reflexes which belied his size, Trog brought the wolf carcass round in an arc, thrusting it into his assailant's muzzle. The creature shied away, frustrated, trying to shake the matted fur from its mouth.

Trog calculated how long it would take him to put the dead wolf down, place a foot on it, and withdraw his sword from its bloodied flesh. About the same time, he decided, that it would take four(ish) hungry wolves to shred him to pieces.

He took another swipe at the nearest creature. Fortunately, the centrifugal force sent the dead wolf flying off his blade, and sailing into the branches of a nearby tree.

Trog whirled back round to face his tormentors, a grin of triumph on his face. His sword was free again.

"Come on, then," he invited. "Which of you wants it first?"

The two creatures which had already been bashed by their dead relative remained on the attack, snapping and snarling just out of reach of his swinging blade. Another two remained a few paces back, exchanging knowing glances with one another. They were older and wiser than their impetuous cousins. They knew the danger of this sword, and had no wish to end up dangling from the nearest tree with blood matting their hides. They knew that reinforcements were on their way, and had decided that the time had come to await the cavalry. When the rest of the pack arrived, the end would come quickly.

A howl in the distance told them that they would not have long to wait.

Rana was regretting taking Trugga with her. She may have been the strongest Amazon in the village, but she was particularly thickset for her race, and was not really designed for travelling cross-country at speed. Without her, Rana could have overtaken the other Amazons before they had even come in sight of the Forest. As it was, she had missed out on their battle with Leofric and his companions, and all the prisoners had vanished by the time she arrived on the scene.

Her warriors had gone, of course. They knew the price of failure – especially against a group of men! – and, in the Amazon way, they had stripped naked and walked into the dense, brooding Forest to end their lives. All they had left behind was a neat pile of squirrel skins, and a bear-claw necklace. The Shamen was still there, though, much to Rana's surprise. She explained that she had stripped off with the others, and strode into the trees after them, but for some reason the woods had spat her back out again, making a sort of "urgh" sound in the process. She assumed that the trees could simply not digest her, in view of the amount of magic which crackled inside her, and indeed even now she could sense a spell brewing. Rana, who was forced to face the naked old hag as she gave her account, was tempted to tell her the more likely explanation for the Forest being reluctant to swallow her bony arse, but contented herself with cuffing the useless crone and sending her back to the village.

The prisoners trail was still fresh. She shook her head in disbelief upon discovering that they had made no effort to hide it. They were almost begging to be caught. They now outnumbered her three to one (five to one if you counted the wizard and Takina, which she didn't), but she was still confident. If they wanted her to catch them, then she didn't mean to disappoint them.

She caught sight of them in the far distance just as they disappeared into the Forest. They showed no signs of noticing her behind them. She urged on Trugga with increasing frustration, as the big Amazon stumped her way awkwardly over the grass in pursuit. She was desperate not to lose her prey now they were almost within her reach. Grimly, Trugga laboured on by her side, anxious not to let her Queen down in her moment of need. She was not at all keen at having to strip off and walk into the Forest, and was not at all sure that she would fit between the trees in any case. The idea of being wedged between a couple of oaks, her bare butt protruding into the grassy meadows outside, was too horrendous to contemplate. Especially with cellulite like hers!

They reached the grass track which the prisoners had taken into the Great Forest, encountering the dwarf twins shortly afterwards. One of them sat sulkily with his back to the other, his head in his hands as he scowled into the distance.

"Horace and Hubert!" Trugga exclaimed in wonderment. "Then the legend is true!"

"No it's not," Hubert snapped at them irritably. "They left years ago. I'm Pigeonscratch, and this is my uncle, King Wilbur Pus-head the Third. How can I help you?"

"Did you tell those men the safe path through the Forest?" Rana asked.

"Yes," Horace chipped in.

"Which is it, then? Which way's safe?"

"They're both safe now," Hubert assured her, "but the safest is the one on the left."

"That's what I figured, Rana told them. That's where the tracks go."

Trugga was still breathing heavily.

"We couldn't just wait here for a minute or two, could we?" she asked. "Just until we've got our breath back?"

Rana snorted dismissively.

"Well never catch them if I have to keep stopping for you. You stay here, and watch my back. I'll go after them on my own. Make sure no-one comes in after me to help them."

The tracks where the pathway divided were starting to blur. It was almost as if the Forest were trying to obliterate them. Rana knew that she would have to press on quickly, and catch the prisoners before all trace of them was gone. She was outnumbered, but she had the element of surprise. Besides, Leofric was the only one of them who was likely to pose any danger to her at all.

She disappeared into the great Forest, leaving Trugga on guard behind her. They would never see each other again.

Thane sat alone in the chamber which earlier that week had been used for Halfshaft's duel with the Grand Wizard. A noisy crowd had gathered outside, staring curiously in at him through the open door. Everyone wanted to see the man who was foolish enough to take on the most powerful wizard the Castle had seen in centuries, as long as it left them enough time to buy a toffee apple before the contest started.

"He doesn't look simple, Arthur," one ruddy-faced woman remarked to the man standing by her side. "You can usually tell the simple ones, you know."

"That's true enough," he agreed. "But my name's not Arthur, and never has been to my knowledge."

"No, I can see that now," she told him. "Arthur's my husband, and now I come to think of it, you're a little taller than him. And you haven't got his nose at all."

"I don't suppose I have," the man nodded sagely, before lapsing into silence.

"Where's the wizard anyway, Arthur?" the woman persisted. "He should be here before the King. It's traditional. King Spartan won't like it, if he's kept waiting."

On cue, the King crossed the courtyard towards them, the Grand Wizard striding along beside him. They were arguing between themselves, the King doing his best to suppress his anger, and keep his voice down. Those in the crowd who felt they could get away with it winked at their neighbours. They had heard the rumours that the two men had fallen out. There would be plenty of scope for gossip when they were a safer distance from the King.

The bickering couple reached the crowd in a few more strides, and it parted like the Red Sea before them, allowing them to pass through its midst to the mouth of the duelling chamber. Cyrellius, grasping his infamous pipe, took his place inside, whilst his monarch took the opportunity to regain his composure.

Spartan raised his hand, demanding silence of his subjects. Since they could no longer talk about him, there was nothing much they wanted to say in any case, so they had actually been silent for some time already.

The King had his speech prepared. The Grand Wizard had duelled on several previous occasions, and he had introduced each duel in much the same way. However, the respectful awe of the assembled crowed towards their sovereign was in such stark contrast to the arrogant treatment which he had received from his friend of late, that he decided that an edited version of the speech would suffice. He did not feel inclined to dwell for long on the attributes of the wizard who seemed so intent on using those attributes against him.

"We all know why we are here. One of our number claims to have been wronged. He has challenged the person responsible to a duel. Let God be with the man who is in the right."

"God be with him," approved the assembly, knowing this part off by heart.

"On my right, we have Cyrellius, the Grand Wizard, Guardian of the Gates, and holder of many other honourable titles."

A slight frown crossed the wizard's face, as he tried to master his irritation at his numerous splendid titles being summarised in such an arbitrary fashion. He hadn't even mentioned him being a prefect, for goodness sake!

"To my left, we have Thane. He is here on a secret mission, of which I can tell you nothing at this stage."

Further meaningful looks were swapped by those about him, and he smiled broadly, pleased at the intrigue he had skilfully introduced to the proceedings. Just as he was about to capitalise on this, Rufford appeared at the edge of the crowd, pushing his way roughly through it towards him. Spartan glared at him as he came to a halt at his side, message in hand. The King coughed meaningfully, and all eyes returned to him at once.

Once again, the King raised his hand into the air. At the click of his fingers, the door of the chamber would be closed and the duel would commence. He was determined not to hurry the moment. His subjects watched on in uneasy anticipation.

"May the best man win," he said.

"Thank you," Cyrellius replied.

His fingers clicked, the chamber door slammed shut, and Thane was plunged into foreboding darkness.

"Hang on," he heard a man cry out from outside. Was it the King? Would Spartan stop the duel after all?

"I reckon," the voice continued, "that I might be Arthur after all!"

T he Forest path had narrowed, and they had no option but to walk in single-file. Leofric covered the front of the column, wary of ambush, followed by Rod. Doon insisted on walking behind the biker, refusing to let him out of his sight. Halfshaft followed at a slight distance, loathe to get too close to the corpse, with Takina just behind him.

Halfshaft was not surprised to discover that he had developed a fear of trees since the incident earlier that day. He kept as far as he could from the branches which bordered both sides of the path, but now that it was so narrow, he was finding it increasingly difficult to keep his nerve. He had discovered, however, that he could just about keep a grip on things by keeping his mind occupied with something else. For this reason – why else? – he had for the past hour been experimenting to find out how loudly he could say the word "bastard" without Doon overhearing him. It had only taken three attempts before he was first overheard, but he decided to carry on anyway. He was going to vary the exercise later on, in any case. Rod had taught him the word "git", and it would be a shame to waste it.

After a while, he realised that Takina had come to a halt behind him. He returned to her side, and followed her gaze. Doon glanced over his shoulder as he dropped back, but said nothing to discourage them from separating from the others. It was for the best; he wasn't about to take orders from a git-bastard corpse, anyway.

Through the trees, he could just about make out the wall of a log cabin. His surprise at seeing the cabin was only matched by his shock that it was made of wood. It would take a pretty brave person to go wood chopping in these parts!

"I think we should stop here for the night," said Takina. "It won't be light much longer. It's dark enough here during the day-time, but if we press ahead at night, we could wander off the path, and you know what that means."

Halfshaft nodded, happy to trust her judgment. He liked her warmth and honesty. Even more to the point, he sensed that she had taken an instant dislike to Doon and that was enough in his book to mark her out as a friend for life!

"Can you bring the others back here?" she asked.

"Leave it to me."

He selected a stone from the pathway, and lobbed it at Doon's departing head. He cursed in disappointment as Doon came to a sudden halt, the stone arching over his shoulder and dropping heavily to the ground a yard or two ahead of him.

"I'll try again," he assured her, stooping to the ground to collect some more ammunition.

"Something's wrong," frowned his new Amazon friend. "Why've they stopped?"

"They've realised we're missing, I expect."

She raised her eyebrows enquiringly.

"Do you really think they'd wait for either of us?"

"Maybe not," he conceded. "So what's going on, then?"

As he spoke, Doon turned around, and dashed frantically back down the path towards them, with Rod and Leofric hard on his heels.

"Leg it!" shouted Rod

Takina and Halfshaft stepped back involuntarily into the trees to allow the others to pass them by. Both knew they should run, but felt an overwhelming urge to find out what they were actually running from before they took flight. Their line of vision was at first blocked by the fleeing threesome, and it was not until Leofric had scampered past them that they were afforded an uninterrupted view of the cause of his concern. Their mouths fell open in unison.

"I think we'd better run," Takina suggested.

"Yes," agreed Halfshaft wisely, surprising himself how calm his voice sounded. "And pretty bloody soon, too!"

Less than one hundred yards in front of them, an eight-foot troll-cross bounded down the pathway towards them. A large pack of wolves swarmed along behind him, their fangs bared and hackles raised. Looking back over his shoulder as he ran, he swatted the nearest of them with his sword, knocking it off balance just as it was making a lunge for his right thigh. Sweat poured from his brow as he thundered on in their direction.

Takina seized Halfshaft's wrist and hauled him away from the path, heading for the cabin she had spotted earlier. At first he resisted, pulling away from the twisted tree trunks in horror, but as the troll bore down upon them he gave in and followed her lead. They stumbled forwards through the dense undergrowth, keeping their feet more by momentum than design. Seconds later, Trog shot past the spot at which they had been standing, still trying to keep at least one sizeable troll stride ahead of the score of black creatures which snapped at his heels.

Two of the wolves banked off from the pack in pursuit of the wizard and the Amazon, sensing easier prey. Halfshaft had almost reached the cabin when he caught his foot in a twisted vine, sending him sprawling forwards on to the ground. Takina still had hold of his wrist, and as he fell, he jerked her backwards. For a second, she twisted in mid-air, before landing heavily on her right side and stomach, the wind knocked out of her. They lay on the ground together, helpless and vulnerable, as the wolves hurtled through the trees towards them.

Things were not looking good.

Thane knew he would have to act quickly. He could not afford to kill the Grand Wizard, if he was going to get paid at the end of the day. Instead, he would have to immobilise him. It was, he knew from experience, quite impossible to immobilise a fire-breathing dragon, and his only hope was therefore to set upon the wizard before he had the chance to shape-shift. That meant acting pretty quickly.

Before the duel he had done his homework. The Grand Wizard changed shape by stamping his feet. Best to make sure, then, that foot stamping was impossible.

He went into action straight away. Leaping across the chamber, he seized the surprised wizard by the scruff of the neck, and pitched him roughly to the floor. Cyrellius cried out in outrage, as he tried to get back to his feet, but before he had got to his hands and knees, Thane was upon him again. With one hand, he tugged the belt from the wizard's gown, using his other arm to keep Cyrellius pinned to the ground.

The Grand Wizard tried to make a stamping motion with one foot. It did not matter that he was lying on his stomach, and that the sole of his foot would not strike terra firma. It was the stamping motion itself which would activate the spell. In an instant, he would be a griffin; half lion, half eagle. In the next, the mercenary would be pleading for his life.

Thane was one step ahead of him. The moment Cyrellius' leg moved, he seized it and pushed the ankle hard against the wizard's upper thigh, the other ankle following it immediately afterwards. Leaning on these limbs to keep them firmly in place, he grabbed the Grand Wizard's wrists, forcing them behind his back. He then held the various struggling limbs together by pinning them down with his chest, whilst he set to work with the belt, lashing them all tightly together.

Cyrellius rocked back and forth on his stomach, bound like an indignant pig on an abbatoir floor. Once again, he was prevented from stamping his foot to set his spell in motion: first as a cobra, then as a shark, now as a wizard hog-tied hand and foot. But this time, he was ready for it. In view of his recent practice, the spell came to him effortlessly. Two sentences and he would change shape into a griffin, whether he could stamp or not. And then Thane would learn that duelling with a first-grade wizard was a very serious undertaking indeed.

"Farwani Dias Arg..." he began. Sadly, the sock which Thane unceremoniously shoved into his mouth prevented the spell from reaching its natural conclusion. The Grand Wizard's (muffled) scream of frustration told the mercenary all he needed to know. His plan had worked. The duel was won.

He tore off the excess cord from Cyrellius' belt, and used it to tie the gag in place. The wizard glared up at him, his eyes oozing impotent malevolence.

"And for your information," Thane told him, "he wasn't my real father, anyway. But I don't suppose you want to make any comment about that, right now."

Without further ado, he rolled the trussed-up wizard neatly into a corner, threw the chamber door wide open, and went in search of the King.

Once the duelling chamber doors were closed, Spartan turned his attention to the message which Rufford had brought him. He was still seething at the wizard's decision to fight the mercenary. Why should Cyrellius risk the Earthman's life when he had admonished his Sovereign for doing the same thing hours earlier? There could be only one answer. The Grand Wizard was indifferent to what happened to Thane, and his only purpose in intervening on his behalf must therefore have been to humiliate the King. If that were so, then this could not go unpunished. But how, he wondered, could he ever hope to punish the Grand Wizard of Spartan? And even if he could manage it, who would that leave to protect the Castle? Not his guards, that was for sure. He could not even be certain of their loyalty after their refusal to obey his orders earlier that day, and if there was one thing worse than incompetent soldiers it was incompetent soldiers who would not do what they were told.

The interruption by Rufford had not been welcome, either. He enjoyed duels. They were state occasions, which helped him show his majesty and power to the people. Rufford had stopped him in mid-flow, which was never a good thing to happen. But for the fact that his acting Captain of the Guard was probably the only half-decent soldier left under his command, he might have had him executed on the spot. He consoled himself with the thought that when Trog returned, he could still have Rufford executed on the spot. It would be a different spot, granted, but you couldn't have everything.

He read the message that was handed to him:

"Your Highness,
We have captured a tradesman. Under gentle torture, he has confessed that he has news of the escaped prisoner. Do you require an audience with him, before I take his stomach out?
Yours very respectfully indeed,
J.Hacker (Chief Torturer, and Purveyor of Novelty Thumb Screws)"

Intrigued, Spartan sent Rufford to fetch the tradesman, and bring him (or what was left of him) to the throne-room. The King went on ahead, positioning himself magisterially on the throne, so as to leave his guest in no doubt of the severity of his position. The tradesman arrived within minutes, looking disappointingly healthy. He stood sandwiched between Rufford and Hacker, fidgeting nervously as he waited for Spartan to speak.

"And who are you?" enquired the King.

"They call me Nik'Nak, your Honour, Sir. It's not my real name, just a nickname. A Nik'Nak nickname, so to speak. My real name's Nik'Nak'Natius. After my Dad, Bob Biggleswade."

"What do you do?"

"I trade in furs, your potent Magnificence. Nothing else. No spying or nothing. Just furs. Sir."

"Who said anything about spying?" asked the King, triumphantly. "Do I sense a guilty conscience?"

"Why he did, your Abundance. That kind gentleman there, who has just been whacking me about the testicles with a garden fork. He mentioned spying on a number of occasions, unless I'm very much mistaken, begging your pardon, your Royal Whatsitness."

Hacker spluttered in indignation at his side. He stuck his thumbs in both Nik'Nak's ears, and gouged them for all he was worth. The tradesman writhed miserably in a futile attempt to fend off the onslaught without giving offence to his torturer.

"That is a lie, your Highness!" Hacker exploded. "I whacked him about the testicles with a pitchfork. I wouldn't whack someone's testicles with a garden fork if you paid me!"

"I do pay you," Spartan pointed out wearily, "and I have no more interest in your garden spade or pitchfork than I have in this man's testicles. Neither are of any significance here."

"I wouldn't say my testicles were insignificant, your Stupendousness," Nik'Nak interjected, a touch hurt. "I've had some very complimentary remarks made about my..."

"Enough," the King told him, in a voice of which Simon Cowell would have been proud. "Tell me why you are here. Start from the beginning. Speak slowly, but not so slowly as to bore me. Lie, and you die. Go."

Nik'Nak started speaking, but stammered in panic when he realised that he was going too fast, and contorted in terror when he

101

decided that his stammering fit might bore Spartan. Eventually, he took a deep breath, covered his ears to prevent a further assault by Hacker, and tried again.

"I'm a merchant, your Majesty, as I've said. I trade with the Amazons. They need squirrel skins, you see, and all those furry little devils have got too much sense to hang around near the village. So I trap them, and sell them to the Amazons for gold. I don't make much, you understand, Sir. They don't need me often. They only want just enough squirrel to cover their modesty, and seeing as how they've got so little modesty, then it doesn't take many squirrels to cover it up."

Spartan yawned threateningly, and the trader scurried on with his tale.

"Anyway, I went to the outskirts of the village this morning. They won't let me enter it. Tell me that if I set foot in it, I'd be mated with and slaughtered. My wife's not keen on them girls taking advantage of me, you know. Gets jealous. I'm not insignificant, no matter what you might have been told, and she wants to keep me all to herself."

"Hang him," interrupted Spartan. "He's boring me, already."

"No, no wait, I'm coming to the point now, your Mighty, Magnificent, Eminence, Sir. Whilst I was standing nearby waiting for someone to come over to barter with me, I had a bit of a listen. As you do."

"I have people," the King told him testily, "who do that for me. What did you hear?"

"From what I could gather," Nik'Nak went on, "they captured a wizard yesterday. He had a couple of friends with him. He fought against their mightiest warrior, and they had to carry her off on a stretcher. And then he escaped overnight. With Leofric, his two companions, and he even took one of the young Amazon girls with him as well, just in case he got a bit frisky on the way. Rana herself has gone after them."

"Did anyone mention a troll?" Spartan enquired.

"No," Nik'Nak apologised. "Wish they had done, if that's what you wanted, but unfortunately no-one said anything about that at the time. I can go back and ask, though."

"Never mind. You have done well to tell me all of this," the King assured him. I will release you in two years time, as a token of my generosity."

"Thank you, your Highness," bowed Nik'Nak, genuinely grateful despite having been captured, tortured, and having his pride and joy pitch-forked/garden-spaded. It was all part of the job. He could claim on his insurance (this had to be worth at least two goats and a sheep-skin rug), and if nothing else, it would make a very entertaining story to tell any children he might still be capable of having. Things weren't so bad after all.

"In the meantime," Spartan went on, "I'm sure Hacker here can find some where for you to stay, where you won't get into too much mischief."

Hacker gave a wide grin, put a friendly arm around Nik'Nak's shoulders, and helped Rufford escort the tradesman from the chamber. The merchant was clearly having trouble telling the difference between one garden implement and another, and Hacker was just the man to help him. He had two years to teach him all he knew. Secateurs might be a good place to start.

As they left, Spartan made his plans. He had always known that there was more to Halfshaft than met the eye, but Cyrellius had always talked him down. Now, the reason was clear. The Grand Wizard was frightened that he might not be so indispensable after all. So Halfshaft had defeated an Amazon in combat, and led his friends out of the tribe's village stronghold? By magical means no doubt. And all of this after vanquishing the Grand Wizard in front of the King's very eyes. Cyrellius never had, he realised, ever explained this defeat to him.

Could it possibly be that Halfshaft was superior to Cyrellius in wizardry? If so, then he could be the new Grand Wizard and he – the King – would have a new, pliable magician at his side again. It would, however, be a terrible risk to cross Cyrellius, especially in view of his recent treacherous behaviour. If Halfshaft was not up to the task of usurping the Grand Wizard's position, then Cyrellius' revenge would be swift and sure. Still, if he played it right, he could always blame everything on Halfshaft, and insist that it had had nothing to do with him personally. That might work.

Whilst he pondered these matters, Rufford returned.

"Grave news, your Highness. The mercenary has defeated the Grand Wizard."

"Defeated? Again? But they've only been in there for fifteen minutes! Where is Cyrellius now?"

"Still in the duelling chamber, Sire. Bound, gagged, and helpless. I was just about to order his release."

"No, stop," commanded the King. "Leave him where he is for the time being. I have some serious thinking to do."

Leofric, Rod and Doon fled wildly down the path, closely pursued by the flailing troll. He gained on them with each huge step, just as surely as the wolf pack was closing in on him. In a matter of seconds, he would mow them down, leaving them to the mercy of the wolves.

Leofric decided that further retreat was futile. As they retraced their steps, the path widened again, and he judged that there was now enough space for the three of them to stand side by side to fight for their lives. He had his sword, Doon had his knife, and the stranger seemed to be pretty good at improvising. They wouldn't stand a great chance of survival, but it had to be better than being flattened from behind by a fleeing troll.

He came to a halt, bidding Doon and Rod to do likewise. Doon carried on running, ignoring him completely. Rod paused only long enough to tell him to stop being a "pratt", and to "leg it."

Assistance came from an unexpected quarter. Instead of trampling him into the ground, Trog stopped beside him, spinning round to face the fast approaching pack. The two of them stood shoulder to shoulder, Captains of the Guard past and present, united in their determination to take the fight back to the enemy. They exchanged glances. Each knew instinctively that whatever their differences, they would stand or fall together.

The wolves were upon them. Razor sharp teeth slashed at them, cutting their limbs and bodies time and time again. The ferocity of the assault drove them backwards step by step, overcome by the sheer numbers of their foes. Every wolf that fell before them was replaced by two others. Grimly, they fought on.

The path continued to widen by degrees, and Leofric became aware that the creatures were trying to outflank him. Although the trees at this point were impenetrable, it would not be long before the path would be wide enough to allow the wolves to pass them by, and once they were encircled they were as good as dead.

They separated slightly, each staying parallel to the nearest edge of the track to prevent the wolves from squeezing through. Within minutes, it struck Leofric that they had wandered too far apart. Tiredly, he tried to fight his way back towards Trog, but all to no avail. Three or four huge black wolves had formed a wedge between them, and were driving their way through the gap to part them forever. The end was in sight.

Suddenly, the wolves faltered, and the wedge loosened and broke amidst snarls of violent frustration. From the corner of his eye, he could see a sword flashing left and right, wielded by he knew not whom. Under this renewed onslaught, the pack lost their momentum. Those in the front line realised that they were now in serious danger, and backed away, incurring the wrath of their comrades behind them. Fighting broke out in the ranks. Before long, the mob disintegrated altogether, taking flight back down the path with a chorus of muted growls and whimpers. The last of them disappeared from view, and all was quiet again.

Leofric turned to his left, curious to see who had filled the breach in such a decisive fashion.

"I should have known," he said to himself, as he identified his rescuer. "No-one else could handle a sword like that,"

"But you came close," came the reply.

He became aware that Trog was staring at the newcomer with the greatest of suspicion, and decided that an introduction was in order before his new troll comrade tried to fight her or eat her. Besides, there was the Soldiers' Code to think of.

"Trog," he announced. "It's my great pleasure to introduce you to Rana, Queen of the Amazons."

When Takina started to pull him towards the cabin, Halfshaft's first impulse had been to resist at all costs. The trees, he reminded himself, were not particularly keen on him. Seeking shelter amongst them would be about as good an idea as a virgin strolling over to a dragon to ask for directions.

His second impulse, however, was to run like buggery. He was, after all, particularly adept at this, having had plenty of practice at it before he had become a great warrior.

It was not until he had collapsed to the ground in terror that it occurred to him that great warriors were not supposed to run like buggery, or to run like anything else for that matter. Lucky I remembered in time, he thought to himself. Otherwise I could have made a total prat of myself.

He struggled back up to his feet. His saucepan was tied to the belt around his waist, and he fumbled with the knot as the wolves came crashing through the undergrowth towards him. As they closed in, the knot loosened, and the saucepan tumbled to the ground. As he bent down to retrieve it, the closest wolf launched itself at him, ready to tear his head from his shoulders with its powerful jaws. Instead, it tasted cold steel.

Halfshaft looked up as he heard the creature yelp. The wolf lay still on the grass before him, its breathing shallow and irregular. Its companion fled, tail between its legs, fearing the same fate.

He turned to Takina to thank her for saving his life again. He was puzzled to find that she was still on the floor. Puzzlement turned to anxiety as he realised that she was staring at something over his shoulder. Anxiety turned to fear very soon afterwards, when he turned round to see what it was.

He was struck most of all by the man's size. He was no taller than Halfshaft, but was as broad as a bull, with a face to match. His fore-arms were the thickest that the wizard had ever seen (not that he had made a study of such things) and the shovel clasped in his giant hands had clearly be used with such force as to knock the wolf out cold. This was not the type of man to tackle with a dented saucepan.

Takina rose to her feet slowly, not wishing to startle him back into action. Halfshaft stayed stock still, not wishing the man to star-tle him.

They regarded each other for what seemed an eternity. What were the man's intentions, he wondered. Would he seize them and drag them into the cabin as helpless captives? Would he set upon them there and then, knocking Halfshaft senseless, and taking advantage of his barely dressed companion (or worse still, knock out Takina, and take advantage of *him*)? Just how hideous was their fate to be?

"I'm Harkwell," their intimidating rescuer replied. "Pleased to meet you. Fancy a cup of tea?"

Several seconds passed before either of them thought to reply, such was their surprise at this unexpectedly friendly greeting.

"I'm Takina, and this is my friend, Halfshaft. We really are very grateful for your help, but we must be on our way. The others may need our help."

"Good," he beamed. "The wife will be so pleased to have company. We've been on our own since we lost our daughter."

"No, I'm sorry, you don't quite seem to have heard me. We have to be on our way."

"You want it strong today? I bet you do, my Dear. I can tell that from your boyfriend here! No, only joking, you were talking about the tea, weren't you? You can have it strong as you like. Now come on in, we can't stand out here all afternoon chatting like fishwives, can we? The wolves might be back, and I hate them bloody things. Make my flesh crawl, they do."

Takina and Halfshaft exchanged glances, as Harkwell looked benevolently on.

"We might as well go in," he resolved. "There's not much the two of us can do against all those wolves. Maybe we could chat up his wife, and get her to send him out to help Rod."

"Okay," Takina told Harkwell. "But we can't stay long."

Harkwell gave her a playful slap on the back, which nearly knocked her off her feet,

"That was a bit cheeky," he remarked, winking theatrically. "And me a married man!"

On this strange note, he turned, and led his two reluctant guests into the cabin.

Spartan received Thane into the throne room about an hour after Nik'Nak's departure. Thane was surprised at the King's change of mood. He had expected him to be even colder than before, now that his champion had been dispatched in such effortless fashion. Instead, he was all smiles, greeting him in such a familiar fashion that he almost forgot that Spartan had been trying to set the guards on him earlier that day. Almost forgot, but not quite. As usual, the more friendly someone was to him, the more the bone-crunchers in the Black Orchard came to mind. The King was not to be trusted.

"I'm so pleased that you succeeded in your duel," Spartan purred. "It shows that my faith in you was justified. I have chosen well."

"Congratulations," Thane replied, trying not to sound too sarcastic.

"I have spoken with the Grand Wizard since your contest, and he now realises that he is not as strong as he thought. He will be unable to accompany you to the Black Mountains after all. I'm sure you will not mind travelling alone."

"And when I get there?"

"You will be assisted in your labours by another wizard. His name is Halfshaft. The Grand Wizard may not have spoken highly of him, but there may be a touch of shall we say "professional jealousy" there. I have proof that he is actually a very powerful magician indeed. When you leave, you must take with you a letter addressed to Halfshaft. You should overtake him on your way, since I have reason to believe that he is travelling to the Black Mountains as well. The letter tells him everything he will need to know to assist you."

"I need another letter from you," Thane replied. "I wish to save the stranger you found recently, the one who escaped from your dungeons. I want to send him back to his own world. Trog must be told to spare him, and return here."

A flash of panic sparked in the King's eyes, but was mastered in an instant. He did not want the mercenary to see it. But deep down, he was shaken. He had forgotten all about Trog. What if the troll had already caught and killed the wizard? All the plans he had made since Cyrellius' defeat would go to waste. If Halfshaft was dead, then he would have no choice but to reinstate the Grand Wizard, and since he had left him bound and gagged in the duelling chamber for the past hour, this might not be the easiest of things to do. Cyrellius would be very, very angry by now. And Spartan was scared.

"You will have your letter," he promised. "It will guarantee your stranger will go unharmed, if he is still alive by the time you find him."

It will also, thought Spartan, instruct the troll to keep away from Halfshaft. Surely the wizard could not have been killed already? If he was as good as the merchant would have him believe, then he should have been able to survive an attack from a lumbering troll cross!

A new thought occurred to him. Trog should have returned by now. Maybe he had already attacked Halfshaft, and been killed in the process. He breathed a sigh of relief, comforted by the idea. It showed that there was hope for his plans yet.

"There is one other thing which I would like you to take with you. I have here a phial of Cyrellius' healing potion. It was found in his chamber. I mean, he found it in his chamber. It protects against all injuries, save for those inflicted by magical means. You may find it useful. We wouldn't want you dying before you even reach the mountains, would we?"

"How weak is the Grand Wizard? I don't want to sound mercenary, no pun intended, but he's the one responsible for arranging payment of my fee."

"He will live. You will be paid. But you must complete your task first. Cash on delivery, I believe that those are your terms?"

Thane nodded

"Then we are agreed. You'll have your knives back. You can set off at dawn. And I will see it to it that you are paid, if you come back alive."

"I'll come back, all right," the mercenary assured him. "I always do."

Harkwell showed them proudly around his cabin. It was dark inside – the only light coming from a couple of candles which were arranged tastefully around the living room – but Halfshaft and Takina could see well enough to convince themselves that their host was very house-proud.

The table was – rather disconcertingly – set for four, as if he had been expecting them. Each item of cutlery had been placed into position with perfect precision. The plates remained on the dresser (an item of furniture which was unfamiliar to both the wizard and the Amazon), each stacked carefully at precisely equal distances from the others. Even his selection of picks and shovels had been secured neatly to the wall on hooks, running from left to right in strict order of size. The only thing in the room which might be said to be untidy was the skeleton which had been propped up on a seat by the stove, and even this had its legs placed primly together, its hands positioned one on top of the other in its lap.

Harkwell took his place at the table, motioning for the others to join him.

"She keeps this place so tidy," he told them in a whisper, as if afraid that the skeleton might overhear. "I keep telling her that she needn't spend so much time on housework, that she should get out more, but she won't listen. I think she's at her happiest when she's about her chores, you know."

"Where is your wife, Mr Harkwell?" Takina asked politely, resisting the urge to tell him from bitter experience that no self-respecting woman would want to do housework when she could be out fighting battles instead.

"That's probably her in the corner, by the stove," Halfshaft joked inappropriately, nodding towards the skeleton. Harkwell noticed the gesture, and leapt to his feet in agitation.

"How very rude of me!" he exclaimed. "We don't get many visitors here, as you can imagine, and I sometimes forget my manners. I should have formally introduced you from the start. Please forgive me."

Without waiting for either of them to confirm their forgiveness, he dashed across the room, hugged the skeleton tenderly to his waist, and brought it back to the table with him. He positioned it carefully on the chair between his and the wizard's, resting its bony hands on the spotless tablecloth.

"Boy, girl, boy, girl," he grinned, pointing at each of them in return. "That's the right seating plan for a dinner party, isn't it? Now then, this is my wife, Bonnie."

"Bony, more like," quipped Halfshaft.

Harkwell spun round to face him. For a second, Halfshaft was convinced that he had been overheard. Once again, his big mouth had dropped him in it up to his neck. He had seen what this man had done to the wolves. Despite his new found confidence in his fighting abilities, a punch-up with Harkwell was not the most appealing of prospects. In fact, it was about the least appealing prospect he could think of, short of an intimate game of Twister with the Grand Wizard and Doon.

Harkwell's face cleared almost as quickly as it had clouded.

"Know me?" he asked incredulously. "Of course she knows me! We've been married for twenty years!"

He gave Takina a quizzical look.

"Is this wizard friend of yours always this slow on the uptake? Anyway, who's for tea, then?"

Halfshaft was beginning to wonder whether he would have been better off taking his chances with the wolves. The same thought had obviously occurred to Takina, as she fidgeted uncomfortably by his side. He was quite relieved that she had drawn the short straw and was sitting next to Harkwell. He much preferred sitting by the skeleton. It had a much lower capacity for acting strangely than her husband.

"Pour the tea, Dear," Harkwell bid his long dead spouse.

They sat there awhile, the skeleton showing no sign of doing what it was told. Embarrassed, Takina went to stand up to fetch the kettle from the stove, but Harkwell placed a heavy hand on her forearm, and pushed her firmly back down to her seat.

"Best leave it to the wife," he confided. "She'll get jealous if she thinks you're trying to take over her kitchen. Besides, you're our guests. Aren't they, Dear?"

"Dear" didn't answer. Harkwell seemed to have heard some sort of reply, though, for he chuckled merrily at her silent riposte, and went to fetch the teacups from the dresser himself. He positioned them symmetrically about the tabletop, and took his place again at his wife's side.

"You've got some very interesting furniture here," said Halfshaft, trying to steer the conversation back to sanity. "And these cups are unusual, too. I've never seen anything quite like them before."

Harkwell did not reply. Instead, he gazed to his left, staring Takina full in the face. Half a minute passed without him taking his eyes from hers, and she shifted uncomfortably, searching the room for a potential weapon. Her eyes lit upon the row of shovels on the wall-rack. She pushed her chair back a few inches, to give her the space she needed to make a break for them if she needed to defend herself. But when she looked back towards Harkwell, it struck her that he now appeared to be staring at her right ear. His eyes had not followed hers when she moved. It occurred to her that he had not been looking at her at all, but was simply in some sort of trance.

Halfshaft reached the same conclusion at much the same time. They exchanged glances, like two little children ready to simultaneously feign illness so as to be excused from the dinner table before the sprouts came out.

"Do you think he'd notice if we go?" he whispered.

"I don't know. What do you think?"

"Well he certainly won't hear us!"

They sat still, neither having plucked up the courage to make the first move.

"I will, if you will," Takina promised, nodding towards the door. She was not the first woman to have told him that, and it got him into trouble every time.

They got slowly to their feet, and crossed to the exit. Halfshaft twisted the handle. It refused to budge. He tried again, a little harder this time, without success. He turned to her, a look of stifled panic on his face.

"I think he's locked it!"

Takina pushed past him, took the handle, and twisted it to one side, pushing hard at the door at the same time. It stayed closed. She pushed again, and this time Halfshaft threw his weight against it, in a frantic attempt to force it open. It remained securely shut.

She cast her eyes round the room, searching for something she could use to lever it open. As she did so, she realised that Harkwell was staring her full in the face again. She stepped to one side, to see if his eyes followed her. They did. She tapped the wizard on the shoulder, but he shrugged her off.

"In a minute. I'll just give it another go, first."

He launched himself at the door, rattling furiously at the door handle, trying to kick his way out through the wooden panels at the same time. She tapped him on the shoulder again, and he spun round in frustration, his hand still on the doorknob, to find out what she wanted. She inclined her head towards Harkwell. His eyes followed hers, until they alighted on the powerful man sitting at the table. The ominous expression on their host's face told him that he was not happy.

"What the Devil's going on, there?" Harkwell thundered.

The wizard gulped, swallowing down the lump of pure guilt in his throat.

"Just admiring your handles," Halfshaft assured him. "Interesting choice of wood. Lovely finish."

"Candles made of wood? Are you mad?"

He turned to Takina.

"I hate to say this, young lady, but you really could do better. Your boyfriend's an idiot."

"He's not my boyfriend."

"And I'm not an idiot," Halfshaft added. "The only stupid thing I've ever done was to come into this damn cabin when I could have taken the safer option and stuck my head down the wolf's throat when I had the chance."

"See," said Harkwell, shooting a sympathetic look at Takina. "He wants a dance! At this time of night. Idiot. Complete idiot. Take my advice, and find yourself someone else, first chance you get."

He collected the four clean cups from the table and placed them neatly in the sink.

"It's getting late. Will you stay the night, or do you have to be on your way?"

"We have to be on our way," Halfshaft and Takina chorused loudly, delighted at this unexpected opportunity to escape.

"You'd like to stay for a day! Beamed Harkwell. "Excellent. The wife and I don't get the opportunity to entertain guests overnight too often. Well, if you'd like to follow me, I'll show you to my daughter's old room."

"He should not have told her," Doon insisted as they sat together at Crow Hill. "This is supposed to be a secret mission. But first of all your friend told that servant girl everything, and then Leofric has explained our entire plan to Rana. To the Queen of the Amazons, of all people! Why does everyone find it so difficult to keep their mouths shut, just because some girl's flashing her fur at them?"

Rod ignored him. Halfshaft and Takina were missing, presumed eaten, and all Doon could do was to whinge on and on about Leofric's indiscretions. He couldn't give a toss about their plan any more. He had lost his mates, he had lost his way, and he had long since lost his last shred of patience with the wizard's apprentice.

The previous day had been the most traumatic yet. First, they had run into (and nearly been run over by) the troll and the wolves. Then they had passed Rana on the pathway, and – fearing that she might attack Leofric from behind – he had doubled back and followed her, with Doon fussing along behind him. She had little trouble in outdistancing them, though. By the time they caught her up, she was engaged in a far from regal clinch with Leofric, practically straddling the pathway with her 40 inch legs, as the soldier cavorted on top of her. Trog lay unconscious on the ground nearby, hemmed in by maimed wolves, his hands and feet bound together with Rana's bowstring.

"You've been busy," Rod remarked, referring to the carpet of wolves around them.

Rana misunderstood him. Extricating herself from Leofric's embrace, she approached Rod with sword drawn, ready to punish his impertinence.

113

"You've been hard at it," continued Rod, trying to clarify his earlier remark, but failing miserably. "I wish I could have been here to see it. I would have joined in if I had a weapon like his."

This also failed to pacify her. She raised her sword above her head, and stepped within striking distance. Leofric intervened, placing a restraining hand on her sword arm in a silent plea for lenience. She lowered her blade reluctantly, and waited for him to give her one good reason why this impudence should go unavenged. Much to Doon's consternation, Leofric gave her a very good reason indeed: he told her the official reason for their quest. He told her about the sword, the Warlock, the Grand Wizard. Everything she could have wanted to know, and more. And Doon had not stopped complaining about it ever since.

Rod was finding it increasing hard to resist the urge to punch his new friend's lights out. He was not helped by the tactful way that Doon had broken the news to him that Halfshaft and Takina were dead.

"Let's go and find the others," Rod had urged, shortly after Rana had consented not to skewer him.

"There's no point," came Doon's reply. "I saw them being dragged into the Forest by the wolves. Neither of them were moving. They looked pretty dead to me." His tone was completely matter-of-fact. "Still," Rod had half-expected him to add. "Mustn't grumble."

They were now at Crow Hill, the scene of the first great battle between the Warlock and Harold all those centuries ago. Rana had insisted that they travel throughout the night, refusing to make camp whilst they were still on the pathway. They were, she reasoned, too vulnerable there. Instead, they pushed ahead until they reached the relative safety of the hill. Rod and Doon now sat at the bottom of the slope. Rana and Leofric had disappeared, the former announcing casually that they were going off to mate, to make fearless Amazon babies.

"Everything was going so well," Doon grizzled. "But just when we get rid of one interfering woman, we end up with an even worse one!"

Rod's patience shuffled a step or two nearer to breaking point.

"Shut it," he told the wizard's apprentice, "or I'll strangle you with your own tonsils."

Doon seemed stunned.

"What did you just say to me?"

"You heard."

"Is that my reward for rescuing you from Spartan Castle? Or maybe it's your way of saying thank you for telling you how you can get back to your own world? Without me, you'd be buried in an unmarked grave in the castle dunghill by now. I don't expect gratitude, but you could at least try being courteous."

"Shut up about Leofric, then. So what if he told her your little secret? She's on our side, now. If this Warlock's as bad as you all seem to think he is, then we need all the bloody help we can get!"

"But she'll take charge. Amazons are like that, and she's the worst of the lot of them. I'm not taking orders from a woman."

"Well sod off, then."

"All right. I will."

Doon got to his feet and started marching purposefully up Crow Hill. It was fairly high, but the slope was gentle, and he would make good progress. Still, Rod reckoned that it would take the little corpse an hour to make it to the top, and Rana would be back by then. She'd get him back down again pretty damn quickly. And it wouldn't be for making brave Amazon babies, either.

As he watched Doon striding up the hill, he noticed that a thick band of grass ahead of the apprentice was changing colour, turning from green to dark grey. Before the transformation was complete, the grass behind him started to darken as well, the metallic grey leaping from one blade of grass to the next like a contagious plague of wet ash. Doon stopped, and eyed the ground warily, conscious of the fact that the two discoloured strips had sandwiched him between them. They joined at the edges. He was surrounded.

The grey grass started to bubble, raising like giant blisters into the air. Dark forms struggled inside each, like ravenous insects trying to break free of their cocoons. The blisters higher up the hill rose to eight or nine feet, a good two or three feet higher than those below. As Doon ran around the oval, seeking a way out, the blisters started to burst open, and a soldier struggled from each of them. The taller ones were trolls, whereas the ones nearest Rod were humans and dwarfs. Doon stood between them, looking from one group to the other, his face impossibly white, as he started chanting half-remembered spells that he knew would be useless. The die was cast.

The cocoons decomposed almost as soon as the soldiers stepped out of them, sinking easily back into the ground. The soldiers faced one another, blinking the earth from their eyes, separated only by an ex-wizard's apprentice who was now desperately regretting his recent decision to storm off in a huff.

An eerie silence fell on the hill. There was a sense of complete inevitability about the two forces closing in upon each other, crushing Doon between them. The apprentice was aware of this. His lips formed one soundless incantation after another, but he no longer searched for a gap in the massed ranks to make his escape. Instead, he stood there, frozen to the spot, his face drenched in icy sweat, waiting for them to engulf him.

Rod acted quickly. Scouring the ground around him, he caught sight of a weighty stone. It would not do much damage against chain mail, but it might at least distract a few of them long enough for Doon to make his escape. He seized it, and hurled it at a gaggle of spectral dwarfs close by. His aim was good. The stone arrowed towards one of the knights, who was in the process of withdrawing his sword from its sheath. Unfortunately, it shot right through him, and came to rest a yard or so from Doon's feet.

The sudden noise startled Doon into action. He turned to his left and raced away, hoping to squeeze between the two forces where their flanks met. But as soon as he started to run, they sprang into life, the two armies rushing towards each other with the blood-curdling cry of battle on their lips. Before he had covered five yards, the spectral combatants had engulfed him. He cowered on the floor, knees drawn up to his chest like an embryo, his arms clasped over his head in a pointless attempt at self-preservation.

The ghostly soldiers wheeled about him, broad sword striking long sword, mace striking shield. Between the heavy clangs of iron against iron, Rod could hear their shouts of anguish and screams of pain, as they fought to gain the upper hand in a battle which had been fought and lost a thousand years before.

Nearby one of the trolls brought his sword crashing down upon his opponent, shattering the man's armour. The soldier squealed, thrashed about wildly, and then sank back into the ground, disappearing without trace.

Seconds later, the same thing happened to a wood dwarf, then a troll, and then to another troll. The numbers on the battlefield steadily decreased until only a handful of spectres remained.

The last troll fell, and the remaining men and dwarfs rallied together. They grouped around Doon, who was now lying on the grass, blood trickling from a slash wound to his temple. They grabbed at his clothes, and slowly began sinking into the ground, ready to take him with them.

Rod looked on in an agony of uncharacteristic indecision. His instincts told him to go to Doon's aid, however much he disliked the man. His brain told him that to do so would be suicidal. He could not hurt these spectres – the stone he had thrown at them proved this – but the blood on Doon's face told him that they were more than capable of hurting him. Now, they were trying to pull the wizard's apprentice down into the ground, to some dark grave below. Becoming part of some human compost heap was not really his idea of the perfect way to end this little hike through the woods.

Despite his fear, he resolved to act. He took a step forwards, just as Leofric and Rana arrived back, flushed and breathless, at his side. At the same moment, Doon broke free of his captors, and ran wildly down the hill towards them, his face convulsed in abject terror.

The spectres caught him almost instantly, and dragged him down into the sodden earth. Each of them seized hold of him, and sank into the ground, pulling their horrified victim with them.

Leofric rushed forwards, determined to free his friend. Rod followed him, his mind made up. Whatever the risks, he knew that he could not stand idly by and watch the man die.

Rana stayed behind. Her warriors had passed down stories of these Forest ghouls from generation to generation. She sensed their power. No queen would be in their right mind to challenge the Dead to save the skin of a man. Especially a man who by all accounts had previously been dead himself, and therefore had less to lose than the rest of them.

Rod and Leofric reached Doon just as his shoulders disappeared into the earth. Only his head and forearms were above the surface now. Although clearly in deep shock, his eyes registered no pain. He tried to speak to them, but made no sound, the pressure of the earth below having crushed all the air from his lungs.

They seized one hand each and strained to pull him free. Their task was hopeless. He continued to sink downwards, as if in quick-

117

sand. Before long, his hands disappeared below the surface, Rod and Leofric releasing their grasp just in time to avoid following him into the earth themselves. His fingers wriggled for an instant, and then were gone. There was just his head left now.

Doon opened his mouth again, still fighting to speak to them, battling to demand their aid. But as he sank lower, his mouth filled with earth, and only his wide, imploring eyes remained to give any clue of the horror below. Before long, even these had gone, and the ground closed seamlessly above him, leaving no trace that he had ever been there.

They stood facing each other, looking down at their feet. They knew that even though he was out of sight, he was still beneath them, sinking further and further into the muddy grave below.

But they could not reach him.

For better or for worse, Doon was lost to them forever.

Horace and Hubert stopped about fifteen yards down the path from Trugga, and watched her curiously. It was not often that they took the trouble to leave their mound to examine strangers, but then again it was not often that a seventeen stone warrior woman clad only in squirrel skins paced up and down all day across the pathways to the Forest.

"She must be hungry," Horace remarked. "Why doesn't she go and find something to eat?"

"I reckon she's dead," lied Hubert, implausibly, as he watched her march to and fro. It was not one of his best efforts.

"You'd still fancy her even if she was," Horace teased him. "I've seen the look on your face since that first Amazon whispered that stuff to you. I reckon you're in love. And now you've got a taste for bigger women, why not go the whole hog, and get yourself some of that one over there?"

Hubert winced. Ever since the blonde Amazon had offered to do all sorts of foul and unnatural things for him in exchange for him pointing out the correct path, he had been besotted. Horace knew him too well not to notice this, and had been making remark after remark at his expense ever since. The only consolation was that, as it was his job, he could with a clear conscience lie again and again that he would not have touched her with a barge pole.

But deep down, both of them knew that he would not have been able to keep his barge pole away from her, given half a chance. The girl was obviously obsessed with his dwarfly good looks, and any fool could see that she would have offered herself to him even if she had not needed his help. After all, who could resist a huge bushy grey beard such as his? The real irony, though, was that it was his inability to tell the truth that had stopped him taking advantage of the proposals which she had made. When she had said, "you do want me, don't you?" he had had no choice but to tell her that he wasn't in the least bit interested. He had said this through gritted teeth and with crossed legs, but maybe she hadn't realised that he hadn't really meant it. He had even done a little jig to show her how much he was looking forwards to all the things she had promised to do to him. Surely she must have got the point then? Little jigs meant only one thing in dwarf circles, everyone knew that.

His reflections were interrupted as Horace gave him a violent elbow in the ribs.

"Ouch," complained Hubert. "That didn't hurt a bit."

He followed Horace's gaze. A stranger was coming along the path towards them. Not that there were many guests who were not strangers to them. Very few people came to ask their way into the Forest, and it was virtually unheard of for anyone ever to come back again.

They moved aside to allow him to pass, but he came to a halt beside them.

"Has a wizard passed this way?" asked Thane.

"Yes," said Horace decisively.

"No," Hubert denied, in a tone more decisive still.

"If I asked your friend which path the wizard took, what would he tell me?" Thane enquired.

"The right hand path," Horace informed him, with a truthful nod of his head.

"The right hand path," Hubert lied through his teeth.

"Thank you," the mercenary replied, heading for the left hand path. Ahead of him, Trugga stood immobile, blocking his way forward. The irresistible force was just about to meet the immovable object, and – like Trugga herself – it wasn't going to be pretty.

"You're losing your touch," goaded Horace to his twin. "You gave the game away. You're mind's not on the job. She wasn't interested, so just forget her, will you?"

That's where you're wrong Hubert wanted to retort. She was interested. If I could tell you what she said to me without lying through my teeth, then you'd know. Being a liar could be so bloody frustrating sometimes. He opened his mouth to proclaim that the woman was clearly gagging for it, but all that came out was what he truly believed to be a gross falsehood.

"That's right. I probably made her stomach heave."

Horace was jubilant. He did not know why he had not thought of this before. All he had to do was to lay it on thick about how the attractive young Amazon had adored his brother, and the poor lying wretch would have no option but to deny every word of it. This would be good.

"You're being too hard on yourself," Horace chided. "I'm sure you didn't really make her feel physically sick"

"Yes I did," protested Hubert miserably, shaking his head to illustrate the point.

"You seem to think that she promised herself to you, after all."

"Who did? I never even met the woman. And she'd hardly be interested in a little runt like me, anyway."

"She must have known you had real feelings for her."

"I expect," explained Hubert, practically spluttering with rage, "that my manly jig must have put her off!"

They paused for an instant, distracted by the burly Amazon's clumsy attempt to punch Thane into oblivion. He had tried to pass her, but she was having none of it. She swung a meaty fist at his head, putting all of her weight into the blow. He ducked beneath her arm, grabbed her by the wrist and elbow as they passed over his head, and pulled them sharply downwards, causing her to lose her balance and fall heavily to the floor.

"Do you fancy that one over there?" enquired Horace innocently. "Any risk that you might try to get into her furs if she stays another night?"

"You better believe it," Hubert confirmed, shaking an outraged fist at his brother. "If she put another ten or fifteen stone on, then she'd be pretty much my ideal woman!"

"You'd chase practically anything in a pelt," added Horace, going in for the kill. "In fact, even the squirrels round here have started looking a bit nervous when you're around!"

Horace justified this last remark by telling himself that he really had seen some very worried looking squirrels of late. The cause of their concern, of course, had nothing to do with any sexual deviancy on his twin's part, but he had not specifically claimed this to be the case. As far as he was concerned, he had told the truth, and the Prophecy was not affected. And for the same reason he could be sure that his brother would now have to contradict him, and tell him that he found the squirrels very attractive indeed.

"Don't say that again!" said Hubert, challenging him to repeat himself.

He was happy to oblige.

"You're right, of course," Hubert confirmed, practically weeping with anger. "I've shagged every one of them twice."

Trugga was on her feet again. Her opponent could have struck her whilst she was down, but had decided against it. Funnily enough, she did not feel that he had backed off through some sense of fair play. No, it was almost as if he was using the fight as a practice bout to sharpen his reflexes for some more serious contest later on. The idea that he was not frightened of her was galling enough, but the possibility that he was using her as a warm-up was infuriating. When Trugga became infuriated, she always did the same thing. She lowered her head, roared, and charged. She may have been better off charging without giving a warning roar, but that was just the kind of girl she was.

"Do you see that great big Amazon over there?" Horace enquired. "The one with a face like a sackful of afterbirth?"

"No."

"Tell me you don't fancy her, as well. The first sign of a flash of bare flesh, and you're away. And that's an awful lot of flesh that she's flashing, unless I'm very much mistaken!"

Hubert's shoulders dropped in defeat.

"Yes," he denied miserably. "I'd like her to be the mother of my dwarflings."

Trugga hit the ground again, Thane having used her momentum to toss her over his shoulder. Her brow creased into a frown. She had to kill the stranger if she was to avoid letting her Queen down a second time. But how to kill him when she couldn't even catch him? With another roar, she lowered her head, and charged at him like a rabid rhinoceros on drugs.

Horace meanwhile pressed home his advantage:

"Would you want all of your children to look like her? That way, they wouldn't all have to have a horrible greasy grey beard like yours."

121

He paused again to watch Trugga run headlong into a tree. She sank groggily to her knees, and then collapsed on to her stomach on the ground. Thane stepped over her, and disappeared along the path which the object of Hubert's affections had taken the previous day.

"Do you think he's going after that woman of yours?" asked Horace, thoughtfully.

"No! He can't! I'm going after her!"

Without further explanation, Hubert dashed into the Forest after Thane, with a flurry of little legs.

"Don't you do it!" Horace yelled after him in astonishment. "Don't you go after her! Remember the prophecy!"

He sat down heavily on the ground, his face ghastly pale, his mind reeling with the enormity of what had just happened. Hubert had said he was going in after the Amazon, and go in after her he had. He had spoken the truth! This was terrible news indeed. If the prophecy was true, then he and his entire race were doomed.

It was not a thought that appealed to him.

Things were getting worse. They had been awake all night, neither Halfshaft nor Takina trusting Harkwell enough to risk sleeping. The cabin had no windows, and they had no way of knowing when it would be morning again. All they could do was pace the floor, and wait for their host to give them their wake-up call.

They had both objected loudly when Harkwell had locked them into the bedroom. Indeed, they must have been loud, because Harkwell had actually heard them.

"Sorry, but it's best I lock you in," he had said. "There are wolves around," he added, inexplicably, as if afraid that they would creep up the stairs and open the door if it was not securely locked.

They had just one candle between them. The flickering light revealed a double bed (its blankets tucked in with hospital corners), a large chest, and a bookcase. All were made of wood. They each offered the other use of the bed, but both politely declined. After a long awkward silence, they eventually agreed that they would both use the bed, but keep to their respective sides. "No mating," Takina stressed, as she sat on the edge of her half of the bed.

"No," Halfshaft agreed. "No mating, tonight."

"No mating any night," she added, to clarify the point.

"No," he conceded. "None at all."

As the night wore on, the candle wore down, and another problem became apparent. They were discussing their dreams at the time. Halfshaft wanted to become an all-powerful wizard, inherit the crown of Spartan Castle, become immortal, and legalise brothels. Takina was just telling him that her only wish was to be treated as an equal by her fellow Amazons, when he made the frightening revelation that he had been trying to keep from her for some time. He needed the toilet.

"It was bound to happen sooner or later," she consoled him. "We've been in here for hours."

He shook his head miserably.

"I don't think you understand the full scale of my....problem."

Now it was her turn to have a miserable headshake.

"You don't mean?"

"Yes!" he confessed, writhing in embarrassment. He was locked in a room with an attractive member of the opposite sex, whom he was keen not to disgust in any way, desperately needing facilities which might not be available to him for several hours, if at all. This would be a pretty demanding test of their friendship, he thought wryly.

The candle had all but burnt out, and his face had gone clammy with the effort of holding everything in. To take his mind off things, he explored the room. He tested the bed (much to Takina's mistrust), rolling around upon it and commenting upon the soundness of the mattress. He leafed through the books, but the light was too poor for him to see if he had them the right way up, yet alone read the things. Eventually, as the flame flickered towards oblivion, he gave in. He opened the lid of the chest, hitched up his robes around his waist, and stuck his bony bottom over the edge.

Takina got up from the bed, and paced around on the far side of the room, keeping as much distance between the two of them as possible. She sung to herself, hoping to distract herself sufficiently to forget the predicament she was in. Of all the horrors she had faced- the fights with the Amazons, the wolves, and Harkwell himself – this had to be the worst.

"Urrgghhh!" the wizard exclaimed. "What on earth was that?"

"I really don't want to know," Takina told him.

"Hang on," Halfshaft insisted. "Pass me the candle."

"No way," she told him, am I coming anywhere near you until you've pulled your robes back down, and shut that chest! Does it matter what it looks like, anyway?"

He snorted impatiently, and fetched the candle himself. It was now little more than a blob in a pool of molten wax, the wick protruding limply from the centre. Shielding the flame, he scurried back over to the chest, and held the flame above it to give him enough light to peer inside. She could see him squinting into the dark interior, analysing the contents in increasing agitation.

"Come over here," he beckoned. "Look at this!"

She resisted the temptation to heave. She had got on really well with the wizard up until now, but this was too much. Her tribe had always said that men had habits so sick as to defy description, but she had dismissed the rumours as ridiculous. But now, as the crazed wizard bent over the chest, apparently intent on giving her a guided tour of his stools, she wondered whether perhaps they knew best after all. This would not be considered acceptable behaviour for a woman.

"Oh for goodness sake!" he insisted. "Would you come here? You know he said he's lost his daughter?"

"Yes," Takina acknowledged, failing to see the connection.

"Well," he explained, pointing into the chest, "I think I've just found her!"

Trog was not in the best of moods. He shivered in the damp mists of early morning as he surveyed the gap where his left thumb had once been. It was not a pretty sight. And it looked even worse now it was gone.

He had lost count of the number of times he had cursed himself that night, so it must have been at least three. He had been given a perfectly routine mission by the King, but would fail it unless he could chew off the rest of his hand within the next few minutes. And just eating his thumb had stung quite a lot.

His big mistake, he knew, was failing to realise what the dark-haired Amazon woman was planning. Leofric had introduced the two of them. Since he had just been fighting side by side with the former Captain of the Guard, the eggy-cut of the Soldiers' Code provided that he should shake him by the hand. The Trolls Code, of course, provided that he was free to eat both of them straight afterwards.

Unfortunately, Rana – being a woman – knew nothing of eggy-cut. As he was sticking out a big paw to greet her, she knocked his feet from beneath him, and bound him tight with her bow string in the time it would have taken him to count to one (about eight seconds).

He had spent the night trying to gnaw his way through the bowstring, but without success. He had then come up with the alternative plan of biting his hands off, so that his bonds could simply slip off at the wrists. He could then, he reasoned, untie his feet. The fact that he would have no hands to untie them had not yet occurred to him. Once free, he would set off after Leofric and his woman, to show them just what an angry, handless troll could do to them.

He had just been on the point of tucking into his left hand, when he heard the first of the howls. The wolves were coming back! He had to get free quickly or he would still be bound when they arrived. He was not the most mathematically minded person in the world, but when it came to fighting he could work out odds with the best of them. The odds of a tied up troll successfully resisting a hungry wolf pack were, he felt, probably on a par with the chances of him becoming a vegetarian concert pianist with an interest in stamp collecting. Not all that high, in other words. Probably only about forty-twelve to three, in fact.

He crunched deeply into his left hand, severing the thumb. He chewed it quickly at first, but then slowed down when he realised that it had a taste to be savoured. His mother would have killed him if she had seen him bolting down good food without chewing it thoroughly. Mind you, his mother would have killed him anyway, had his father not restrained her. She was a complete psychopath, he reminisced proudly.

A wolf howled again at the same moment as his teeth cracked into his thumb bone. He looked up, sensing the creatures were nearer than ever. Damn wolves, he thought resentfully. I taste far too good to share myself with them.

He forced the rest of his hand into his mouth. He had big hands, but a mouth to match. Blood from his severed thumb pumped down his throat, as he steeled himself to sever the bone and tendon which constituted his wrist. Better bite quick, or the blood would choke him.

It was then that he noticed a man walking down the path towards him. As the man drew closer, he could see that he was smiling.

"Mm-mm-mu-mm-mm-murgh?" Trog demanded menacingly. He then withdrew his hand from his mouth, and tried asking the question again.

"What are you smiling for?"

Thane glanced behind him, and nodded towards a grey-bearded dwarf who was trying to follow him inconspicuously along the pathway. As they turned to watch him, the dwarf dived behind a tree, with only his beard and belly protruding beyond the trunk.

"Impressive shadowing, huh?" the mercenary commented. "That dwarf's a natural."

"Help me or you die," responded the troll, conversationally.

"You are Trog, then."

"Yes," Trog replied, amazed at the man's stupidity. Of course he was! Even he knew that!

Four wolves cantered on to the path fifty feet away. They hesitated for a second, wary of men from bitter recent experience. They would not take on three of them again. But one was tied up; there were none of those scary fur-clad men with breasts around; and one of their prey was just a portly dwarf hiding behind a tree.

Thane fished the King's letter from his pocket, and flashed the royal seal at Trog like a police detective showing his identity card.

"Recognise that?"

Trog nodded. Behind him, Thane could see the wolves breaking into a trot in their direction. He did not really have time to talk. Hoping that the seal would convince the troll that they were both on the same side, he used a knife to slice through the bowstrings which bound the troll's hands and feet, and hauled him to his feet.

The wolves came to a halt again. The smell of freshly spilt blood reached them, and urged them forwards, but the big troll intimidated them. They churned around, waiting for one of their number to break the deadlock, and lead the attack. None of them would commit himself.

Their indecision was broken as Trog snatched up his sword and charged down the path towards them, slashing the blade wildly around in front of him like some demented 300 pound troll lawnmower. They scattered, tails between their legs, the last of them melting into the trees an instant before he steam-rollered past them.

They slunk off into the Forest, drenched in disappointment. They would have liked to taste troll-flesh again; none of them had tried it in years. Still, they could always pop out for a dwarf or two, and wait for night to set in again. Sooner or later, the strangers would have to sleep. And then the wolves would feast.

T akina rushed over to him, and looked in the chest. She then remembered what Halfshaft had been doing before making his gruesome discovery, and instantly regretted her rash turn of speed. She backed away in distaste, just as the candle went out.

"Are you sure it was his daughter?" Takina asked him, once she had recovered herself.

"It looked like him in a dress," came the unsettling response. "Only with blood all over her. If it wasn't his daughter, then he had a son who needed a really good talking to."

The discovery did not help the time to pass any quicker. Halfshaft refused to go anywhere near the chest, and took a turn pacing the far corner of the room. This may not have been the brightest way of burning off nervous energy, because he kept bumping into the walls in the darkness.

Takina's native superstition (not to mention acute sense of smell) obliged her to close the chest, and she sat upon it to prevent the soul of the deceased girl escaping. Better it stayed in the chest, she reasoned, than to share a room with them.

The hours dragged by. The wooden lid felt cold against her bare legs, but she stayed put, unwilling to give Harkwell's daughter the opportunity to put in an appearance.

"How old was she?" she asked eventually, as much to break the silence as anything.

"About your age, I think," replied Halfshaft.

The answer did not please her, and the conversation lapsed for a while. In the silence, she thought about all they had been through already. She couldn't let it end here. No way was she going to end up in a chest with a dead girl, a wizard, and a pile of...well, she just wasn't going to end up there, that was all. They had to escape.

"Sooner or later," she said, "he's got to open that door. I've still got my knife, you know."

"And I've got my saucepan," Halfshaft reassured her. "And boy, do I know how to use it!"

"Okay," she agreed, sounding as impressed as she could manage. "So when he opens the door, we kill him. Agreed?"

"Kill him? Couldn't we just stun him a bit?"

"We kill him."

"Okay, then. Kill him, it is."

They waited. Then they waited some more. An eternity passed, but still nothing happened, and they waited some more for a third time. Eventually, they heard a tuneless whistling, followed by the rattle of a key in the lock.

"This is it," Takina prompted. "We've got to take him down, before he tears us to pieces."

Harkwell threw open the door.

"Wakey, wakey, rise and shine," he greeted them cheerfully. "Who's for a cup of tea, then? You've got a long journey ahead of you, and it's best to start the day with a cuppa, I always say!"

Non-plussed, they filed out the room after him, taking the places which he offered them at the table.

"I thought you were never going to get up," he chided them play-fully. "It's three o'clock in the afternoon! The wife was getting quite worried about you!"

Halfshaft nodded in understanding. "Yes, she didn't look too happy when we saw her yesterday, either."

"Right," said Harkwell. "A cup of tea, and then I expect you'll want to be on your way."

Escape at last, Halfshaft thought. And the sooner they got away, the better. Their host had treated them pretty shoddily, he reflected. And he wanted to be as far away from the cabin as possible when Harkwell discovered that one of his guests had dumped all over his dead daughter.

Harkwell jumped up from the table and fetched the cups. This time, he made the tea himself. Best to give the wife a rest, he explained. She was looking a bit peaky lately.

They downed their tea hastily, and made for the door, thanking him at the top of their voices for his kind hospitality. He seemed touched at this display of gratitude, and told them that if they ever wanted to drop in on him again, then he and the wife would certainly make them welcome.

As Halfshaft stood aside, waiting for Harkwell to unlock the front door, he noticed that the room was starting to slip out of focus. He turned to Takina to remark upon this strange phenomenon, just as she collapsed to the floor.

"The tea!" he exclaimed indignantly "You drugged the tea!"

"No I didn't" replied Harkwell defensively, shaking his head in protest. "It was the wife!"

Horace bowed low, his forehead almost touching the ground in deference to the wood dwarf elders. He would upset them enough with his news. There was no point making things even worse by giving them a sloppy half-bow in the process.

"You may rise," Arkon told him. "Why have you left your post?"

Horace shifted uncomfortably from foot to foot. How do you tell your leader that all dwarfkind was doomed?

"It's Hubert," he explained. "He's gone to find the Amazon."

"Which one?" enquired Arkon. "My spies report three of them in the Forest."

"The first of them. The one with the wizard."

"She was with a wizard?"

Arkon looked shocked. He went into a tight huddle with the elders, and they jabbered excitedly away to each other for a quarter of an hour or so. Horace took the opportunity to look about him whilst he waited. It was not often that he got the chance to leave his mound, yet alone to attend the Grand Assembly Cavern. Hubert would want to know all about it later, if he was ever allowed to return to his post, that is.

They were about twenty feet below the Forest. The roots of some of the larger trees protruded through the ceiling of the underground cavern, making strange twisted shapes above him. The only light came from the surface shafts which punctuated the perimeter of the roof at each compass point. No fire was ever lit here. The trees would never have allowed it.

As well as the shafts which led up to the sky above, a number of downward spiralling tunnels were scattered around the chamber floor, leading to the wood dwarfs living quarters. These formed a complicated maze in the earth and rock beneath the Forest, like some giant ants' nest. Occasionally, Horace caught a glimpse of a dwarfling peering out at him from the cover of one of the tunnel openings. As one of the dwarf twins who guarded the Forest pathways, he was, he knew, something of a celebrity in these parts.

The elders stopped whispering, and resumed their positions.

"He was with the Amazon, you say? The two of them together? As friends?"

"Yes," nodded Horace. "But there's something else. Hubert has spoken the truth!"

The elders gasped as one. A couple of them nearly fainted, and had to be steadied by the others. Arkon himself looked shaken, but managed to retain his composure better than the others.

"Are you certain of this, Horace?"

The dwarf nodded.

"This is dreadful. We all know the Prophecy."

There was a collective clearing of throats as the dwarfs prepared to recite the well-known lines from the scriptures:

> *Two dwarfs shall guard the Forest gates,*
> *And one shall to all questions lie.*
> *The second dwarf shall speak the truth*
> *To all who pass him by.*
> *But if these dwarfs shall fail their roles*
> *The Forest will come to an end,*
> *Unless a troll shall kill the girl*
> *The Wizard does befriend."*

"There's only one option, then" announced Arkon, his face creased with worry. "We must capture the Amazon who is with this wizard, and hand her over to the trolls."

A seedy looking wood dwarf oozed from a dark corner of the chamber just a few feet from Horace's right. He had not noticed him before, but this did not surprise him, for this was none other than the spy-chief Stainwright. Since the dwarfs had no other spies, being spy-chief was no great accolade, but it made the slimy little thing happy.

"There may be a problem with that," the spy-chief announced. Horace was mildly surprised that Stainwright had not bowed before speaking. Even spies should have respect for the elders, he believed.

"Stainwright!" Arkon exclaimed. "I didn't see you there!"

"Thank you," the spy replied, taking this as a compliment.

"What's this problem, then?"

"The Amazon has already been captured by Harkwell. She will be dead soon."

Arkon pondered this latest development, wriggling a hand through his bushy beard to stroke his chin.

"Harkwell is a troll of sorts. He's got some troll blood in him, on his mother's side, I believe. Maybe it would be okay if we let him kill her. But then again, the Prophecy doesn't say "unless a troll-of-sorts", does it? It specifically mentions a troll. Best not to take any chances. You'd better try and save her, and bring her back here."

Stainwright evaporated into the darkness.

"And remember..." Arkon continued.

Stainwright reappeared with the petulant sigh of a bored teenager.

"...The fate of the Forest is in your hands."

T he two knights were clad in suits of armour, their visors pulled down to protect their faces. They stood opposite one another, exchanging fearsome blows in their duel to the death.

As Halfshaft approached them, he realised that they had different weapons. The knight in silver was throwing bolts of lightning, which crackled furiously in his mailed glove as he took aim and hurled them at his adversary. The other knight was clad in black, and wielded a double-handed sword, with a ferocity that was frightening to behold. This was clearly a battle between a powerful wizard and a great warrior, but which of them would win?

Halfshaft approached the feuding knights, determined to see just who these men were. They seemed oblivious of his presence, and he stood at the silver knight's shoulder without being challenged by either man. He reached out falteringly towards the silver visor, astonished at his own audacity. The sword swung through the air behind him, just a hair's breadth away from cleaving him in two. Unperturbed, he grasped the visor, and raised it. A familiar face stared back at him.

131

"That's me!" he cried, his mind reeling in confusion.

He whirled round, and threw open the black knight's visor. Again, he saw his own face staring back at him.

"They're both me!" he shouted, to no one in particular. But deep down, he knew it was not so. Only one of these men could be the real Halfshaft. But which of them was he? The great warrior, or the all-powerful magician?

"Wake up!" Takina hissed.

He looked around him in puzzlement. He was sure he had heard her voice, but there was no sign of her anywhere. Where was she, and what was she doing here?

"Wake up," she demanded again louder this time.

The knights disintegrated, and he awoke. He was lying on the grass in the Forest. He was tied up, as was Takina, who lay at his side. Nearby, Harkwell was digging a pit in the ground to one side of a large oak tree.

Halfshaft shook his head to clear his thoughts. It did not work.

"That looks like a grave," he observed.

"It is," she replied.

"For us?"

"For us," she assured him. "Unless you can think of some way out of this."

"Of course I can. I've got an idea."

He screamed for help as loudly as he could. Takina squirmed with embarrassment. Harkwell stopped digging.

"It's no use calling for help, you know. There's no-one around to hear you but the wolves, and they won't be much use to you, believe you me!"

"You heard me!" exclaimed the wizard, forgetting his predicament in his surprise.

"Of course," Harkwell replied. "I'm not really deaf. I just pretend to be. That way, I can ignore people when they ask to leave my cabin, and they're always too polite to insist. It works every time. And drugging's far nicer than violence, I always think."

"What are you going to do with us?" Takina asked.

"Oh, bury you, of course. You make good compost for the trees. And in return, they let me take wood from the one's that die. To make my furniture. It's a very convenient arrangement for everyone. I get my lovely furniture, and they get you."

132

"It's not so convenient for us though, is it?" remonstrated Halfshaft, trying to suppress the panic in his voice. "Being murdered, I mean."

Harkwell stopped digging, and shot him a hurt look.

"Murdered! I'm not going to murder you, what do you take me for? If I wanted you dead, I would have left you to the wolves, and salvaged your bodies after they'd killed you. No, all I'm going to do is to pop you into this here hole, and fill it up again. Anything that happens to you after I've buried you is nothing to do with me, is it? I won't even be here by then."

Takina tried to keep him talking. She didn't have much hope that it would save them, but – bound and gagged, and stacked by a freshly dug grave – there did not really seem to be many other options open to her.

"Tell me about your daughter."

A profound sadness descended upon Harkwell, and he brushed away a tear with the back of an earth-encrusted hand.

"The wolves got her a few months back. I hate them for that. I'll have to keep her in the trunk until she's fully decomposed, of course. I won't let the trees have her. That would be awful. She might be dead, but I've still got to look after her, you see. She's all I've got."

"That's why you've not buried your wife, then?" Halfshaft enquired, changing the subject quickly. If Harkwell was willing to bury them just to get wood for is furniture, he hated to think what the man might do to them if he knew that the wizard had dumped on his daughter earlier that morning.

"Why would I want to bury the wife?" came the puzzled reply. "She's not even dead!"

"See," Halfshaft whispered to Takina. "He really is mad."

"He'll be even madder when he opens the chest in his spare bedroom," she replied. "Not that we're likely to be around long enough to see that."

Harkwell carried on digging, removing earth from the hole one methodical shovelful at a time. Only when he came across the tree roots did he slow down. He knew better than to risk marking them with the spade.

When he had finished, he crossed over to his two captives, and tucked one under each arm. They wriggled furiously, but his grasp was too firm for them to break free. He returned to the grave, and positioned them at the bottom with surprising care, even moving Takina considerately when she complained that she had a root sticking in her back.

"Is that okay?" he asked, anxious that his guests should be as comfortable as possible in the circumstances. He took his responsibilities as a host very seriously, after all.

Halfshaft continued to stall for time.

"Why wait 'til this afternoon to do this?"

"You didn't touch the tea the wife gave you yesterday, so I had to wait until today. I didn't want to use force. I don't like hurting people, you see. The wife always said that I 'm too soft."

"Gentle as a lamb," the wizard agreed, as the first shovel-load of earth hit him full in the face.

Harkwell scooped up another spadeful, and dropped it on Takina's pelvis.

"Sorry," he blushed. "I wasn't aiming at that bit!"

As he filled in the hole, his face became more and more troubled. Before long, he had covered their entire bodies, leaving only their faces relatively mud-free. He scooped up enough earth to fill over Halfshaft's face, but seemed to have a change of heart, placing the shovel back on the ground without dislodging its contents.

"I hate this part," he told them. "People always look so sad when they see I'm going to bury their faces. I just want you to know that I'm very, very sorry."

"Oh, that's all right," Halfshaft assured him bitterly, sarcasm being his only refuge from blind screaming panic. "You just go right ahead. Don't you worry about us!"

Takina shook her head from side to side to throw off a worm which was trying to seek sanctuary up her left nostril.

"Pay no attention to him. He's twisted. Listen, Harkwell, it's not too late to let us go. You don't want to do this, do you? Untie us, and let us on our way. Please!"

"I'm afraid it's not as simple as that," said Harkwell sorrowfully. "I'd like to release you, I really would. But I've just started work on a lovely little nest of tables, and I've run out of teak. What choice do I have?"

He picked up his shovel, ready to finish the job.

"It's going to be a beautiful nest of tables. Quite exquisite. I just wanted you to know that. You will not die in vain."

Halfshaft unsuccessfully tried to suppress a hysterical giggle as Harkwell gave them a farewell wave.

"Goodbye, my friends. Than you for doing this for me."

With a grimace, he raised the shovel and tossed enough earth into their grave to cover them completely.

L eofric and Rana spoke in whispers. They were anxious not to awaken Rod until his fate had been decided. He filled in the gaps. She now knew that he was in league with the Warlock, who had wanted two right-hand men to help him conquer the whole of the known world, and beyond. Now that Doon was dead why not offer him the services of a right-hand man and right-hand woman instead? He had wanted to involve her from the start, but Doon would have none of it. If he could no longer share his power with his best friend, then there was no one else he would rather share it with than her.

Rana was not so sure. Her natural tendency was to conquer and to dominate. She would be more than happy to rule the world, but to do so as the vassal of the Warlock was not so appealing. How could she serve so evil a being? And more to the point, how could she serve a man?

Eventually, Leofric persuaded her to join him. They then went on to discuss Rod. Why, Rana asked, were they deceiving him into accompanying them to the Black Mountains? She had no wish to lie to him, for this was hardly conduct becoming to a Queen. No, it was far better to stick a sword to his throat, march him off to the Black Mountains, get him to free the Warlock, and then dispose of him as she thought fit. Which would probably be quite painfully, because he was annoying her no end.

She expected Leofric to give in to her, but for once he argued the point. Deep down inside, she was pleased that he was finally showing some backbone by standing up to her. She had been impressed by his swordsmanship against the wolves, and he was at last acting like the sort of man who would be worthy of a warrior like her. Despite this, she was still not used to being contradicted, and it required a great effort of will to keep her temper in check. She was still trying to batter it into submission when she heard the noise.

"What was that?" she asked edgily.

135

"What?"

"That noise. Didn't you hear it?"

He shrugged. He knew her senses were keener than his. He had heard nothing, but trusted her hearing more than his own. He drew his sword, and scoured the trees around him.

"Keep an eye on him," she cautioned motioning to Rod. She sprang to her feet, and stalked into the undergrowth, reminding Leofric more than ever of a lioness: beautiful, sleek and savage. He was a lucky man, he thought, as an oblivious Rod shifted restlessly in his sleep nearby.

The minutes passed by, but Rana did not return. He started to fidget, genuinely worried about her. He tried to convince himself that he could press on without her if she did not return, but knew that he could not. Now that she was part of the quest, he would do whatever it took to keep it that way.

The tension mounted. Half an hour passed by. Then an hour. Then two. Finally, he could stand it no longer. He disappeared into the Forest, leaving Rod asleep and vulnerable on the ground behind him.

One moment they were spluttering on the suffocating earth; the next, they were being pulled to their feet by a man they had never met before. With a flick of his trademark knife, he released them from their bonds, and they were free.

"Watch out for Harkwell," warned Takina urgently, once she had coughed up sufficient earth to speak. She cast an anxious eye around her, worried that their mad host might appear out of his cabin and set upon the three of them at any moment. She was glad to be free, but not to keen on having to go through the whole burial-alive thing again. Especially as there would be even less room in their grave this time if there were three of them in it.

"He's all taken care of," Thane assured, as he helped her from the pit. Halfshaft surprised himself with a little pang of jealousy as he watched their rescuer place a hand on her bare back, and guide her gently on to the bank. He and Takina had come to depend upon one another, and he was uncomfortable with the knowledge that despite all his powers as a warrior and magician, he had failed to protect her, whereas this man had succeeded. He was grateful that she was safe of course but he would have given anything to have been the one to have been the one to rescue her.

Nearby, they saw two figures struggling on the grass. Halfshaft turned pale as he identified the two combatants, and almost shrunk back into the grave for safety.

"Goodbye frying pan," he muttered unhappily to himself. "Hello fire."

Harkwell lay on his back on the ground. Trog leaned over him, forcing the sharp-edged shovel blade towards his throat. Sweat ran down Harkwell's face as he fought to keep Trog at bay. The two were not unevenly matched, but the Captain of the Guard had had the element of surprise when he set upon his foe, and now he was on top he was too good a soldier to lose the advantage. The shovel descended a fraction of an inch at a time, slowly but surely bearing down upon the unprotected throat beneath it.

"Help him!" cried Takina, in distress. "He'll hurt him."

"Don't worry," Thane assured her. "Trog's got everything under control."

"Not him," she retorted. "Help Harkwell! He'll kill him!"

Thane stared at her incredulously as she hurled herself at Trog, bundling him away from the prostrate grave-digger.

"Leave him alone," she shouted. "He doesn't deserve this. He needs help. You can't kill him!"

Trog had had enough. First, he had been tied up by an Amazon he had just saved from the wolves. Then he had received orders from the King to help a total stranger rescue the very people he had earlier been instructed to kill. And now he had been set upon by some mad woman whom he had just rescued from being buried alive, who was upset that he was fighting the man who had been trying to bury her. Snarling ferociously, he slapped her hard across the face, sending her sprawling backwards to the ground.

With a shriek of indignant rage, Halfshaft vaulted out of the grave in which he had sought refuge, and cannoned ineffectually into the troll-cross' legs. Trog seized him, and hauled him into the air, ready to hurl him against the nearest tree. Thane dealt Trog a blow to the stomach which doubled him over, dropping Halfshaft unceremoniously to the grass in the process. Takina had by now regained her feet, and closed in crouching panther-like to the ground, determined to avenge herself and protect the wizard from further assault. Thane wheeled round to intercept her before she could launch herself at Trog. Halfshaft, meanwhile, pushed himself up on to his hands and knees, preparing to set upon the troll's ankles.

The atmosphere bristled with confrontation. Thane positioned himself between the troll and the two people he had just rescued, hoping to deter them from attacking one another, but also conscious of the risk that Trog might set upon him in retaliation for the blow to the stomach. The troll unsheathed his sword, deliberating which of the three he should slice up first. Takina stood panting, still in the Amazon attack crouch, ready to pounce upon the troll as soon as he made a move. And Halfshaft knelt on the grass snarling like a deranged animal, puffing out his chest in a desperate effort to make himself look large and ferocious. Whenever someone made the first move, it was going to kick off big time.

The first move never came. Instead, a noise rose up above the snarling, growling and panting of the antagonists, causing each of them to stop in their tracks. It was the sound of Harkwell weeping.

"The wife!" he cried in anguish. "My daughter. They're dead! Dead! They've left me here on my own. I can't cope without them, I just can't cope. Why did they have to die? Why did they have to leave me all alone?"

Bitter tears rolled down his face as he sobbed uncontrollably. Takina felt a lump in her throat, and even Trog seemed to be touched by the depths of the man's despair.

As Harkwell started to grind his teeth in misery, Halfshaft approached him and placed a comforting arm around his shoulders.

"I hate to be the bearer of bad tidings," he told him, "but I'm afraid you've lost your nest of tables as well!"

Rana awoke lying face down in the dark. Her head hurt, and her wrists ached where they were pinned behind her back. She felt cold stone against her stomach. Her legs were numb with inactivity, but she guessed that they were tied together, too. The darkness was impenetrable, but she did not need any light to tell her that she was in very serious trouble.

"Good. You are awake," observed a sinister voice near her right ear,

She tested her bonds. They held firm. She remained silent, biding her time.

"Please don't insult my intelligence by pretending you're still asleep. You're awake," persisted Stainwright. "I can tell by your breathing."

"If you want to keep breathing," she hissed at him, "you'd better untie me now."

He sniggered, apparently amused.

"I'm afraid you're in no position to make threats, my dear. But don't worry, you'll be untied eventually. Once the trolls have you. Now tell me, are you a close friend of this wizard, or just a travelling companion of his?"

"What wizard?"

"Don't play games with me. I want to know if you two are intimate."

"Oh, so that's your game, you sad little man! You capture women, tie them up, and ask them suggestive questions for your own perverse sexual gratification. Typical man! That explains why it's so dark in here. You're probably touching yourself up right now, aren't you?"

Stainwright slapped her hard across the face, outraged that she had tried to put him on the defensive. Okay, so maybe he did touch himself sometimes when he was interrogating the ladies, but that was one of the perks of the job. There was no need for the horribly big young woman to try to make him feel guilty about it.

"How dare you speak to me in this fashion! I am Stainwright, Chief of Spies!"

"And how DARE you strike ME," she spat at him. "I am Rana, Queen of the Amazons!"

His brow creased into a nervous frown. Amazons rarely lied; it was against their code of honour. But this one must be. Her story was impossible. Well, pretty much, anyway.

"Your queen is at Crow Hill. You were captured miles from there, at Harkwell's cabin. I have spies everywhere."

"I was abducted from Crow Hill!" she responded icily. "I have never heard of Harkwell. And you are in SO much trouble!"

She heard him scuttle out of the room. Within half a minute, he had returned with a flaming brand. He examined her briefly, his expression turning from anxiety to fury in the process.

"You've got the wrong colour hair!" he cried. "Why aren't you blond? You're supposed to be blond!"

"Blond is an inferior colour. Takina is blond. I have black hair, as befits a queen. Now release me, imbecile."

"I delegate this one little task to my second in command," he screeched at her, covering her face in dwarf spittle, "and look what happens! She's with Harkwell, I told him. Harkwell. And what does he do? He brings me the wrong bloody woman!"

"You have ten seconds to untie me, cretin. If you take one second longer than that, then this bloody woman is going to chop you into so many pieces that your children will be able to use you as a jigsaw!"

"I don't suppose you're friends with a wizard, too?"

"Seven seconds," she informed him. "And counting."

Surprising himself at his own speed, he released her before she got down to five. Surprising herself at her own restraint, she only punched him twice. She did, however, compensate for her over-generosity by kicking his testicles several times when he fell to the floor.

She was still kicking him when Arkon entered. The dwarf elder seemed amused.

"I've heard you've introduced new forms of torture, Stainwright, but forcing prisoners to kick you while you lie whimpering on the floor is a bizarre method of interrogation even for you! I dare say her feet will be pretty sore by the time she's finished kicking you around the room, but I fear that your private parts may be in an even worse condition by then. Have you managed to beat the truth out of her yet, then?"

Stainwright struggled to his feet with difficulty, his world in ruins. It had taken him many years to build up a reputation so sinister that even the elders were wary of him. Now, his leader had seen him cowering pitifully on the ground whilst being beaten mercilessly by a big girl-without-a-blouse. To make matters worse, this half-naked mad woman wasn't even the right half-naked mad woman. This would not look good on his dwarfish CV.

"Well?" asked Arkon, smirking.

"Never felt better," replied Stainwright, avoiding the issue.

"Are you in charge here?" asked Rana, her voice heavy with menace. She would be quite happy to kick two of the horrible little men around the room if she had to, but thought she would give the newcomer one brief chance to redeem himself by doing everything she told him to do. "Are you responsible for this oaf?"

140

"I'm not an oaf!" Stainwright protested. "My men brought me back this woman instead of the Amazon we wanted. But this one assaulted me in the execution of my duties. In the penal code I'm drawing up, that's an automatic death penalty. Will you order her execution or shall I?"

He awaited Arkon's reaction. Perhaps this show of authority and decisiveness would save his reputation. Keep shouting and making unreasonable demands he told himself. If you shout long enough and loud enough, people will listen. No, more than that, they will positively jump at your command. And once you've got them jumping, you're safe.

"I am Rana. I'm sure you've heard of me. If you so much as mess my hair up, our people will be at war. Do you imagine that the Amazons will allow their queen to go unavenged?"

"There's no question of you being harmed in any way," Arkon assured her. "As a royal guest, you will be treated with the greatest of respect. I'll escort you from the Forest personally, wherever you wish to go. All I ask is that we can take your Amazon friend captive."

"Have her," Rana nodded. "She betrayed me. Do with her as you will."

"Leave it to me," interrupted Stainwright, fading into the shadows.

"Come back here!" Arkon ordered. Stainwright bashfully reappeared again. Arkon took him to one side. "I'm sending someone competent this time. You have brought us to the verge of war with one of the most powerful tribes in the known world. Make your peace with her, or you'll be back on mining duties for the next eighty years."

Stainwright miserably bowed his head in understanding. He turned to Rana, his pride and self-respect crumbling to nothing. Without looking her in the face, he gave her a grovelling apology, and asked what he could do to earn her forgiveness.

With a grin which betrayed an ironic sense of humour that rarely saw the light of day, she picked up the ropes with which she had been bound moments earlier.

"Strip down to your underwear and lie down on that stone slab over there. I want to show you how interrogation should really be done."

The repentant Harkwell led the way, showing them the safer route through the Forest. Thane, Halfshaft and Takina followed close behind him, with Trog covering the rear. Thane told Halfshaft and Takina everything about his mission, but nothing about himself. He explained that he had been brought in from "outside" to kill the Warlock, he outlined his discussion with the King, and told Halfshaft that Spartan had selected him to replace the Grand Wizard on the quest. He produced the healing potion and bade them all drink from it to protect them from all save magically inflicted injuries.

"Is Trog coming with us?" asked Halfshaft, casting a suspicious glance over his shoulder at the hulking troll-cross. "I've seen what he does to people. Rips them in half, and juggles with the pieces. I don't trust him."

"He'll be fine," said Thane. "He's acting on the King's orders. You've got nothing to fear."

"I wasn't afraid," the wizard corrected, catching Takina's eye. "I'm a warrior. I was just being cautious, that's all."

They travelled on in silence. Evening was drawing in, and they eventually came to a halt to make camp for the night. Thane and Harkwell went off in search of food, leaving Trog to stand guard. Before the mercenary left, he handed Halfshaft the message from Spartan.

"He wanted me to give you this. He thought it might help you."

The wizard waited until Thane had gone off foraging before opening the note. It consisted of two sheets of paper. The first of them read:

"We have received conclusive proof of your prowess as a magician. We know that you are more powerful than even Cyrellius. Accomplish the task which Thane gives to you, and you will be our new Grand Wizard upon your triumphant return here.

We know that you have had precious little time to prepare for such an immense task, and do not wish you to be at a disadvantage. We therefore enclose the spell which Cyrellius was to have used against the Warlock, before We chose you to take his place. Use it wisely.

Your ever approachable King,
Spartan"

Halfshaft smiled widely, suddenly exuding confidence.

"Proof of my prowess as a magician! Recognition at last. I am a wizard! And now I have a proper spell to work with," he declared, waving the piece of paper around above his head, "people better start showing me some respect around here!"

Takina looked stunned.

"You don't believe all that rubbish Thane told you, do you?"

"What do you mean?" asked Halfshaft, irritated at being side-tracked into a question and answer session at this moment of revelation. He was a wizard! A real wizard! How cool was that?

"Everyone knows what your king is like. We don't say "liar" in our village, we say "Spartan"! We don't know that the mercenary hasn't just made everything up to put us off our mission. And even if he hasn't, you can bet your life that Spartan has. He wants you dead. He'll do anything to stop us getting to the Black Mountains. I say we sneak off, just the two of us, and carry on without them."

"No. I thought he was bad, but he's a good man after all. He's the first one who's ever believed in me. Even I didn't believe in me, but I do now! I can save the whole world with this spell! We don't even need Rod, as long as I've got this. Why are you trying to take that away from me?"

Takina was getting increasingly desperate. Spartan's trap, she believed, was perfect. By pandering to Halfshaft's ego and playing on his insecurities about his abilities as a wizard, he had convinced him that he was the next Cyrellius, instantly winning him over to his side. He was her friend, and she would do anything for him, but she was under no illusions that his powers as a magician were practically non-existent.

She tried once again to convince him of his folly.

"Do you think it's coincidence that Trog's here?" she asked, hoping that the troll would be unable to hear her from his post nearby. "Don't you see that he's here to protect the Warlock? As soon as we look like killing him, then he'll stab us in the back."

"Thane wouldn't let him."

"Why not? Who is this Thane? What does he want? We know nothing about him at all. Why place our trust in a total stranger, eh? Besides, he won't be here all the time. He's off looking for food now. Trog could kill us whenever he wants to."

"But he hasn't, has he?" countered Halfshaft, pointing out the flaw in her argument. "If he's so intent on finishing us off, why did

143

he save us from Harkwell? And why isn't he beating us with our own body parts now?"

Takina scrunched up her face in frustration. It was so obvious to her. Why couldn't Halfshaft see what was going on here? If she lost him, then that would just leave her and Rod to finish off this quest, assuming that the biker had survived the wolves. She was determined to leave before Thane returned, come what may, for everything depended on her finding Rod and escorting him safely to the Black Mountains before the troll and the mercenary had a chance to kill them. But the last thing she wanted to do was to leave her friend behind. Who knows what would happen to him.

"He's obviously waiting for something," Takina persevered, "He's probably hoping that Rod will turn up. He's using us as bait. Don't forget that it's Rod he really wants. He's the important one."

"Thanks very much," he huffed.

"I'm going," she told him. "Come with me. Please."

He froze. He liked her a lot more than he could admit to her. She took him seriously. He would do almost anything for her. But she was asking him to turn his back on his place in history, on his chance to save the world using magic which until now he had never really been sure he possessed. He had finally realised his own self-worth, and if he succeeded in his quest he would gain the respect and adulation of others that he had craved for as long as he could remember. She was asking him to throw all this away. He valued her friendship greatly, but this was just too high a price to pay.

"I can't," he said.

She smiled at him sadly, and gave him a hug.

"I do understand," she told him. "But I still have to go. I can't abandon what I believe in."

Whilst Trog's back was turned, she crept quietly into the Forest, leaving Halfshaft staring vacantly after her into the trees.

"I know you can't," he said quietly, when he was sure she could no longer hear him. "But I thought that you believed in me."

Crug, Lord of the Trolls, was bored. Rock-throwing had long since lost its appeal, and – in the words of Runt, the great troll philosopher – "if you're tired of rock-throwing, you're tired of life." But he would not be bored forever. Soon it would be Thursday, the day the virgin would be sacrificed. There were but two problems with this. The first was that no one could find a virgin (virgins having become something of a rarity in this day and age). The second was that nobody was quite sure when it would be Thursday. However, the great troll philosopher was confident that he would be able to find solutions to both these problems, and indeed had managed to identify the first three days of the week already. It was only a matter of time.

His realm stretched from the outskirts of the Black Mountains almost to the Great Forest itself. At its centre was Mount Doom, at the top of which stood his magnificent castle of Urknor. In fact, Mount Doom was more a hill than a mountain, but Hillock Doom just did not have the same ring to it. Furthermore, Urknor was not so much a magnificent castle as a pile of rocks (which got smaller every time someone started lobbing them at passers-by, because the lazy sods never put them back again when they'd finished with them) with a few chambers crudely cut into the ground below. Still, it was home.

For centuries, the trolls had inhabited the taller mountains in the area, some of which stood nearly as high as those in the Black Mountain range itself. However, fewer and fewer travellers had passed through them, and without them the troll population had dwindled dramatically. There had once been tens of thousands of them there. Crug wasn't sure how many that was, but he knew it was more than a hundred, and that was quite a lot by all accounts. Now, there were- well, a lot less than that. Without travellers to hunt down and feed upon, the trolls could not survive.

And then came Runt, the great troll philosopher. With a genius which overwhelmed his contemporaries, he conjectured that the reason why travellers no longer passed through the mountains was that they knew there would be a bunch of bloody great trolls up there. By moving to flatter country which they had not hitherto populated, Runt postulated, they would open up new hunting grounds, and gain access to sources of food and sustenance which had previously been unavailable to them. They would, in short, "catch the buggers by surprise."

The plan had worked. Passing travellers seemed to be totally oblivious to the possibility that a troll might come galloping towards them across a daisy-covered country meadow, and therefore wandered round completely unarmed and off guard. It was true that you couldn't get quite the same satisfaction rolling rocks down a gentle slope as you could from hurling them down a gaping precipice, but then again mountains were much colder and draftier in the winter, so it wasn't all bad. "Location, location, location," Runt would say. And Crug would nod wisely, wondering what the hell he was going on about.

The great troll philosopher also explained that it was necessary to make regular sacrifices to the Gods to thank them for the plentiful food supply which was now theirs for the taking. Each and every Thursday, he stated, a naked virgin would have to be thrown from the hill (or at least rolled down it very quickly). He, in his capacity as great troll philosopher, would obviously do the throwing, and would also "be in charge of handling the naked virgins generally". This had caused a jealous uproar when he had first said it, until he had reassured them that the words "generally" and "genitals", though sounding a little similar, meant two different things entirely.

The search started for the first virgin to be sacrificed, whilst Runt set to work on calculating when it would next be Thursday. This was about three weeks ago. They had captured twelve travellers since then who looked as if they might be virgins, but when the trolls' predicament had been explained to them they had all claimed to be sexual active (whatever that meant). Two of them had been suspected of lying (after Runt had noticed that they had crossed their fingers when making their denials), but when the great troll philosopher had taken them into the castle for further questioning, he had apparently satisfied himself that they used to be virgins but were not any more. Despite this, he had taken the disappointment better than most.

Crug sighed. One day, he would find his virgin. And if that day was Thursday, then his luck would be in. Hers, of course, would not.

He decided to ponder the subject for a while, but – as always seemed to be the way when he got to the good bits – he was interrupted in mid-ponder by the arrival of Runt. The philosopher had a carrier pigeon cradled in one large hand, and the flapping bird had a message tied to one leg.

"Give me that," commanded the Lord of the Trolls.

Runt handed him the bird. Crug detached the message and regarded it thoughtfully, nibbling on the pigeon as he did so.

"What is this?" Crug asked.

"It is writing," replied Runt informatively.

"I thought as much," said Crug. "What does it say?"

"I don't know," the great troll philosopher responded with a shrug. "I can't read."

Lord Crug waited patiently, confident that Runt would find a solution to this unforeseen problem.

"I think," said the philosopher, "that I may have a solution to this unforeseen problem."

Crug nodded indulgently, as Runt hurried away. The philosopher returned moments later with a haggard old woman.

"She's not a virgin is she?" asked the Lord of the Trolls.

"No," Runt confirmed.

"Thank goodness for that. Take her away and bite her head off."

"No!" the woman screamed. "I'll do anything, if you'd just spare me."

"We don't want you to do anything," he replied. "Not unless it was to volunteer to bring your granddaughters here. I don't suppose you have granddaughters, do you? I don't suppose they're vir..."

"No, they're not," she wailed. "Not since that Michael Humpendecker moved into the hovel next door."

"I thought," Runt interrupted, "that she might be able to read the letter for us."

Crug handed her the missive, licking away the dripped pigeon entrails from it first. Humans could be funny about that sort of thing. She took it gratefully, relieved that she had not suffered some worse fate. What could be worse than reading in public, though, he found it very difficult to imagine.

They waited for her to begin.

"No, no, no!" shouted Crug, after several silent minutes had passed. "Read it aloud!"

"Sorry," she apologised. "I didn't realise. I can't read all of this here message anyway. It's got pigeon liver smeared across some of the words."

"Paraphrase the bits you can read," suggested Runt, resisting the urge to give the letter a good lick.

"No, no," put in Crug impatiently. "Just give us a rough idea what it says."

"It's from someone called Hench. He hopes you are well. He's been told by some dwarfs that they've caught an Amazon, and he'll buy her for you if you're interested. On the usual terms."

"Is she a virgin?" asked Crug, hopefully.

"Yes," replied the woman, without even consulting the note. "Definitely. Has been all her life. Unlike me."

The Lord of the Trolls clapped his hands together in glee.

"Excellent. Fetch this woman a quill. Write a letter back to Hench, and you will go free. Tell him to buy this virgin. We'll pay him all the gold we have. Runt will call upon him to collect the woman himself. Oh, and tell him I hope he is well. Say that at the beginning. I like that bit. It's got class."

She scribbled down these things as instructed. When she caught up, she looked up at him, awaiting his further command.

"Anything else?" she enquired.

"Yes," Crug stated purposefully. "Ask him if he knows when it's Thursday."

It was not a pleasant experience waking up in a strange, hostile forest to find your companions had vanished without trace. Rod knew. It had just happened to him. It was even less pleasant to see a pair of malignant yellow eyes gleaming in the undergrowth a mere stone's throw away. It was less pleasant still, though, to have your eyes become accustomed to the poor light, and to make out the shape of the large bristling wolf to whom those eyes belonged. Still he thought. Mustn't grumble.

Rod considered his position as calmly as was possible in the circumstances. His Aunt Maud kept dogs. One had attacked him when he was twelve. Okay, so it was only one of those sausage dog things, but the principle was the same. Don't show them any fear. Show them who's boss.

"Bugger off," he told the wolf.

It snarled at him, pulling its lip back across its fangs. He could tell it was not just a warning snarl, either. It was more of a "I'm-going-to-rip-you-to-pieces-for-treating-me-like-a-sausage-dog" type snarl, which had a different meaning entirely.

Rod changed tack. He rummaged through his pockets and found his key ring. He jangled it around for a few seconds to catch the creature's attention, and then threw it as far into the trees as he could.

"Fetch!" he commanded, more in hope than expectation.

The wolf's hackles raised. Its snarl increased in volume, and it rocked back on its haunches, ready to spring. If there was one thing it hated more than being treated like a sausage dog, it was being treated like one of those bloody retrievers.

"Great," said Rod. "Now, even if I get out of this alive, I won't be able to get back in my flat when I get home."

The wolf stopped snarling. It was ready to move in for the kill.

"Don't worry about it, though," Rod reassured it. "I'll go and fetch those keys myself."

He ran. It sprang.

Four dwarfs appeared from nowhere casting a net over the airborne creature, and bringing it crashing to the ground. It struggled there helplessly, growling in anguish and frustration as they pegged down the edges of the net.

"You want to get yourself a cat," Rod advised. "Your dog's bloody mental!"

Once they had finished securing the wolf, they retreated back into the forest, beckoning for him to join them.

"We're taking you to our leader," one explained.

"Yeah," Rod nodded. "I thought you might be."

Try as she might, Takina was unable to sleep. The tree in which she was perched was uncomfortable, and whenever she changed position she felt sure she could hear groaning in her head. It was almost as if the tree was complaining of her weight. She wondered how much it would complain if it had been Trugga up here instead.

For the umpteenth time that night, she considered descending to the Forest floor and making her bed there. It would be softer than the bough of the tree, less precarious, and less noisy. Once again, she came to the same decision. The ground was too dangerous. There were too many predators down there. Uncomfortable though it was, the tree was the only safe option.

As if to illustrate the point, her sensitive hearing picked up a shuffling noise from below. Some creature – a wolf, perhaps – must have picked up her scent, and was circling the base of the trunk to track her down. It could smell her, and it could probably even see her, but as long as it couldn't reach her she was safe.

"I'm coming up," the creature called up to her.

She nearly fell down the tree in surprise. This was unexpected. It could climb, it could talk, and it didn't feel the need to catch her unawares. What manner of beast could it be?

"Leave me alone!" she called back, aware of the inadequacy of the response, but uncertain what else she could say in the circumstances.

"Don't worry," came the response. "I'm nearly there now."

The voice sounded vaguely familiar. She tried to place it without success. As she did so, she caught the sound of claws digging into bark. Whatever it was, it was on its way up.

"What are you?" she asked in trepidation. As she waited for a response, she slipped her knife from the waistband of her fur. She was not used to fighting in trees – or anywhere else for that matter – but would defend herself as best she could. She was an Amazon, after all.

"It's me!" came the less than informative reply. "Hubert!"

For a second, she was at a loss for words. Hubert was supposed to be guarding the gates of the Forest. Legend had it that he had been doing so for centuries. What would he be doing shinnying his way up a tree, miles from his post, in the early hours of the morning? More to the point, what was he doing shinnying up HER tree? What could he possibly want from a penniless serving girl all alone in the woods, at this time of night? She thought it best to ask.

"What are you doing?"

"Climbing a tree."

Another thought occurred to her.

"You can't be Hubert. Hubert always lies. If you were Hubert, you'd say you were rowing a boat or something."

She received no response to this for a while. All she could hear was his laboured breathing, interspersed with the occasional curse, as he hauled himself up the tree towards her.

"Answer me!" she commanded, "or I'll plunge my knife into your chest when you get here."

The sound of climbing ceased, though the heavy breathing continued unabated. It was not a very attractive noise.

"That's charming!" the dwarf protested. "But you might as well cut out my heart, if you must. I've lost it to you already."

"Are you drunk?"

"Drunk with love."

She paused, uncertain where to go from here. What was the little man going on about? If he was lying, should she kill him? And if he was telling the truth, should she kill him anyway? The thought of being anyone's bitch horrified her, but the thought of being the bitch of a depraved and asthmatic dwarf was almost too much to bear. And best not to even get her started on that beard!

"I've been following you since you made that promise to me," he explained. "It's been very dangerous, but I'd do anything for you, such is the depth of my love. I'd storm the very gates of Hell if I had to. That's how much you mean to me!"

"If you've been following me since then, why didn't you help me when we got chased by those wolves?"

"Don't do wolves," he explained. "Terrified of the buggers, always have been."

"And when Harkwell buried me?"

"Have you seen the size of him? I'm only little. I love you and all that, but there's no point in getting killed over it, is there? What good would that have done you? There's other ways I can prove my regard for you, in any case. Come down here, and I'll show you!"

There was a sudden noise below her, which sounded suspiciously like a dwarf falling from a tree.

"Hubert? Are you all right?"

He gave a muffled reply. It sounded like "three".

"Three what? Are you hurt?"

He could not have been, since she could hear him scaling the tree again. She sat astride the bough and edged further along it to make room for him. A misshapen dwarfish head loomed out of the darkness beneath her, and she felt rough cloth against her thigh as two stocky arms closed around it, locking tightly on to it to prevent her escape. She did not recognise the face, but one thing was for sure. This was definitely not Hubert.

"Your boyfriend's okay, just a little bruised," the dwarf informed her smugly. "And he didn't say "three", he said "flee". But I wouldn't worry about it, if I were you. You'd have never escaped alive anyway."

Leofric stood in the chamber in which Stainwright had interrogated Rana the day before. He could see nothing; no torches were lit in the wood dwarfs' caverns at night

151

for fear of burning stray tree roots whilst the brands were unattended. He had therefore been feeling his way from room to room in his quest to rescue the queen.

He was determined to find her as soon as he realised that she had disappeared. Things had seemed different between them since they had fought together against the wolves. They had been closer; more intimate. The social gap between them had narrowed, and he had finally felt that she really needed him. No sooner had this happened, then she had been snatched away from him. He meant to get her back again, whatever the cost.

He had found signs of a struggle, and by the look of it there had been quite a lot of people involved. The size of the footprints suggested dwarfs, maybe twenty or thirty of them, and the blood on the grass told him that she had taken a few of them out before they had subdued her.

The trail they left had been easy enough to follow. It had led back here. He had incapacitated the two guards at the entrance without difficulty and had worked his way through the maze of underground tunnels, a chamber at a time, hoping to chance upon the Amazon queen. Though the wood dwarfs had excellent night vision, they would all hopefully be asleep at this time of night, and if any awoke he would have to deal with them before they raised the alarm. He appreciated that his chances of success were not high, but what else could he do?

The main problem, of course, was that he could not see Rana in the dark. For all he knew, she could have been asleep or gagged in one of the rooms he had visited already. All he could do was quietly whisper her name in each chamber, hoping that her superior Amazon hearing would catch his words without any interfering wood dwarf rousing the colony against him. There had been one or two close calls already.

He called her name again, and paused in the hope of catching her response. He thought he heard a whimper. He started to retreat. This could not be her. She was not the whimpering type.

"Don't go," a voice called out after him. "Help me!"

He ignored it, and continued to feel his way along the packed earth wall towards the exit. He did not have time to get sidetracked.

"Help me!" the voice shouted. "Don't leave me like this!"

"Sssshhhh!" he cautioned, irritated. "You'll wake everyone up. Keep quiet, and I'll come back and help you later."

It was too late. Light flickered in the tunnel outside. Someone must have awoken from their sleep further down the corridor. No doubt they would come and investigate, and within minutes the whole place would be in uproar, with dwarfs running around all over the place. He'd be caught like a fly in a spiders' web. Mind you, at least this fly had a bloody big sword, and the ability to chop off a few legs before they got anywhere near him.

He crept back into the chamber, toying with the idea of taking the occupant hostage. The light from outside got brighter as someone came down the passage towards him, and he could now make out a large stone slab in the centre of the room, to which a half-naked dwarf had for some incomprehensible reason been tied. It occurred to him that this could be Rana's handiwork. It was just her style. He should know; he had been there before, under somewhat happier circumstances. He realised that he was allowing his mind to wander, and pushing this distraction to the back of his mind for later enjoyment, he hid behind the stone, motioning the dwarf to silence.

The shadows on the wall changed shape, and Leofric knew that the torchbearer had entered the chamber. Others were with him. By the sound of their footsteps, he estimated that there were at least three of them in all, possibly more. He heard them approaching the dwarf on the slab, and prayed that he would keep silent. If the dwarf said nothing, then he might still get out of this alive.

"He's down here!" the bound dwarf cried out. "Down behind this slab!"

Leofric leapt out from the shadows, ready to take as many of the dwarfs with him as he could. His sword left its sheath and sliced through the air in one fluid movement, arcing towards the nearest figures without giving them the slightest chance to leap aside. They would barely have time to glance towards him, before the blade would cut into them, lacerating their flesh. Only half way through the stroke, he realised that they were not warlike dwarfs at all. One was Rod; the other, Rana!

He froze, the sword puncturing the skin of her exposed belly to a depth of barely half a millimetre. A thin trickle of blood ran along the edge of the blade, and congealed there. He had come that close to killing her.

Her reaction surprised him.

"No-one has ever managed to mark me before. You ARE the man for me."

She hugged him to her, as she introduced him to her companion, Arkon. As she spoke, a cross little voice piped up from the stone slab.

"That is SO unfair," wailed Stainwright. "I give her a tiny little pat on the head, and I end up like this. You try and chop her in half, and she gives you a cuddle!"

The sun had barely struggled above the level of the treetops when Hubert found them. Harkwell, the wizard, the troll, the warrior; they were all there. Between them, they would surely be able to save Takina from the fate which awaited her.

"Stop! I must speak to you!"

Halfshaft regarded him suspiciously.

"Sod off. We've got problems enough already."

"It's Takina. She's in danger."

Halfshaft came to an abrupt halt, the colour drained from his face. He seized the dwarf by the arm.

"What's happened to her? Tell me!"

"She's been captured by the dwarfs. They mean to give her to Hench, the slaver. She'll end up dead unless you help me."

The wizard fought back panic. She had asked him to go with her, and he had refused. What if anything happened to her? It would all be his fault. He should have gone with her. He should never have let her wander off into the Forest alone.

"Follow me," said Hubert. "I'll tell you all about it as we go."

He turned to leave, but found his way blocked by Harkwell. The big man did not seem pleased to see him.

"What has he been telling you?" Harkwell asked Halfshaft. "Whatever it is, ignore it. He's never told the truth in his life. I can't abide liars."

"You're staying with us," Thane ruled.

"It's all true," Hubert insisted. "Come with me. She'll die if we don't save her!"

Halfshaft stared at him for a few seconds, floundering in indecision. He knew the dwarf was a liar; that was the whole point of his existence, as far as he could make out. But he seemed so sincere. And Takina's life could be at stake here.

"You're her only hope," appealed Hubert. "Please don't let her down now."

154

He made up his mind. "I'm going with him."

Harkwell seized the dwarf and shook him roughly from side to side.

"What's your game?" he shouted. "I'm trying to make amends here, and I'll not let you spoil it for everyone. I don't believe in violence, everyone will tell you that, but liars make me so angry! Tell me what you're up to, or you'll answer for it!"

"Don't you rough me up!" protested Hubert, wagging an indignant finger in Harkwell's face. "For once in my life, I'm telling the truth. Now leave me be, or I'll tell your wife that you let Takina escape. She wouldn't like that, would she? She's an attractive woman, Takina. She's bound to think you had an ulterior motive for letting her go."

"The wife!" howled Harkwell. "I'd forgotten about her!"

"Your wife's dead," said Halfshaft, placing a supportive hand on his shoulder. "She's gone. You know that."

"You haven't left her on her own, have you?" Hubert asked. "All alone in the woods. With all those wolves poking around outside. You know what those wolves are like. They get into everything, don't they? I wouldn't be surprised if they were scratching at your door even as we speak."

"I've got to go to her," Harkwell fretted. "I'm sorry everyone. I've got to go."

"We need you to guide us through the Forest," Halfshaft told him. "Don't listen to him. There's nothing you can do for your wife now. Except maybe give her a good polish once in awhile."

Hubert theatrically placed one hand to his ear.

"Did you hear that?" he asked. "It sounded like scratching to me. I hope your front door's nice and sturdy."

Harkwell's face crumpled completely. With a wail of terror, he turned and crashed his way back through the Forest, returning to a wife who had long since died. Thane and Trog looked on in disbelief.

"I didn't want to do that," the dwarf announced, "but it was self defence. You saw how agitated he was getting with me."

"I thought his wife is..." began Thane.

"She is. Rumour has it that he killed her, you know. She was a nasty piece of work. Deserved everything she got. They say it was self-defence. She kept picking on their daughter, and he just couldn't

155

take it any more. Finished her off with the shovel in the kitchen. It's driven him completely mad, of course. So much guilt. It's a shame, because he was really quite nice before she died. When he wasn't burying people alive, that is."

"Excuse me," interrupted Halfshaft. "Haven't you forgotten something?"

"No, I don't think...Oh, you mean Takina. My beloved! Yes! Follow me!"

The dwarf disappeared into the woods, with Halfshaft in hot pursuit.

"I'm coming!" the wizard called after him. "But I'm not your beloved!"

With a shrug of resignation, Thane followed the two of them into the trees, with Trog close on his heels. Now that they no longer had Harkwell as a guide, there did not seem to be much of an alternative.

Takina drifted in and out of consciousness for much of the day. She remembered a bunch of surly dwarfs hauling her from the tree, and seeing Hubert (or was it Horace? She could never remember which was which!) struggle free from a second group of surly dwarfs and make a run for it, blowing her sticky wet kisses as he waddled quickly away. She even remembered one of the nasty little men whacking her on the back of the head. After that, her recall was a little vague.

Between her short periods of consciousness, she had the same recurring dream. She saw a man wandering through a grey feature-less desert. There was powdered rock beneath his feet, like ash, and this stretched for miles in every direction. The wind whipped the rock up into his face, and she felt it in her own eyes, leaving her blind and disorientated. She knew he was in desperate need of something. She assumed it was water. She ran her tongue over her own parched lips, craving a drink.

She came to, and discovered that she was in the back of an uncovered cart. In the far distance, she could see a blanket of green – the Great Forest perhaps – but everywhere else she looked she could see the same grey rock-ash as that in her dream. She lapsed back into sleep again.

Now the man had a goat with him. A nanny goat, she somehow knew. All of a sudden, it struck her that it was not water this man wanted, but love. Goat love, to be precise. The man reached out tenderly towards the creature, but it recoiled in disgust, and fled from him.

Again, she awoke from her slumber. She was still in the cart. Her throat was dry and painful, her lips cracked and bleeding. She lifted her head a few inches, and looked about her. A fat man sat at the front of the cart, spurring on his horses across the grim wasteland. Ahead of him, she could see some sort of encampment, an oasis of tents in a sea of powdered granite. She tried to focus on it, but the effort was too much for her. Her head started to swim giddily in all directions at once, and she lapsed back into unconsciousness again.

The man now stood on the crest of a rock-dune. The goat grazed nervously nearby, but he was paying it no attention. Something had caught his eye on the horizon. She squinted, relying on her keen Amazon senses to pick out whatever it was he had spotted. With a shock, she realised it was her. She could see herself in the distance, stark naked, and bound to a post in the middle of nowhere, for reasons she could not even begin to imagine. She wracked her brains to remember how she had got there, but her mind was blank.

The man ran towards her. He reached the foot of the dune of crushed granite, and clambered up towards her, breathing hoarsely as he struggled towards her. She was naked, vulnerable, at his mercy. But he was her only hope of salvation. She must persuade him to release her, or she would die.

He reached the pole, and stood before her, surveying her with a satisfied smile on her face. Despite her position, she blushed, flattered by his attention.

"Untie me," she told him, "and I will be very grateful."

His grin widened. "You would show me your appreciation in any way I ask?"

"Any way at all," she assured him. She was not used to being provocative. It felt strange. Humiliating and empowering all at once. "You won't be disappointed, I promise you."

He seized her ropes, and started to untie her. It took an age before he could calm himself down sufficiently to unpick the knots, such was his excitement. She grimaced as his nails cut into her wrists, but held her tongue, impatient to be free. At last, the bonds dropped loose from her wrists and fell to the ground. She stood before him, nude but proud, ready to fill her part of the bargain. She had never actually mated before. Now was to be her time.

"What would you have me do?" she asked, her voice vibrant with yearning.

His eyes sparkled with a depth of passion which both aroused and frightened her. He pulled her close to him, and brought his mouth close to her ear.

"I would be forever in your debt," he whispered, "if you would help me catch that nanny goat over there."

Although still upset by the deaths of Halfshaft, Takina and even Doon, Rod had decided to make a conscious effort to return to his usual cheerful self. This, he quickly discovered, had the added advantage that it wound Rana up something chronic.

"We'll reach the edge of the Forest within the hour," Arkon announced encouragingly as they struggled through a band of trees so dense that only the dwarf was able to pass between them unscathed. Rana was doing her best to give the impression that she could easily weave her way through the chaotic web of branches that barred her path, but even her agility was insufficient to protect her from the myriad of scratches which criss-crossed her body. Leofric was faring no better. The closer they got to the Forest boundary, the harder it became to penetrate the trees around them. It was almost as if this was some ancient bulwark to keep enemies out. And, more to the point, victims in.

Rod – whose fondness for lager, pizza and kebabs made him an even easier target for the trees than his companions – laughed loudly each time a spiteful thorn-laden branch raked his face.

"This," he declared the most irritatingly cheerful voice he could muster, " is the bee's knees."

Rana glared at him, wishing that it wasn't quite so much in her best interests to keep him alive. One swing of her sword would be enough to split his skull clean in two. Just one swing. Life was so unfair.

"The cat's whiskers," he added, to illustrate the point.

She had no idea what cat's whiskers had to do with getting torn to pieces by a thousand obstinate trees, any more than she knew what sort of bees had knees. What she did know, however, was that one more such remark from the freakish alien would probably be enough to ensure she hacked his brains out with his own toenails.

158

"The dog's bollocks," pronounced Rod, with relish.

She swung round to face him, almost poking out her eye on a protruding branch in the process.

"Thus far I have tolerated you. But even queens have their limits. Your next word will be your last. Understand?"

He winked at her, and gave her a thumbs-up sign.

"I love it when you're rough with me. Makes all the veins stand out on your forehead, though."

For a second, he thought he had gone too far. Her hand shot out for his throat at a speed which caught him totally off guard. But no sooner had her fingers clenched hold of his windpipe than they relaxed again.

"Later," she hissed at him. "We'll have this conversation later."

Rod knew better. There would be no "later". All of the fun had gone out of the quest since Halfshaft and Takina had gone, and now he just wanted it over as soon as possible. They were almost out of the Forest, and he felt that he no longer needed any help from Leofric. He certainly didn't need any from Rana. As soon as he got the chance, he would go it alone.

The warm hand on her forehead awoke Takina with a start. She sat bolt upright, trying to get her bearings. At first, she could think of nothing but goats, but the unpleasant images fortunately faded quickly into oblivion. In their place, she saw a man who looked disconcertingly like a toad. His eyes were bulbous, his face wide, and his jaw rounded. All of this atop a blubbery body which had only narrowly lost the contest with his legs as to which of them could get closer to the ground. Had he stuck his tongue out to catch a fly, she would not have been in the least bit surprised.

"It's a good job we already have a buyer for you," said the toad-man. "We wouldn't get much for you on the open market. Hardly an ounce of flab on you anywhere. Still, we might have got something for your squirrel-skins at a push."

"Begone, foul beast" she retaliated groggily. "I will not be insulted by a fat tadpole like you!" She smiled, pleased with the remark. Even Rana would have been proud of that one.

"Excellent!" he applauded. "You're alive. There's nothing worse than dead merchandise, it puts the punters off something rotten.

Fever is so debilitating, don't you find? And I can't have debilitated women on my books, even with a buyer lined up. I have my reputation to think of."

Takina still felt very much debilitated, but was loath to admit this to a toad. Her head was pounding, her throat was sore, and to cap it all an uncomfortably large quantity of sand had found its way into her furs, and was rubbing her up the wrong way, so to speak. All in all, she was not in the mood for a cosy chat.

"Have you any water, Toad?" she asked.

"My name is Hench," he replied, "and I have plenty. You, on the other hand, have none. I do not feel inclined to share any with such a rude creature as you, but I suppose I have little choice. I don't want my stock dehydrated. Though it's food I should be giving you really. Why, I bet you've never been twenty stone in your whole life, you miserable looking creature!"

He poured some water grudgingly into a bowl, and shoved it into her hands. She took it from him, and drank deeply. It occurred to her that although she was clearly a prisoner, he had made no effort to tie her up. She shivered in guilt and embarrassment, as the thought of ropes brought her dream back to her.

He looked at her condescendingly. "You are my product. A commodity, to be bought and sold. For a profit, of course. Your buyer waits outside. I thought I ought to check on you before admitting him to the tent. Make sure you're of merchantable quality. Even a troll wouldn't be stupid enough to accept delivery of damaged goods."

"You're selling me to a troll!"

"It's part of the bargain. I got you at a discount on that express condition. I like to keep my word if it doesn't cost me anything. Always keep the customer happy, if you can. You're more likely to get repeat business that way."

She made a break for the door before he had finished his sentence. He was fat and slow, and it seemed like a good idea at the time. She pulled back the cloth covering the exit, and came to an abrupt halt. A troll barred her way. She doubled back towards the rear of the tent, hoping to crawl beneath the canvas to safety. As she passed Hench, he shot out a chubby arm, encircled her waist, and reeled her in, thrashing and kicking, to his side.

"This toad," he told her smugly, "has caught a fly. Now stay there quietly like a good item of merchandise. I don't want to tie you up –

your wrists will get shop-soiled – but I'll do it if that's what it takes to make you behave yourself. It would not do to risk losing my stock beneath the customer's very nose!"

She sank to the ground, overcome by hopelessness and fatigue. She needed time to think. She would not get it.

The troll entered the tent.

"Runt, my old friend!" Hench beamed.

"That's no way to speak to a customer," interrupted Takina, refusing to go without a fight. "Fancy him calling you a runt! If I were you, I'd take my business elsewhere!"

"Runt is this gentleman's name," Hench explained patiently. "I'm surprised you did not know that. He is renowned throughout the land as the greatest philosopher the trolls have ever produced. He is to be your new master."

Runt nodded to confirm all this. To show that he was not unfamiliar with the etiquette of the outside world, he decided to exchange pleasantries before getting down to business.

"Hello, Hench," he greeted the merchant, in a well-rehearsed tone. "I hope you are well."

"I am in excellent health," replied Hench enthusiastically. "Just like this feisty young woman, here. And your good self?"

"Fine, fine," Runt responded impatiently, feeling that the pleasantries were being a little overdone. Some people just didn't know when enough was enough. It was time to get down to business.

"Is she a virgin?"

"Very much so. That's why the charming creature has so much energy to spare. Have you my commission?"

Runt looked blank.

"My fee."

Still no joy. Hench stifled a sigh.

"Have you brought the cash?"

"Ah! Your fee! Of course!" he replied, nodding his head wisely. "It's outside." As he pointed in the relevant direction, he caught sight of Takina, who was inching her way over towards the exit. He glared. She retreated back to her place. No wonder there weren't many virgins around, he philosophised, if they kept trying to escape all the time.

Hench made his way to the door with difficulty, his massive body almost dragging on the ground as he went. He pulled back the cloth expectantly. His face fell.

161

"I see no gold out here."

"Gold?"

"Yes, gold. It was in the message I received from Crug. He agreed to pay me all the gold you have."

"Gold? I thought he said goats! All the goats we have. They're all out there, all twenty-seven of them. It took me hours to herd them here on my own. Obstinate little buggers, they are. You can count them if you like."

"I already have. There are not twenty-seven of them. There are four. But that is immaterial. I am afraid that you have wasted my time. Our contract states that I should be paid in gold, and gold I must have. You can't change a contract, you know that as well as I. Take your goats away."

Runt glared at him maliciously. For a moment, Takina thought that the troll was going to set upon him, and she prepared to start shuffling towards the exit again whilst they were fighting. Hench caught sight of the ferocious outrage on Runt's face, and decided that a bit of backtracking was in order.

"My stock is well protected, as am I. I have seventy armed men outside, willing to do my bidding. But let's not fall out over this. Bring me the gold by sunrise tomorrow, and the virgin will be yours."

With a parting look at Takina, Runt stalked moodily from the tent.

"Trolls are so temperamental," Hench complained when they were alone again. "But don't worry, you won't have to work for him for long. Troll slaves never last more than a day or two at most."

L eofric shook Rod awake. "Your turn for guard duty," he informed him. "We may be out of the Forest now, but we must still be vigilant."

Rod sat up, and rubbed away the sleep which encrusted his eyes. Rana slumbered restlessly nearby. Even in her sleep, her movements were fluid and elegant. Despite his dislike of her, Rod had to admit that in terms of her appearance the woman was a work of art. Personality-wise, however, she was more of a spoilt child's scribble.

"She's something special," Leofric remarked, as he watched her shift into a graceful foetal position.

"Too right," Rod agreed. "There's certainly not many more like her around."

Leofric smiled, apparently pleased by the remark.

"I think you can safely say," Rod pushed his luck," that she's in a class of her own."

"You now she doesn't like you?"

"Hates my guts," Rod grinned. "I'd be gutted if it was any other way."

"I'm glad you feel like that. I wouldn't want to think that anything would jeopardise our mission. We'll be in the Black Mountains in the next day or two, so you haven't got long to put up with each other anyway."

Rod saw the opportunity to find out more about where they were heading. If he was going to go off on his own, he had to have some idea of the direction he should be taking. Leofric seemed to be in a pretty talkative mood, and Rana was still sleeping. If they were now only a couple of days away from their destination, this might be his best chance to get the information he needed, and slope off.

"Whereabouts in the Black Mountains are we going? No-one's ever told me that"

"Mount Leiden. It's just the other side of troll country. It's a shame. If it wasn't for having to skirt round that, we could get their even sooner. But it's best not to take the risk. You don't mess with trolls if you can help it. And once we're there, it's over to you. You've done really well so far. I'll be sorry to lose you."

"Lose me?"

"Yes, I..." Leofric began. "I mean, when you go back to your world."

"You really think I can find my way back home through this tunnel?"

"Definitely. Believe me, once you go into the mountain, there'll be no need for you to come out here again."

Rod stared at the fire in silence, digesting this reply. He had felt uneasy ever since Halfshaft and Takina had died, but the feeling had intensified today. Something was being kept from him, he was sure of it. All the more reason, then, to leave while he still could.

Leofric's eyelids started to droop. He had gone without sleep the night before, yet had still volunteered to take the first stint of guard duty tonight. Now that he was idle, his body started to relax, and he knew that he would be unable to stay awake much longer.

"You look knackered," Rod observed. "I'd get your head down if I were you. Busy day tomorrow."

Leofric did not feel inclined to argue the point. He lay down, and was asleep almost immediately.

As soon as he was sure that neither of his companions remained conscious, Rod slipped quietly away into the darkness. He was frightened, but knew he was making the right choice. He had to finish his journey alone, whatever the risks might be.

The day was still in its infancy as Halfshaft peered over the peak of the ashen rock-dune towards the confused mass of brightly coloured tents on the plain below.

"It's down there, all right," he reported, as he crawled back to join the others.

"I told you it would be," Hubert protested moodily. "When oh when will you start believing me?"

"When we can be sure you're not a lying little toe-rag," Thane advised him.

"Are you sure she's there?" the wizard asked.

"Positive. I heard them say they were selling her to Hench. That is his encampment. She'll be there, I'm telling you. No go and rescue her, and be sure to tell her that it was me who sent you."

"Let's go, then."

Thane shook his head. "It's not that easy. It's a big camp. Until we know how many guards they've got, and how good they are, it would be too dangerous for you lot to go storming in there."

"We could wait until dark," Trog suggested.

"She might be dead by then," Halfshaft pointed out, with a shudder. "And we don't know what they're doing to her in the meantime. We've got to act now. Has anyone got any bright ideas?"

"I have!" cried Hubert.

"Has anyone else get any bright ideas?" asked Halfshaft in desperation.

"No, trust me, it's a good one," Hubert insisted. "Traders come in and out of the camp all day. There's a road on the far side. Why not just hijack the first trader who passes by, steal his clothes, and trick our way in? It doesn't even matter what shape he is. His clothes are bound to fit one of us."

"It might work," the wizard pondered.

"It won't work," retorted Trog. "But if it means killing someone for their stuff, then I'm all for it."

They circled warily around Hench's camp. Once they reached the track of which Hubert had spoken, the wizard, dwarf and troll buried themselves into the grey powder at the margin of the road, and settled down to wait for a trader. Thane took refuge behind a nearby dune, trying not to laugh. This was undoubtedly the saddest attempt at an ambush he had even had the pleasure to witness, and he had only managed to distance himself from it by pointing out that someone would be needed as back-up. Hence, he was perched in relative comfort behind the nearest dune, whilst the others were playing at human sand-castles close enough to the track to leave them at serious risk of being crushed by the first wide-axled cart which came their way. C'est la vie.

Fortunately for Trog's patience and Halfshaft's arthritis, they did not have long to wait. Within half an hour, a cart was spotted trundling along the track towards them, borne by two dispirited looking horses. They pounced as it passed them by, springing from their hiding places like rabid jack-in-the-boxes on speed. Hubert seized the bridle of the nearest horse, bringing the animals to a halt. Halfshaft and Trog leapt into the back of the covered cart, the weight of the latter nearly fracturing the rear axle. To the troll's great disappointment, all the occupants fainted before he had a chance to terrorise them.

Hubert climbed with difficulty into the rear of the cart, and looked at the three unconscious travellers in dismay.

"Oh dear, oh dear. Still," he said, "we did say the first ones who passed by."

Trog shook his head violently. "No," he said firmly. Not even for the King,"

"Takina is in danger," Halfshaft retorted grimly. "I'm afraid we have no choice."

The Warlock's smile broadened. His plan was nearing completion. Leofric was bringing the alien to free him. His army of corpses was ready to march. Everything was ready. He gave the order, and the corpses around him sprung to life, trundling determinedly towards the tunnel which led from the mountain. There, they would wait in the shadows for the sword to be pulled from the stone. Then they would march. First on the trolls, then the wood dwarfs, the Amazons, Spartan Castle, and anything beyond. He would resurrect any who fell in battle, perpetuating his army for as long as it took him to conquer the world. And once they had killed and mutilated all before them, he would be avenged for the insults and defeats of centuries past.

The wheels had been set in motion. He had been waiting for this moment for close on a thousand years. And now it was Time.

The Grand Wizard froze in mid roll. He had lost count of the number of days he had been shut up in this foul cupboard, with no one but the rats to keep him company. Still bound, and still gagged, he was not in the best of moods. How could someone of his stature have been brought to this, rolling around in his own urine in an unused larder full of impertinent rodents? And then that cackle from the corner. A laugh that froze his blood with fear.

He squirmed around to catch a glimpse of he knew not what. To his surprise, he found that he was now sharing his larder with a hideous old woman. Quite how she had got in was anyone's guess. The door had not been opened for days. That could only mean one thing. She was a witch. And a particularly foul-smelling one at that, he thought (somewhat hypocritically for someone who had been lying in their own excrement for so long).

The witch began to feel his back and arms, as if assessing his strength in some way. He shuddered at her touch, but knew with outraged frustration that there was nothing he could do to fend her off. Instead, he contented himself with watching her with hate filled eyes, trying to convey to her the peril of her position. Touch me again, those eyes said, and you will pray for death by the time I've finished with you. But the stupid old cow was too busy touching him up to notice, and all the hard work he put in to his scowl was wasted.

"Bit bony," she commented, "but you'll do, I suppose. I need someone to ride, and you magicians always make a pretty good mount at a push. That Shamen was none too steady, I'll grant you. Had to give her the elbow after just a week or two. But you look like you'd last for years."

She muttered something under her breath, and touched his legs. To his horror, he felt the magic drain from his body. What foul spell was this? What was she doing to him?

"There, that's your magic gone, Dear. We don't want you using your spells to escape now, do we?"

She pulled the gag from his mouth. In a flash, he muttered the words to free him from his bonds, but nothing happened. He watched in misery as she unbound him, knowing that the hag spoke the truth. She had stripped him of his powers. He was a wizard no more.

"Why?" he asked, crushed with self-pity. "Why have you done this to me?"

"Because," said Martha Catwort, "I'm sick of trying to catch people the nice way. You invite them back to your hovel for a chat and a cup of drugged potion, and they push off the moment they realise you want to use them as a donkey for the rest of their lives. Well that's fine for them, but what about me, eh? I'm not getting any younger. Why shouldn't I have a bit of help getting around at my time of life?"

"But why me?" the ex-Grand Wizard screamed at her.

"You were lying in a cupboard unused," she told him. "I do hate waste. Now come with me like a good boy, and I'll give you your powers back when I'm sixty."

He brightened up.

"How old are you now?" he asked.

She ran her fingers coquettishly through her matted grey hair, giving him an enormous, hideous wink as she did so.

"Why, twenty one, of course. Now get a move on, before I lose my patience."

She hustled him out the cupboard, and into the disused kitchens in a long empty wing of the castle. She waited there, apparently expecting someone else to turn up.

"Mabel will be along shortly," she explained. "She insisted on coming. Her knees are going, so she wants a donkey, too. Just make sure it's someone who won't be missed, I told her. Check the cupboards first. No one who'd bring attention to us, like when she pinched the Shamen from the Amazons. I think she got the message."

There was a commotion from outside. Galloping footsteps, interspersed with the occasional inexplicable shout of "giddy up, a ding-dong, giddy up!" Within seconds, Mabel rode into the kitchen astride King Spartan. The King had a bridle shoved unceremoniously into his mouth, and looked on the verge of tears. A sob wracked his body as he came to a halt beside the fireplace.

"Stop snivelling, donkey!" Mabel complained, whipping him across the buttocks with a riding crop. She turned to Martha, a triumphant grin on her face.

"Doubt they'll miss this one!" she exclaimed. "I think he's some sort of convict. There were guards all over the show outside his room!"

She wheeled him round, and galloped away. Martha leapt on the Grand Wizard's back, noticing with dissatisfaction the way his legs buckled under him when she did so. She'd have to break him of that habit pretty quickly if she was going to compete with Mabel during donkey derby week in March.

With a crack of her whip, she sent him down the corridor off in pursuit.

B y the time they had finished pulling on the slave girls' garments, even Hubert was starting to have second thoughts about the wisdom of his plan.

"I'm not so sure about this now," he said, his face creased up with concern. "Too many things could go wrong. What if they fancy us or something? They might make demands of us, that I for one would be very reluctant to satisfy!"

Halfshaft surveyed his companions in silence. The outfits were fortunately not as revealing as some he had seen (and dreamt about). These must have been senior slave girls, entrusted with the work of bringing fresh recruits to the harem for their masters. Still, the costumes were scant enough to expose areas of flesh which no self-respecting wizard would ever wish to put on general display. Altogether, the three of them made a very unappealing batch of slaves indeed.

His only consolation was that Trog looked even worse than he did. He towered above the other two, looking the least likely sex-slave ever. He had insisted on keeping his trousers on, and Halfshaft had little choice but to agree to this since none of the slave-girl's outfits reached below the troll-cross' waist. He had fashioned a bodice out of one of the women's skirts, which was wide enough to cover his hairy back but fell about twelve inches short of stretching across his chest. This gave him a plunging neckline that would have confirmed to anyone unfortunate enough to notice that he was not a slave-girl with an over abundance of cleavage. He had covered his face with the girl's veil, but the huge expanse of muscle and sinew on show was still more than enough, in Halfshaft's view, to give the game away.

Hubert was little better. His expansive stomach spilled out over the waistband of his outfit and his stubby little legs turned the short skirt into a long one (which was probably for the best). The chest of the bodice was too large for him – its owner, Mammary L'amour, having been by far the bustiest of the three girls – and he could only keep it up by holding it in place (always an inconvenience at the best of times). His veil covered his beard, but bristly stray hairs protruded through the silk all over the place. All in all, he was not a pretty sight.

By comparison to his two companions, Halfshaft felt that he must have actually looked rather fetching himself. His beard sat neatly below his veil, without him experiencing the same problem with errant bristles as his hirsute dwarfish counterpart. It was true that he had been forced to tuck the end of it in his bra to stop it peeping out from under his top, but what woman did not use a little artifice in her make-up from time to time? Besides, the ticklish sensation was rather pleasant.

The three of them moved off down the road towards the large cluster of tents ahead. Thane stayed behind, theoretically to come to their aid if so required, but in practice to wet himself laughing. He was also entrusted with keeping an eye on the slave-girls they had divested, something which Hubert had been doing ever since divesting them.

To the wizard's surprise, they entered the camp unchallenged. There were still few people about, and those who were present seemed to be too busy erecting signs by their tents to concern themselves with the three battle-axes who passed through their midst. This was market day. They had to sell their wares to survive, and this task had to take precedence over jeering at the ugliest slave-girls they had ever seen.

"How will we know which tent she's in?" Halfshaft whispered.

"Look at the signs they're putting up," Hubert told him. "They describe what's on sale. It shouldn't be too difficult to work out which one's her."

They stopped at he first sign they came across. Trog looked at it blankly, before announcing that he could not quite make out the handwriting. Hubert read it for him:

> *"Although this slave's not very clean,*
> *And some might call her dirty.*
> *A dirty woman's highly sought*
> *By all men over thirty.*
> *Besides, her mileage is quite low,*
> *The logbook's here for all to read.*
> *She'll last you for a thousand nights,*
> *And that, my friend, is guaranteed."*

They moved on to the next tent and waited impatiently for the tradesman to finish his sign. This one was shabbier than the last, and clearly aimed at the bargain-basement end of the market:

> *"Give me your sword, bow, arrows and pike,*
> *And my slave-girl will give you one as oft as you like."*

Hubert looked distracted.

"You two go on ahead. I'll just hang around here for a bit."

"We all know what bit you're after!" retorted Halfshaft. He then noticed the puzzled expression on the face of the trader. Anxious to protect their cover, he thought he ought to give Hubert the chance to find some plausible excuse for his remark.

"Besides," he addressed the dwarf, in as high a voice as he could manage. "Why would you want to go in there to see another woman?"

"Another woman?" repeated Hubert, mystified. Then, cottoning on, he continued shrilly:

"Oh yes, of course. Another woman. Well, I just wanted to tell her that she shouldn't despair. She should be loyal to her master, and one day, she could end up just like us!"

"I very much doubt it," muttered Halfshaft under his breath as he pulled the dwarf on to the next tent. This one was larger than the others, and it was this that attracted them to it. As Halfshaft started reading the sign, Hubert glanced around to see if he could spot any other notices of interest. How frustrating was this? He felt like the kid with the key to the sweet shop, who had just been diagnosed with diabetes. Surrounded by candy, and he wasn't allowed to have a suck.

"This has got to be it!" announced Halfshaft.

"Here," Hubert interrupted. "Do you see that one over there? "Masochistic lover" and "Hit her with a shovel" doesn't even rhyme, does it?"

"Never mind that, now," snapped Halfshaft. "Look at this one:

Nubile girl for sale or rent
A slave for work or vice.
Could do with fattening up a bit,
So yours for half the price.

Comes free with log book, neck collar,
Instruction manual, too.
But since the poor girl's got no flab,
She's sold as seen to you."

"I think we've found our girl," the dwarf agreed. "Let's try to rescue her. And if we don't get anywhere, maybe we should rescue the one with the shovel."

Halfshaft ignored him, and led the others to the entrance to the tent. He tried to knock on the door through habit, but found that knocking on billowing fabric does not actually achieve very much. Trog pushed him impatiently aside, and strolled inside. The wizard got the impression that the troll was for some reason keen to get this over and done with. Maybe it was because his outfit was a drab yellow, whilst Halfshaft and Hubert were wearing costumes coloured in a much more fetching purple. Jealousy was an ugly thing.

A man gave them an oozingly warm welcome inside. He reminded Halfshaft of a fat swollen frog. Takina lay sleeping on the floor nearby. She did not look well.

"How much for the woman?" asked Trog gruffly.

"Our fellow woman," Halfshaft chirped, nudging Trog in the ribs with a well-raised elbow. "How much for our fellow woman? We're all women here, you know. Not a man amongst us, I'm glad to say."

"Yes," agreed Hubert emphatically. "Nasty hairy things. I can't stand the sweaty little buggers. Clawing at you all night, making degrading demands of you, expecting you to...."

"I think I've got the point," Hench interrupted discreetly. "So you three beautiful ladies would like to buy this girl here, would you? A wise choice indeed. And it's your lucky day! She was reserved for another buyer but he hasn't come up with the money. She's all yours for just twenty gold pieces."

Halfshaft fished out the moneybag he had taken from the slave-girls they had ambushed, and counted out the contents into Hench's fatty palm, one coin at a time. There were seventeen gold pieces in all.

Hench's face darkened a degree.

"You are three coins short, my dear."

"Twenty pieces is an awful lot of money for one slave," the wizard observed. "And she doesn't look all that healthy to me. Surely you could let her go for seventeen?"

"The price is twenty," Hench insisted. "My original customer may still turn up, and I wouldn't go to the trouble of disappointing him for any less than twenty gold pieces. Trolls can get very upset if they miss out on a bargain, you know."

"You'll find out how upset if you don't sell her to us for seventeen," growled Trog. Hench looked startled at this ferocious outburst from the hulking slave-girl. Halfshaft placed a restraining arm around the troll's back (not being able to reach his shoulders), and tried to smooth things over.

"My friend here didn't mean to upset you. She was an Amazon before she became a slave – hence her size – and you know what they're like when they get agitated! My master likes them spirited, though. That's why we're so keen to buy this one."

"And buy her you shall," Hench agreed, "provided you come up with the extra three gold pieces. And if you find that you can't raise the extra funds, then there's plenty more stock out there, which I'm certain would meet with your master's approval. I'd be happy to recommend a girl or two, for a very modest fee."

"We want this one," Halfshaft insisted.

Hubert had an idea.

"Is it right that you take weapons for payment? I saw a sign out there about swords, and arrows and stuff."

"Of course. They're a very valuable commodity round here"

"Would a good sword...well, a fairly good sword, be worth three gold pieces?"

Hench laughed, his gross belly blobbing up and down before him like a whale carcass in a rip tide.

"Yes, but where would three slave-girls pick up a decent sword, eh? You're hardly likely to have them tucked into your dainty little costumes, are you?"

"You'd be surprised what we have tucked into our dainty little costumes," Halfshaft countered. "We'll be back for the girl in the next half an hour. Promise you'll keep her for us in the meantime."

Hench gave them a wide, ingratiating grin.

"You have my word on it!"

"Mount Leiden!" exclaimed the soldier. "Why on Hedral would you want to go there?" Rod was a great believer in fate. He had left Leofric and the Bitch-queen from Hell, wandered off, and got hopelessly lost. Just when he was starting to resign himself to going back in search of them, he had spotted a figure sitting beneath a gnarled old tree, who was taking long swigs from a bottle. The figure turned out to be a soldier named Jasper.

Jasper, it transpired, was on his way to some market or other. Rod could not really work out what sort of market would set up in a god-forsaken place like this, but found out that the man was off to buy some "camp followers," whatever they might be. In any event, it seemed it was a trip that the soldier was very much looking forward to.

"It's a long story," Rod told him, in reply to his question. "Maybe I'll tell you later. Why pull that face? Have you ever been there?"

"No. I've never been to the sea, though, but I know it's bloody wet there. Why go to Mount Leiden? There's nothing worth seeing in the mountains. Never has been."

Rod thought things over for a while. He was now painfully aware that he would never make it to the mountains without help. He really didn't want to go back to that big butch Amazon pain-in-the-arse if he could help it, so why not enlist Jasper's help? He did not have to tell him the whole story, after all.

"How many of you are there?" Rod asked. "It's not just you, I take it?"

"Oh no," Jasper assured him. "Far from it. There must be about two hundred of us altogether. There used to be more, but our numbers are dwindling a bit now. You know how it is."

"The trolls?"

"No, the trolls have moved. They left the mountains ages ago. They couldn't have gone far, but we haven't been able to track them down yet, more's the pity. If we could, we'd be there like a shot, I can tell you."

"They don't scare you, then?"

"Of course not!"

"This is almost too good to be true! If I told you where you could find thousands of them, do you reckon your mates might be interested in joining me?"

"We'd die for an opportunity like that!"

"Then Jasper, my old mate, I think we're in business!"

"The bad news," Hench declared nonchalantly, "is that the girl has already gone. The troll came back and paid for her while you were gone. She'll be sacrificed tonight."

Halfshaft felt his legs go weak beneath him, and it was as much as he could do to stay upright. Hubert squealed in indignation. Only Trog was unmoved.

"We had a deal!" Hubert cried. "We've got the sword here. You should have sold her to us!"

Hench gave them a reassuring smile.

"My friends! All is not lost. I have told you the bad news; now let me tell you the good. Although the girl has already left the camp, I can take you to her buyer, if you wish. Perhaps he will have a change of heart, and sell her on to you."

Hubert nodded eagerly. "Yes, yes. We want to buy her. Where is he?"

"This way," gestured Hench. "One at a time, please. There's no rush."

Trog pushed his way impatiently past Halfshaft and Hubert, and followed Hench out of the tent. The dwarf scampered along behind

174

him. The wizard hesitated for a few seconds. He did not like Hench, and trusted him even less. He had, after all, just sold Takina as a human sacrifice, so he was hardly the sort of person to whom you'd hand your keys and ask to keep an eye on your house whilst you were away on holiday. Having said this, what choice did he have? If he did not follow the merchant, Takina would die.

With mixed feelings, he left the tent to catch up with the others. His feelings instantly became unmixed again, as he saw them lying in an unconscious heap on the ground. Around them stood nine or ten of Hench's men, each of them wielding sizeable clubs. Runt towered above them, with Takina slung over one massive shoulder.

Before he could react, one of the group heaved a club towards him. It made contact with his head with a sickening thud that sent the wizard plummeting into unconsciousness. His legs buckled beneath him, and he succumbed to the blanket of nothingness which engulfed his fuzzy mind.

Hench and Runt shook hands over the three inert bodies.

"You're sure they're all virgins?" Runt enquired.

"Take a look at them," smirked Hench. "Who could doubt it?"

"Excellent!" Runt exclaimed, overjoyed at the news. "Then we will sacrifice all four of them tonight. This promises to be the best Thursday ever!"

J asper's comrades impressed Rod. He had feared that they might turn out to be a bunch of ill-disciplined bandits – a bit like his mates after a heavy Saturday night – but nothing could have been further from the truth. This was a large, well-organised military unit. Just what he needed to escort him safely to the Black Mountains, and to keep the dead trolls busy whilst he was giving the Warlock a good kicking.

All of them wore the same uniform. Their helmets bore the legend "Bickos", some motto of bravery and honour, no doubt. They were clad in black chain mail, the only distinguishing feature of which was the large circle cut from the front of each tunic that left their hearts exposed. It was almost as if they were taunting their foes, like the boxer who drops his guard to show his opponent how little he fears him. Flash buggers, he thought.

As Rod spoke with their leader, Tiggs, the thing that encouraged him most was the man's total lack of fear. The troll army would run into thousands, but the man seemed to positively relish the challenge. Trog was the only troll Rod had encountered – and that only briefly – but he had seen enough of him to know that they were bloody big, and frightening with it. But the more he emphasized the danger of their mission to Tiggs, the wider the soldier's grin became.

After conversing with Rod in private, Tiggs summoned the whole camp, and invited him to address the army himself. It seemed strange him giving them a talk on military tactics, when the closest he'd ever got to battle was giving his little brother a whack round the head with an Action Man at the age of seven, but they all seemed happy to adopt him as their new leader. Even Tiggs treated him with deference, as if afraid that he might cut them out and continue his mission without them. Growing in confidence in his newfound role as military genius, he told them what he needed.

"Right, I'm off to Mount Leiden to give this evil old sod a good hiding. The word is he's got thousands of trolls to look after him. I need you lot to keep them busy while I sort this bloke out. When I finish him off, they should all disappear, so all you need do is keep them busy 'til I'm done. Who's up for it?"

"I am!" they all shouted in surprisingly harmonic unison.

He was once again taken aback by the enthusiasm of their response.

"When shall we leave?" he asked Tiggs.

This time, the synchronised shouting fragmented. The replies ranged from a bellowed "as soon as we can," to a hoarse "I haven't got a bloody clue." One man at the back suggested that they all set off as soon as soon as he'd had the chance to use the facilities. It soon subsided into a general mumbling to the effect that although this particular question had stumped them, they were still all eager to set off as soon as the order was given.

"We'll get there tonight," Jasper chimed in. "I can guide you, I'm good at that sort of thing."

"You're sure you don't mind taking on all those trolls?" Rod asked, giving them one last chance to save themselves. "It's going to be really dangerous."

"Don't you worry about that," Tiggs reassured him. "We've been waiting for this opportunity for a very long time."

The Lord of the Trolls was ecstatic. "You have four virgins! Four! And they're all here!"

"Yes," nodded Runt proudly. "All of them. They were really cheap, too. That stupid merchant wasn't interested in goats; he just wanted that gold stuff that's lying around all over the place! And better still, it has been confirmed to me that it's Thursday this evening so we can sacrifice them tonight. I'm not sure how long it will last, though, so we'd better do it pretty soon."

"This is great news," Crug enthused. "You really are the greatest of troll philosophers!"

Runt blushed. "I do what I can," he said modestly. "I'm just pleased to have been of assistance."

At last, thought Crug, the sacrifice can take place. It had been far too long since he had had something to occupy his mind. The days had come and gone, each more boring than the last. Trolls needed excitement, and excitement had been very thin on the ground of late. But now the sacrifice was ready, all that would change. And to have four virgins to sacrifice was more than he could ever have hoped for in his wildest dreams (which really was saying something, because his dreams were very wild indeed). Whilst thinking about those dreams, an idea struck him.

"Runt! Let's dress up!"

"I don't do that sort of thing any more," the Great Troll Philosopher replied defensively. "No matter what you may have been told to the contrary."

"No, no, I mean dress up for the sacrifice. Frightening masks, that sort of thing. Nothing girlie. Make an evening of it."

"An excellent suggestion!" applauded Runt, sighing with relief. "We could make them so disgusting that everyone would vomit. In a dignified, ceremonial way, of course. We just have to make a mould of a horrible face."

Crug looked thoughtful. "They could be tricky. What face would be so hideous that even a troll would heave upon seeing it?"

Runt laughed.

"You obviously haven't seen the virgin-sacrifices yet!"

The light was fading fast, but there was no mistaking the ominous shape of the jagged peaks rising up before them in the distance. They were, at long last, within sight of the Black Mountains. Rod shook his head in disbelief at the thought of all the perils he had blundered his way past on the way here, but knew that the biggest danger was yet to be faced. Ahead of him, the Warlock lay in wait. Jasper's crew could keep the trolls occupied, but he was the only man alive who could fight the Warlock and win. It was a daunting thought. He'd had a few punch-ups in the pub car park from time to time, but that was hardly preparation for something like this. The fear of failure finally caught up with him, and clutched its icy fingers round his spine. People were depending on him for the first time in his life. He didn't want to let them down.

He had expected snow, but there was none. Instead, the mountains looked like razor-tipped volcanoes, slashing the murky skyline with jagged rock at irregular intervals. Everything was black, with not so much as a fistful of white ice or a clump of green grass to break the cruel monotony of the landscape. It was not hard to see how the mountains had been named.

"That one's Mount Leiden" advised Jasper, pointing to the tallest of the peaks. It's tucked behind a couple of others, but it doesn't look particularly hard to get there. If we press ahead, we can still reach it tonight."

"You're having a laugh!" Rod retorted. "What sort of psycho goes running around mountains in pitch darkness. We'll all get killed!"

He thought he heard Jasper giggle, but dismissed the notion. He was a professional soldier. The man had no fear. Fearless mercenaries did not giggle like schoolgirls for no apparent reason. Or even for apparent reasons, for that matter.

A soldier approached before he had time to give the matter any further thought.

"Our scouts have reported that we're being followed, Sir. What do you want them to do?"

"Followed?" Tiggs repeated. "By whom?"

"A soldier and an Amazon, Sir."

"Oh great," moaned Rod. "That's all I need!"

"You know them?" asked Jasper.

Rod nodded. He would have loved to have been able to say that he had never seen them before in his life, but that was sadly not the case. With the possible exception of Doon, he doubted he had disliked anyone in his life as much as he disliked the Amazon. It was partly how bossy she was, partly her lack of any sense of humour, but mostly her complete insensitivity at the death of his friends in the Forest. Leofric wasn't so bad, but he was Rana's bitch. What she said, went. Rod knew some pretty tough women, but the idea of following any of them around, and doing as he was told all the time, was just laughable. Unless he was on to a sure thing, and it was just for an hour or so, of course.

"Will they interfere with our mission?" asked Jasper, a worried frown on his face.

"If that's Rana you've spotted back there, then she's bound to interfere with something. She'll probably challenge you all to single combat, and then march me off by my ear for a good talking to."

"Shall we kill them both?"

"Very tempting," Rod told him, "but I think I'd better have a word with them instead. Where are they?"

The soldier led Rod away. Tiggs and Jasper followed, reluctant to leave him in the company of two strangers whose motives were not yet known to them. Whatever else happened, they were determined that there mission should not fail now. Not when they were so close to achieving their goal.

Rod saw Leofric first. He was hiding behind an outcrop of rock at the very outskirts of the mountain range. Rana was more difficult to detect, exploiting the poor light and natural cover to melt into the stone. Both seemed surprised to see him.

"We thought you'd been captured."

"No," replied Rod. "I was trying to get away from you two, and decided to recruit an army while I was at it. Now get over here, and tell me what you're up to."

They emerged from their cover, like two embarrassed children who had been caught smoking in the school toilets. Rod savoured the moment. He did not want to get caught up in power games with the Amazon, but the expression on her face would live with him until the day he died (which, he appreciated, might be quite soon). It was clear that she was desperate to reassert herself, and regain control of the mission, not to mention give him a good beating for humiliating her in this way. But as long as he had two hundred men at his command, then she did not have a Cornetto's chance in Hell of achieving any of these objectives. It was such a shame!

"You can't take all these people to the mountain," she protested. "Send them away, and we'll finish the task ourselves."

"I don't think I need you any more," he pointed out. "Why send them away? They'll be a lot more use than you two."

"You don't even know who they are!" she protested. "Maybe they're working for HIM."

"We've been introduced, actually. This is my mate Jasper, and this is Tiggs. They're the "Bickos". And they're all on my side. To the death. Right, Lads?"

The lads nodded their assent.

"Bickos?" Leofric repeated. "If they want to come along, that's fine by us. You don't mind if we tag along, too, though?"

"Are you out of your senses!" Rana exploded, rounding on him. "Think about what you're saying!"

"There's nothing to worry about," Leofric assured her. "Trust me."

She looked around her. Apart from Tiggs and Jasper, there were at least twelve other soldiers within easy striking distance, each armed to the teeth. Scores more could be on the scene within a minute or two. If Leofric was not prepared to back her up, then this would be a particularly bad time to make a scene. She was conscious of the fact that Rod could order her execution if the mood took him, and she would not put it past the fat, vindictive oaf to do so on a whim. But having put up with him all the way through the Forest, she was not about to risk the whole mission when she was so close to eternal glory. She would think of some plan to get him to Mount Leiden on his own. And once he had released the Warlock from his tomb, she would repay his impertinence with interest. Rod, she decided, would die by her sword.

Four heavy stone wheels stood atop the hill, each of them about six feet in diameter. Four iron manacles had been driven into each, and each manacle now imprisoned the wrist or ankle of one of the ugliest slave-girl sacrifices you ever saw (the feisty blonde one excepted). The light from thirty or forty torches reflected off the highly polished stone casting the slaves in an atmospheric mix of flickering light and shadow. It played across the bare skin of the best looking of the bunch, and what appeared to be the beard protruding from the veil of one of her less blessed sisters. The stage was set for the greatest sacrifice in troll memory (usually about three weeks).

180

"Oooohhh!" exclaimed the Lord of the Trolls from beneath his fearsome death mask. "I do enjoy a good Thursday!"

Around him, the other trolls danced and frolicked in a frenzy of wild abandon. As they circled him in what can best be described as a demented corruption of the hokey-cokey (left legs going in and out all over the place), they wailed ancient rites which had been passed down from generation to generation. Each wore a different mask to identify them to the spirits which raged outside the ring, and each knew that once the ring was broken these spirits would fall upon the sacrifices, devouring them one chunk of writhing flesh at a time. At the crucial moment, they would roll the stones down the hillside, sending both the spirits and the sacrifices to their deaths. It was a simple ritual, but a very effective method of pleasing the Gods. It was also a good laugh to see the virgins stripped naked and sent spinning down the slope.

Runt stepped into the circle, his place at its circumference immediately taken by another drunken reveller to stop the spirits sneaking in early. Crug and Runt had agreed between them that they would strip two sacrifices each, and roll the stones of their selected virgins down the hill once the circle had been breached. Runt's only complaint was that he had been allocated the two slave-girls with beards. Still, any port in a storm.

Thane lay hidden in the grass nearby. In theory, he should have been torn to pieces by the multitude of frenzied spirits who were supposed to be wailing and shrieking around him. In practice, he just felt a little bit chilly.

He cursed himself for his lack of judgment. He should have rescued everyone during the journey from Hench's camp to the troll castle. There had only been three trolls to guard them, and he had the advantage of surprise. But he had chosen to wait, expecting that he would have a better opportunity later on. As it was, he had somehow to break into the circle, untie the four prisoners and get them out in one piece under the noses of thirty or forty extremely hyped-up (and tanked-up) trolls. It wasn't going to be the easiest task he had ever been set.

Runt approached the first slave-girl. Take off her clothes one item at a time, that was the way his father had taught him. Play to the crowd, and prolong the moment. He knew how to put on a good sacrifice, all right! He gripped the veil of the large girl, deciding to save the good-looking one 'til last, and ripped it from her face with a dramatic flourish. As he stared at the face beneath it, his expression turned from recognition, to surprise, to total revulsion.

"Trog!" he exclaimed in horror.

It was then that Thane made his move. He slipped silently through the ring of dancing trolls, sliced through the ropes binding Halfshaft and Takina almost in one motion, and moved on to Trog. By now, Crug had ripped the manacles from the stone, and thrown the troll-cross to the floor. He sat astride him, pummelling him violently about the head and shoulders with clenched fists, swearing fearsome curses at him the whole time. Trog lay passively beneath him, his arms raised to protect his head as best he could, but otherwise taking no steps to defend himself.

Thane seized Crug by the folds of his massive neck, and flipped him over to the ground. He moved in, aiming a kick at the troll's head to knock him senseless, but Trog intervened, pushing the mercenary violently away from the prostrate troll.

"Leave him alone!" Trog bellowed at Thane in rage. "That's my Dad!"

They had arrived at long last. Before them stood the entrance to the tunnel which led into the very heart of Mount Leiden. Leofric recognised it with an excited shiver even in the darkness. Their quest was nearly at an end.

Rod would have preferred to have made this final leg of the journey in the morning, when everyone had rested. He was tired, and did not feel in any fit state to take on the Warlock in this condition. But Tiggs was too impatient to wait, and Leofric – somewhat to his surprise – was all for pressing ahead as well. He had explained to Rod that they were more likely to catch the enemy by surprise at night, but he was not especially impressed by this argument. It would be difficult to be caught by surprise by two hundred noisy soldiers clambering across a mountain with flaming torches in their hands. They must have looked like something out of a Barry Manilow concert!

Rana was all for waiting for the morning. That was all it took to convince him that it was best to press on. There was something going on between Leofric and the Amazon Queen. She seemed desperate to get an opportunity to speak with him in private, and Rod felt sure that any discussion they had would not be to his advantage. Maybe it would be better to press ahead, and find out if there really was a Warlock beneath the Mountain. And, if there was, whether he had it in him to defeat it, and make his way home.

At the mouth of the tunnel, everyone fell silent, waiting for him to take the lead. He paused, apprehensive at the task which awaited him. He was risking his life here. And all the soldiers around him were putting their lives at risk for him. The pinnacle of his achievement in the past had been winning the pub pool competition three years in a row. How he could he possibly go through with this?

He looked around him. Two hundred expectant faces peered back at him, willing him on. He would do it, he decided. Not for them, but for Halfshaft and Takina. They had died in the Forest, just to help him get this far. He couldn't turn back now, not when he was so close to the end of their quest. He couldn't fail them now. He had to finish what they'd started, or die trying.

"Go on," urged Leofric, the voice of temptation behind him. "Pick up the sword. Lead us into the mountain."

"Okay," Rod agreed, without moving an inch.

"When you're ready," prompted Rana.

The soldiers started to get restless, fidgeting from foot to foot. Everyone seemed eager to enter the mountain for their own individual reasons. He knew that there was only one way to go, as well, and that was forwards. He just needed a minute or two to compose himself first.

"Are we going in, or not?" huffed Rana.

"Yeah," he told her. "We're going in, all right."

He felt that a rousing speech was in order to lift morale – not that anyone's but his seemed in need of lifting – and searched his mind for something appropriate. He really should have paid more attention at school.

"Once more into the breach, dear friends, once more. And kick their heads in when you get there."

The soldiers gave a rousing cheer. So much for catching the trolls by surprise, he thought.

The time had come. He stormed into the mouth of the tunnel, and seized the hilt of the sword. He pulled on it, expecting it to slide effortlessly from its stone surround. It stayed put. The soldiers crowded against him, waiting to bundle into the tunnel. He felt faintly ridiculous. How stupid would he look if he came all this way, and couldn't move the bloody thing?

"What's the matter now?" asked Rana. "Why the delay?"

"It's a bit stiff," he told here. "Probably rusted over a bit. It definitely moved a bit, though. I'll give it a good tug, and get on with it."

Relieved that no one had spotted the accidental double-entendres, he placed both hands around the hilt, and struggled to free it. He felt it move a fraction, but that was all. He waggled it from side to side, hoping to loosen it a little, all the time conscious of the withering looks he was being given by the Amazon Queen.

"Tell the tart to move away," he ordered Leofric, "or I'll call it a day. I can't work with her leaning over my shoulder."

Rana seethed, but did as she was bid. Surrounded by two hundred of Rod's soldiers, she did not really feel that she had much choice. Besides, her time would come later.

"Right," said Rod. "One more pull, and it's out."

He grasped the hilt again, and tugged on it with all his might. He felt his hands slipping sweatily around the grip, but persisted. He could sense it becoming looser, and by working it to and fro he was able to free it from its casing one agonising inch at a time.

Dipping into his pocket, he found a bunch of scrunched up paper tissues. He dried his hands on them, and wrapped them round the hilt to gain a better purchase. After five or six more minutes of puffing and panting amidst the throng of impatient warriors, the sword finally slid free.

"I bet King Arthur never had these problems," he remarked to no one in particular. Then, deciding to inspire the soldiers forward to victory, he raised the blade in the air above his head, and roared out his call to battle:

"Do unto others," he cried, "before they do unto you!"

With these inspirational words of wisdom still echoing off the tunnel walls, he ran headlong into the darkness, bidding them follow him.

"Let's go!" shouted Tiggs. As one, the army rumbled forwards, ready to do battle with the mutant trolls inside the mountain fortress, ready to fight for their brave leader to the death. Before they had covered ten yards, however, they cannoned into him as he fled back towards them, a shocked expression on his face.

"Leg it!" he yelled. "There's thousands of the buggers down there!"

Halfshaft and Hubert were very relieved that Thane had brought their clothes with him. They sat quietly, pleased to be back in familiar garments, as they watched Trog being taken to task by his father. It was not a pleasant experience, but they felt better able to cope with it now they were no longer virgins.

They had been brought to Castle Urknor, the trolls' stronghold. Crug and Runt had pulled them from the circle and out of earshot of the other trolls within seconds of Trog announcing his relationship to his father. It would not do for the Lord of the Trolls to air his dirty linen in public. Especially when the dirty linen was in the style of a slave-girl's outfit.

"How could you?" Crug spat at his son. "How could you embarrass me in this fashion?"

Trog looked suitably contrite. He writhed in his chair, avoiding eye contact like some errant seven year old caught with a packet of Dad's cigarettes.

"I'm sorry," he repeated for the umpteenth time. "I don't usually dress like that. They made me do it to rescue the girl."

"To rescue the girl!" Crug exploded. "And you think that makes things better, do you? You're a troll, for goodness sake! Your role in life is not to go around rescuing girls, whether dressed as a woman or otherwise. It's to go around eating them!"

"I wanted to eat her," Trog protested, "but they wouldn't let me!"

"Then you should have eaten them as well!"

"I'm sorry. I'll eat them next time."

"As if I haven't got enough to worry about. I sit here, year after year, bored out of my mind. Nothing ever happens here. Nothing! Finally, the Great Troll Philosopher here arranges a really good night out – a slave girl sacrifice, with four slaves, no less – and what happens? One of them turns out to be my long-lost son! The humiliation of it all! I'll have to resign, of course. You can't treat the Lord of the Trolls with respect if you know his son skips around in a veil and matching bodice!"

"Your father was really looking forward to tonight," Runt chimed in. "If he was bored before, how much worse is it going to be for him when he's not Lord of the Trolls any more? I'll probably replace him, you realise that? Me, whose been his servant all his life, giving him commands, making him cook my breakfast in the morning, making him sing me a song when the mood takes me, maybe a nice ballad or..."

"Yes, I think we've got the general idea, Runt," interrupted Crug testily.

"Boredom's a big problem round here, is it?" Thane enquired casually.

"The biggest," confirmed Crug, with a sigh. "Save, that is, for the problem of how to explain things to your friends when your transvestite son comes out of the closet at a human sacrifice!"

"If," Thane went on, "I could suggest something to keep you and all your friends busy, would you set everyone free?"

"Does it involve dressing up?" asked Runt.

Crug glared at him.

"Just asking," Runt shrugged.

"No, it doesn't," Thane told him. "It involves fighting. Blood, guts, and vengeance."

"And head-biting?" ventured the Lord of the Trolls. "Is there any head-biting involved, by any chance?"

"Plenty," Thane confirmed. "I think the time has come to let you know exactly why we're here."

As the tunnel regurgitated troll after troll, Leofric pulled Rana a safe distance away. Rod's soldiers closed in on the trolls, and the two armies joined in battle. Well, battle might not be quite the right word for it. Rod watched in astonishment as soldier after soldier threw off his helmet and walked towards his opponent with arms invitingly outstretched. A score fell within minutes, each of them neatly skewered on the end of a troll sword which had been thrust through the gap in the chain-mail on their chests. Jasper and Tiggs were amongst the first men down.

Leofric laughed. Rana grabbed his arm, shaking it roughly.

"Tell me what's happening? Why are they doing that?"

"These people are followers of the cult of Bickos. It's a suicide sect. I thought they'd all died years ago, but there must have been a revival or something. Their sole purpose in life is to kill themselves.

That's why they're here. There's not one of them who'll lift a finger to protect himself, believe me. Rod won't have his army for long."

She could see that it was true. They were being massacred with such ease that even she was repulsed. She was a warrior. She was used to killing in battle. But this was not like that. It was more like some twisted abattoir, where the cattle were volunteering to sharpen the knives.

Leofric seemed to find the whole thing hilarious. She wondered whether he might be hysterical. They had, after all, both been under tremendous pressure in the last few days, and it might only take something like this to push him over the edge. She needed him sane. He had proved himself to her on their journey. For the first time in her life, she was ready to share power with a man.

"Rod will die soon," she stated flatly, examining his face closely to gauge his reaction.

He stopped laughing immediately. For the first time, she noticed the pain hidden deep within his eyes. She knew he liked Rod – though quite how anyone could do so was beyond her entirely – and even the immense rewards that awaited them did not make his betrayal any easier. She squeezed his arm supportively to show him she understood.

"We'd better move out of the way," she said. "These trolls are mindless. They won't know of our deal with the Warlock."

He nodded his understanding, and they moved further aside. By the time the last of the soldiers had fallen, they had found a suitable hiding place behind an outcrop of rock. From their vantage point, they could see column after column of walking troll corpses march from the mountain. There was no sign of Rod anywhere.

They waited for a quarter of an hour, until the last of the trolls had departed. They then returned to the battlefield at the tunnel mouth to search for Rod. It did not take them long to find him, lying motionless on the ground amidst a heap of blood drenched soldiers.

"Rest in peace," muttered Leofric almost inaudibly, as he rolled Rod's eyes closed with his thumb.

The Lord of the Trolls marched proudly at the head of his army, with Trog to his left, and Runt to his right. Thane had told him of the Warlock's plans, stressing the indignity to the resurrected trolls who were being used as his over-sized pawns. Boredom alone may well have been enough of an incentive to go on the offensive, but this insult to his long-dead ancestors made his mind up for sure. Crug would lead his people into battle for revenge, and go down in folklore as a warrior king, rather than just someone who knew how to throw a good Thursday.

Thane, Takina, Halfshaft and Hubert marched with them, slightly behind the others. It was several miles to the Black Mountains, but that would not take long at indignant troll marching speed. The pace was a little difficult for some of this following group, though. Hubert in particular was struggling, having for centuries done nothing more energetic than sit on a mound and lie to people.

Takina walked beside Hubert, with Thane striding impatiently ahead, and the dwarf scurrying along behind them. She looked across at the wizard, and saw that he was already glancing towards her. They exchanged a smile. She had missed the stubborn old goat, and was touched at how relieved he had been to see her alive when they had been reunited. He winked at her, and she winked back. She would make sure that they would not be separated again.

As they reached the foot of the first mountain, the cry went up that the troll corpse army had been spotted ahead. It was still night-time, and Halfshaft could see little by the light of the reticent moon, but he trusted the superior night-vision of his allies. The largest battle on Hedral for many centuries was about to commence. And he would have to take a prominent part in it, if they were to have any hope of victory. He felt in his pocket and gripped the spell for reassurance. His moment of destiny was at hand.

Thane approached Crug.

"We'll skirt round them and go to the mountain. Once we kill the Warlock, those poor trolls should all be free again. They'll collapse into dust. All you have to do is contain them in the meantime. Don't let them leave the mountains."

Crug nodded seriously. "I know what has to be done."

Thane clapped him on the back, and led his friends away, minutes before the two armies closed in combat. The Lord of the Trolls and the Great Troll Philosopher watched them go.

"It goes against the grain releasing so many humans," Crug told his companion thoughtfully. "I know chopping up long-dead relatives in battle will be fun, but I just hope we don't regret this in the morning."

"Don't worry, Runt reassured him, ever the philosopher. " If we change our minds about letting them go, we can always eat them on their way back!"

Rod sprang to his feet, coming within a greasy-hair's breadth of giving Leofric heart failure in the process. He waved the sword dangerously close to the soldier, forgetting that he still had it in his hand.

"Leave it out!" he protested. "I nearly lost a contact-lense when you did that!"

"We thought you were dead," responded Leofric in astonishment.

"No. I was just playing possum 'til the trolls had gone."

He gave Rana a wink.

"All right, Darling. Bet you were worried about me, weren't you?"

Before she could answer in the emphatic negative, he had sauntered into the tunnel, leaving her staring after him in disbelief.

"He's alive!" exclaimed Leofric, and Rana noted with irritation the tinge of relief in his voice.

"Not for much longer," she vowed, bringing her partner back to reality. She still sensed, however, the divided loyalties that battled away inside him. She had to be sure of his support before she went after the alien. Rod had the sword, after all. It would take both of them to get it off him, and she could not risk Leofric changing his mind halfway through. They would both end up dead if he did.

"I've left my tribe to be with you. I've sacrificed everything that's important to me, just to accompany you on this quest of you. Please don't let me down now."

He made up his mind. Whether it was in recognition of her sacrifice, or in shock at hearing her use the word "please", she would never know. But she had his support. They would take the first opportunity they got to disarm Rod. And once he was defenceless, she could take her revenge.

They entered the tunnel in pursuit. Though it was still night-time, the passage-way was no longer in darkness. Light emanated from a source at it's far need, sending pulses of colour throbbing along the heavy stone walls, like a spider's web with landing lights.

Thirty or forty yards ahead of them, they could make out Rod's silhouette running like a maniac towards the source of the beam, the sword slashing musketeer-like ahead of him.

"This light. It's magical," commented Leofric, somewhat unnecessarily.

She turned her head towards him to signal her understanding with a brief nod of her head. By the time she looked back, Rod had disappeared. They hurried forwards, stopping abruptly as they reached the top of a steep staircase hewn into the stone. It led downwards into the bowels of the mountain. Though it was lit by the same eerie light as before, Rod was obscured from their view by the downward curve of the spiral. However, the muffled pounding of heel on stone assured them that this was the route he had taken.

"I remember this from last time," Leofric told her. "The Warlock's chamber is right at the bottom of this staircase. This is where our journey ends. I'd like you to meet our new master!"

The first thing that struck Rod was the smell. It was not just the nauseating odour of semi-decayed trolls who until recently had been crammed into the chamber like so many insanitary sardines in an over-populated tin. It was more the overwhelming stench of evil which really upset him, so much so that he nearly parted company with his tea.

The Warlock stood in the centre of the chamber flanked by four of the ugliest creatures Rod had ever seen (and he had seen some real dogs in his time). They looked like trolls who had had their faces cut off with a blunt knife. After studying these terrible monstrosities for a few seconds, he decided that there was a good reason for this. It was because they really were trolls who had had their faces hacked off.

The Warlock was visible only by his lack of form, the dense void of blackness of which he consisted contrasting starkly with the light which pulsated around him. Though the thing before Rod had no eyes, he knew it was watching him. As the air about him started to crackle with magic, it seemed almost as if it was laughing at him as well.

He held the sword in front of him, taking comfort from the feel of its hilt in his palm. Still puffing from the exertion of running down the passageway outside, he advanced slowly towards the Warlock, ready to counter the ferocious attack which he knew his presence would provoke. He was momentarily distracted as Leofric and Rana ran into the room, but pushed all thought of them instantly from his mind. He had to be like that Grasshopper bloke in the Kung-fu series when he was a kid. He could not afford to lose his concentration if he was to have any hope of coming out of this alive.

Even as he was turning his attention back to the Warlock, the creature made its move. It flickered in the place its hands would have occupied had it been human, and as if at some sort of signal the trolls came lurching into motion. One lumbered straight towards him, blocking his path to the Warlock, whilst the others tried to surround him in a clumsy circle, like some giant noose being placed around the condemned man's neck.

He lunged forwards, striking at the nearest troll with his sword. The blade plunged deep into its stomach with an ease which took him totally by surprise. The creature howled in pain and threw itself backwards to escape a second thrust. For one horrific moment, Rod thought that it would take his weapon with it, but he clung desperately on to it, and was relieved to find the hilt still in his hand when the point slid out of the retreating troll's body,

The other trolls attacked him as one. Though possessing very little intelligence, they had sufficient cunning to realise that there was safety in numbers. But for the sword, he would have been torn to pieces within seconds. As it was, the ferocity of their attack drove him backwards, but he somehow managed to keep them at bay. His sword whirled about him as if it had a mind of its own, slicing, hacking, dicing, and parrying as if reliving some old Errol Flynn movie. Even so, defending so inexperienced a master was no easy task even for a weapon such as this, and the deflected blows from the trolls' weapons scorched the air inches from his body time and time again.

He knew that he would not last for long. Though he was deflecting the blows themselves, the force of each reverberated through his body like a sound wave through a tuning fork, each vibration leaving him weaker than the last. He could not keep this up forever. As he retreated from their onslaught, he felt his strength ebbing from him, and he realised that this was not a battle he could win alone.

It was then that he felt Rana and Leofric on either side of him. Just for once, he was very glad to see them.

"It's the cavalry!" he gasped, almost overcome with relief.

"Sorry," Rana replied with a vindictive smile. "Guess again."

She plucked the sword from his grasp, but dropped it immediately, shrieking in surprise as her skin bubbled at its touch. Another flicker of the Warlock's form sent the nearest troll lurching into action. It raised its great sword above its head and brought it crashing down upon its distracted victim. To Rod's astonishment, that victim was Rana. He closed his eyes for a second to compose himself after seeing the mighty blow cleave the Amazon Queen in two. He kept them closed for another second or two, as he felt her body – or at least half of it – brush against him as it collapsed to the ground at his feet.

Willing himself to stay calm, he opened his eyes again. The first thing he saw was Leofric, who had collapsed to his knees and was trying to push the two halves together, as if carrying out some temporary and incompetent repair. The second thing he saw was the Warlock, as he started to change shape.

As they hurried along the tunnel, they heard the heavy clunk of metal against metal, and they knew the final battle had started. By the time they reached the top of the staircase, they heard a scream. Thane took the steps three at a time, with Halfshaft, Takina and Hubert following as best they could. They entered the Warlock's chamber just as his transformation was nearing completion.

"Halfshaft!" shouted Rod his bloodstained face breaking into a huge smile. "Takina! I thought you were dead!"

"Not yet," Halfshaft pessimistically advised him.

Any further conversation was cut short by a gasp from Hubert. All followed his gaze save for Thane, who took advantage of the diversion to seize Harold's sword from its resting place near the foot of the staircase.

The Warlock's shape had altered. He had now taken human form. Even Leofric – who was still huddled on the floor cradling the severed remains of his Queen – looked up, staring wide-eyed at the sight before him. He recognised the face of his old friend and colleague. He was looking in the face of Doon.

Doon lifted his arm, and made a complicated gesture with his hand, smiling as he did so. Without warning, the trolls attacked again.

Thane sprang to his companions' defence, wielding the magical sword with such calm effectiveness that he had beheaded one of the trolls before the others had even got close to their intended victims. He sliced into a second just as the creature was lifting Hubert into the air. The dwarf dropped heavily to the floor, bounced, and came to a rest lying face to face with Rana. Or rather, face to half-face with her.

"Killed by a troll!" he yelped, leaping back to his feet. "She's been killed by a troll! The Prophecy!"

He was then knocked unconscious by the troll who had obligingly fulfilled the Prophecy a little earlier. This troll, though, was having troubles of its own. He had set upon the Amazon with the yellow hair, confident of finishing her off as quickly as he had dealt with her tribeswoman. But she had fought back, showing courage and swordswomanship out of all proportion to her size. The harder he tried to swat her aside, the more difficult it became to pin her down, as she side-stepped, feigned and parried as if she'd been fighting faceless trolls all her life. It was quite a relief when he caught sight of the dwarf, breaking off from his duel with the Amazon just long enough to send him crashing to the floor with a well-timed kick to his little dwarfish-head.

The fourth troll was struggling, too. It had been severely wounded by the human with the magic sword early in the fight, and would have collapsed long ago if it wasn't for the fact that the Warlock's mind control was throwing him in whatever direction it chose. To make matters worse, there were two easy targets practically within striking distance, and the effort expended in deciding which of them to kill first was almost too much for it. Should he go for the soldier, who was trying to squeeze the dead woman's innards back into the severed body he was holding together? Or should he start off with the wizard who was standing nearby, chanting incantations and drawing strange shapes in the air with his fingers?

He had just decided on the wizard, when Thane's sword sliced his head off.

Crug and Trog stood back to back, hacking away at their ancient ancestors with a demented ecstasy borne of the knowledge that they were surrounded, and without hope of rescue. Their comrades had been driven back by the overwhelming numbers of the Warlock's army, and they had been the only two able to stand their ground. Now they were isolated, a tiny island in the sea of living-dead, fighting for their lives against odds which even they knew to be insurmountable. It didn't get any better than this!

"Do you think your friends will kill the Warlock?" Crug shouted over the din of the battle. "Make all these dead trolls turn to dust again?"

"I hope not!" his son yelled back at him, as a shuddering blow glanced off his chainmail, breaking his collarbone in two.

The Lord of the Trolls wiped the blood from his own shattered cheek, and smiled proudly back at him.

"That's my boy!" he said.

Thane dropped the sword to the ground once the last troll fell to Takina. The weapon had burnt his hand to the bone, eating through skin and muscle alike in its struggle to escape his grasp. He was half-human, but that had meant the sword had merely tolerated him. It did not mean that he could tolerate the sword. He would have to find some other weapon to use against the Warlock.

He could see the look of surprise and recognition written deep in the faces of his companions as they stared at the man the Warlock had become. Only the unconscious dwarf and the preoccupied wizard failed to register any emotion at the transformation. The Warlock's tactics were clear. By turning himself into someone they all recognised, he hoped that they would underestimate him, and maybe find it harder to kill him as well. Thane would make neither of those mistakes.

"Pick up the sword," he told Rod.

The biker moved towards him to do as he was bid, but the Warlock was faster. Before Rod had covered half the distance, the image of Doon positioned itself between him and the weapon, bringing him to an uncertain halt. Rod looked to Thane for guidance, feeling as if he had lost all the initiative here. As long as he was fighting trolls, he knew what he was supposed to be doing. Now it was the twice-dead wizard's apprentice there, the rules did not seem so clear.

Taking advantage of their inactivity, the creature seized Takina, and raised her above his head without effort.

"Thank you for releasing me from my prison," mocked Doon, "At the risk of seeming ungrateful, I must now kill you all, one miserable life at a time. I have work to do; Kingdoms to conquer. The girl dies first."

Halfshaft had set to work as soon as he entered the chamber. Whilst the others fought trolls, he fished out the King's spell from his robes, and re-read it silently to himself to remind himself of its contents. Once he had it clear in his mind, he replaced it, and made his preparations.

He chanted, waving his hands extravagantly in the air as he did so. Almost immediately, a tunnel started to appear before him, a tunnel which sprang from a different time and dimension. He smiled contentedly to himself. The spell was working. After all those wasted years of uncertainty, he finally knew the truth. He was a great and powerful wizard after all. And he had it within his power to save the world.

The tunnel grew rapidly in size and substance, a kaleidoscope of light whirling rhythmically within it. Reds, oranges, yellows, greens, blues, indigoes and violets; all competed for supremacy in a stunning blaze of spectral colour that would have left him breathless under any other circumstances. As it was, he worked on, oblivious not only to the beauty of his creation, but also to the battle which raged around him. He had more important things to concern him.

A speck appeared deep within the tunnel, a speck with arms and legs. It expanded rapidly, Halfshaft's proud and triumphant grin growing proportionately with it. Within seconds, it was the size and shape of a man. He had never seen this man before, but knew who he was. The time had come to introduce him to the Warlock.

He turned round to find Doon standing in the chamber, holding Takina precariously over his head. His heart missed a beat, and he had to fight back the urge to rush forwards to wrestle her free. The tunnel behind him flickered for an instant, and the image lost an inch or two in height. But then the wizard's resolve returned, and he stood his ground in the knowledge that his magic was her only hope of salvation. Behind him, the figure regained its substance, and loomed supportively behind him.

"Stop, foul Warlock!" commanded Halfshaft. "Your time is at an end!"

The Warlock froze, leaving Takina suspended in the air above his head, still struggling to escape his grip. He stared at the wizard, astounded that such a puny excuse for an individual should have the audacity to challenge him in this manner.

"I," Halfshaft went on confidently, "am a magician of the highest order. I am unequalled in this or any other world, I know this now. And you shall know it, too. I shall not demean myself by fighting you in person. There is no need. For I have summoned a man who will vanquish you in my place. The one man who can wield the magic sword to defeat you. Warlock, I give you Harold the Invincible!"

Halfshaft stepped aside, revealing the figure in the tunnel to all those assembled. He awaited the gasps of joy and admiration which would surely follow. To his surprise, the overwhelming reaction was actually one of complete puzzlement. He glanced at Doon, only to find that he seemed as baffled as the rest of them. This was not the response he had anticipated. He looked back towards the tunnel to find out what was going on.

The shape in the tunnel had changed. It was no longer Harold, although there remained a very strong resemblance to him. As he tried to work out what was happening, he realised that the figure was walking towards him, attempting to leave the time tunnel. With every step forward the man took, his face changed. By the time he had advanced six paces, he had been four different men, and -more worrying still from Halfshaft's point of view—two different women.

"What's going on?" he wailed. "Is he some sort of quick change drag-artist, or something?"

Doon threw back his head and laughed in triumph, maintaining his grip on Takina all the while.

"Time," he told them. "Time is "going on"."

They stared at him blankly for a while, trying to comprehend the meaning of this strange announcement.

"But he's not getting any older," Halfshaft reasoned. Doon laughed even louder.

Thane was the first of them to work it out.

"This is a time tunnel. You started with Harold, but every time he takes a step forwards, he moves on a generation. That is a direct lineal descendant of Harold. Whoever steps out of the tunnel will be his present day relative."

"You mean like his great grandson?" asked Rod.

"Give or take forty or fifty 'greats', yes."

Halfshaft remained unconvinced that his spell could have gone so disastrously wrong. "Harold didn't have any children," he pointed out.

"Maybe not on Hedral, but he must have had at least one on Earth. Those are Earth clothes he's wearing, round about the 18th century, I'd say. This tunnel leads from England, I'm sure of it. You've summoned up another 21st century Earthling to help you."

Takina coughed. They had forgotten her predicament. She remained hoisted above Doon's head, ready to be sent crashing to the floor whenever he chose. But the man in the tunnel remained her best hope of rescue. Indeed, he may well have been the only hope of survival that any of them had. The Warlock knew this, too. That was why he started laughing at them.

"It's not over yet," Halfshaft persisted. "This man is a descendant of Harold, remember. If he has a fraction of his strength and courage then the Warlock is doomed. And besides, if he's from Earth, he can wield the sword."

Doon stopped laughing. He threw Takina violently to the floor, sending her skidding towards the granite wall by the staircase, and strode towards the tunnel. He would not allow his new opponent the luxury of becoming accustomed to his surroundings before the battle commenced. Best to catch him as soon as he stepped out of it, when he was still confused and disorientated. He would blow him away before the man even knew why he had been summoned there.

Rod and Halfshaft rushed to Takina's side. Blood oozed from a deep wound to her head, and her leg was bent to one side at an impossible angle, but they were relieved to see that she was still very much alive. Her face convulsed in pain as she tried to struggle to her feet, desperate to counter-attack the Warlock whilst he was distracted. Rana would have been proud of her, but she cared nothing for this now. After all she had been through, she was beyond the stage of craving the approval of others. She had finally satisfied herself of her own worth, and that was all that mattered. That, and gutting the Warlock from neck to groin with her knife. But her wounds were too great. She sank back to the cold stone floor, with an animal groan of frustration which would have kept Hubert going for years, if he had only been conscious to hear it.

Her cries sent Halfshaft into an empathetic fury. With a scream of rage, he charged at Doon. The force of the impact knocked the wizard from his feet, and sent him hurtling backwards, tripping over Takina's outstretched legs so that he landed in a heap beside her. Both wizard and Amazon winced in pain, but Doon remained unscathed, apparently oblivious that Halfshaft had even touched him.

As Halfshaft crashed to the ground, the tunnel wavered, and shrank a little. The figure inside it stopped in his tracks, a look of uncertainty on his face.

"Don't lose it!" Thane instructed the wizard. "If your concentration goes, the tunnel goes with it. Think!"

"But look what he's done to her!" shrieked Halfshaft indignantly. "What if she dies?"

"She won't die. She's had some healing potion. Now concentrate, and let's see who comes out of the tunnel."

The figure in the time tunnel took another step forwards as Halfshaft focused on him again. By now, he was a World War II soldier. The uniform and the rifle reassured them. Perhaps this was a warrior after all. A few more steps, and he would be with them. Trying to shut out the sound of Takina's second painful and unsuccessful attempt at regaining her feet, Halfshaft resumed his incantations. He had to succeed in this. Failure was not an option.

Rod went to collect the sword. After seeing the ease with which Doon had brushed off Halfshaft's full-blooded attack, he was none too sure that he would be able to hurt the Warlock even if he got within striking distance. But he could at least make sure Harold's descendant had the chance to use it when he came out of the tunnel. It might make all the difference.

The figure changed again. Now it was a burly man wearing flared jeans and a "Slade" t-shirt. He looked as if he might be useful in a fight, although it seemed unlikely that swordsmanship would be his forte.

"The seventies," Rod remarked. "Only one more generation to go!"

The man took his last step forwards, leaving the confines of the tunnel as he did so. He looked about the cavern, as confused and disorientated as the Warlock had predicted, trying to make sense of his surroundings, but failing completely. Everyone stared at him expectantly. Even Doon paused, as if intrigued by what the newcomer would do next.

"Oh no!" groaned Thane. "Not you! Out of the whole population of Earth, surely we could have ended up with someone other than you!"

"Well, excuse me!" replied Archie Watkins, more than a little offended. "Politeness costs nothing, you know!"

It was early morning, and the dreams of countless Hedralians were tainted by images of bloodshed and wild, uncontrollable magic. Harkwell lay on the right hand side of his bed in his Forest cabin, drifting between sleep and wakefulness, his brow dripping with sweat. His wife lay motionless beside him, cocooned in warm woollen blankets, dead to the world, but not to her husband.

Trugga slept uneasily beneath a large tree within a stone's throw of Horace's mound. She dreamt of returning home back to the village in which she had lived all her life, the village in which she hoped that she would one day die. But she could not go. "Stay here, and watch my back," Rana had told her, and that is exactly what she meant to do. She would stay in the Forest until her Queen returned. She was lonely, hungry and depressed, but she could cope with it. After all, Rana would not be gone forever.

Nearby, Horace dozed fitfully atop the mound, dreaming of his brother. Lying toe-rag that he was, they were still twins, and he missed him. Until his return, any passing strangers would be able to find out the correct path through the woods, and he feared that before long there would be hundreds of day-trippers wandering around all over the place, spoiling the eerie mystique that the Forest had been cultivating for millennia. Nothing would ever be the same again.

Just a few miles from Spartan Castle, the King and the Grand Wizard lay exhausted on the grass, snatching a few hours of sleep whilst they had the chance. The fat old hags who now owned them had galloped them hard, for mile upon mile. The witches remained astride their backs as they slept, chattering happily to one another. Now was a time of great excitement. They sensed the magic in the air, and it couldn't have come at a better time. Tomorrow was going to be a very special day. Witches from all over the country would be calling upon them, and the unsubdued magic which crackled in the air would create a mood of breathless expectancy. What better atmosphere for a donkey derby?

All of them – and thousands more like them – sensed the huge build-up of magical forces in the air, like a sky heavy with ominous thunderclouds before a storm. But this would be the storm to end all storms.

They tossed and turned in their sleep, waiting for the first gash of lightning to tear their lives apart.

"So this," gloated the Warlock, "is your champion? Your saviour? The man upon whom your miserable lives depend? You must be delighted at the hand that Fate has dealt you!"

They surveyed Archie with mounting disappointment. Weak, middle-aged, and seedy, he looked as if he would have trouble lifting the sword, yet alone killing the Warlock with it. This was a man whose idea of bravery was to go out in the cold without his vest on. He was no hero, and they knew it. Worse still, Doon knew it, too.

"Flee, little man!" crowed the Warlock in triumph. "I wish to see the off-spring of Harold run from me in terror. Flee like the cowardly dog you are!"

"Now just hold on a minute," retorted Archie, who was starting to get just a little cross. "That's a bit strong, isn't it? And my Dad's name was Albert, not Harold. I'd get your facts right if I were you, before you start..."

The Warlock grabbed him by the head in mid-sentence, and flung him dismissively across the room. Two loops and a backward somersault later, he came to a halt on the stone floor, sandwiched between the two bloodied halves of a very tall woman in squirrel skin knickers. He leapt to his feet, puffing and panting with ineffectual indignation, and – with all the dignity he could muster – delivered the line which he knew would leave his aggressor begging for forgiveness.

"Right, that's it. I'm phoning the police!"

Feeling that he had at least had the last word (even if it had not had the effect he had hoped for), he ran like buggery.

200

"There goes your champion," taunted Doon the excitement in his voice growing to fever pitch. "There goes your last hope of survival. I have won. I've beaten you all single handed!"

"Too right," agreed Rod. "And here's your prize!"

Using every last remaining ounce of his strength, he rammed the magic sword up what his instincts told him was the must vulnerable part of the warlock's body. Although he did not know this, it was the same line of attack that had killed Edward II seven centuries before. A death fit for a King.

"There," announced Rod with satisfaction, at a job well done. "You're not so hard with a sword up your bottom, are you?"

The Warlock screamed in agony, a sound which could only be compared to the noise an animal might make if an extremely sharp instrument had been forcibly inserted into its posterior (which was not surprising in the circumstances). Before the echo had died out, he had vanished completely.

"He's gone!" Halfshaft cried in jubilation. "We've done it! We've killed the Warlock!"

Thane, sniffing uneasily, did not seem so sure.

"Get everyone inside the tunnel," he said quietly.

Why?" asked the wizard curiously. "What's the point?"

"Just do it. Now."

Puzzled, Halfshaft went to pick up Takina. With Rod's help, they eased her to her feet, and escorted her to the mouth of the tunnel from which Archie had emerged.

"Inside?"

"Yes. Quickly."

They carried her in to it. As they stepped over the threshold, they felt the air being ripped from their lungs for a second, but before they could panic, the sensation passed and they were able to breathe again.

"One step only!" Thane called after them. "Don't go any further than one step into it."

They turned to face him, but had difficulty making him out. Although they could still see back into the chamber, the images were distorted beyond recognition, and the only way to pick out anyone was to watch for signs of movement. Even then, they were all caught by surprise as he burst into the tunnel with Hubert slung over his shoulder. He dropped the portly dwarf at their feet and stepped back out again, only to return seconds later, leading Leofric by the arm.

"Take off your socks," he ordered Rod.

"Is that your idea of foreplay?" Rod replied, trying to lighten the mood a little. The danger was gone. He did not understand why the mercenary was acting like this.

"Halfshaft," Thane went on, ignoring the quip. "Can you make fire?"

"Yes," the wizard nodded. "And water. Not very much of it, though."

"That's fine. Let's see the fire."

Halfshaft duly obliged, snapping his fingers to conjure up a flame. Thane held out his hand towards Rod. Reluctantly the biker surrendered his socks to him. He watched in astonishment as the mercenary set light to one of them, and threw it towards the chamber outside. The flame extinguished itself almost the moment it left his hand, leaving the smoking remnants of the sock to drop limply to the floor.

"Do you want to tell me why you've just set light to my sock?" asked Rod. "Is this some weird celebration at killing the Warlock, or have you just got a foot fetish?"

"The Warlock's not dead," Thane declared. "He's just turned himself to gas to protect himself from further injury. We're safe here; the gas can't get in. There's a barrier across the mouth of this tunnel it can't pass. But if we were out there, we'd choke to death in seconds."

"So what are you doing with my socks?" asked Rod, feeling that it was still a valid question to raise in the circumstances.

"I'm trying to ignite the gas," Thane explained. "If we could get a flame out there, he'd be blown to smithereens. But we can't. The flame needs oxygen to burn, and there's a layer across the mouth of the tunnel with no oxygen in it. As soon as the sock reaches it, the flame goes out."

"Why not try again?" suggested Rod ever the optimist "Maybe there's a gap in it, or something. Pass me back my sock."

He produced a packet of matches from his pocket, and extracted a match from it. He ignited it, and went to put the box back in is pocket.

"I'll look after them for you," Leofric volunteered.

This offer took them all by surprise. Leofric had been in deep shock ever since Rana's death, staring vacantly into space ever since his futile attempts at reconnecting her body had failed. His mind seemed as broken as her body had been. None of them had expected him to play any further part in the proceedings.

Rod threw him the matchbox. At the same time, the heat which singed his fingers reminded him that he was still holding a burning sock. He dropped it just in time to prevent the hair on the back of his hand catching alight. It landed on the floor by his feet.

Catching them unawares again, Leofric seized the blazing sock and leapt from the tunnel. The flame disintegrated the moment he crossed back into the chamber outside.

Remembering his earlier treachery Rod watched him go with concern.

"What's he doing? You don't think he can hurt us from out there?"

"He's avenging Rana," winced Takina from their feet. "In the only way he can."

"The matches!" Rod exclaimed. "He's gonna blow the bastard to buggery!"

"Then we'd better get out of here," Thane told them. "In case the tunnel can't withstand a full scale explosion."

Halfshaft went to take a step deeper into the tunnel, but Thane restrained him.

"Not that way," he said. "Not unless you want to end up as your own great-grandfather. This way. Through the walls of the tunnel."

He threw Hubert over his shoulder and waited for Rod and Halfshaft to help Takina (rather more gently) to her feet. Supporting her weight between them, they followed him through the tunnel walls, disappearing into another dimension in space just as a tremendous explosion tore Mount Leiden into a million jagged pieces.

The Lord of the Trolls stood over his injured son, his sword clasped firmly in both gigantic hands, ready to defend him to the last against an enemy which no longer existed.

Trog had fallen minutes earlier, caught off guard by a wrenching blow from a doubleheaded war-axe that had sent him crashing semi-conscious to the ground at his father's feet. The troll corpses had closed in for the kill, well aware that even Crug could not resist them for long.

Then there had been the massive explosion. The rocks had fallen from the sky, and the troll corpses had disappeared as if they had never existed in the first place.

He relaxed his pose, and formed his broken teeth into a grin of welcome, as he made out Runt limping slowly across the battlefield towards him. There was no other sign of movement elsewhere. All his other subjects had long since fled or fallen (hopefully the latter if they knew the meaning of shame), and their foe had vanished completely.

The two hauled Trog to his feet and stood either side of him, holding him upright. He lifted his head wearily to follow their gaze. Together, they stared fixedly into the distance surveying the gap in the mountain range, which until moments before had been occupied by Mount Leiden.

After a while, they caught sight of a figure approaching them at speed. They watched in silence as he came to a halt in front of them, swaying on his feet as though on the verge of collapse.

"Which way," he gasped, "to the police-station?"

Runt, the greatest of troll philosophers, chose a direction at random, and pointed it out to him. He had no more idea of the meaning of "police-station" than he would have had of "vegetarian" but felt too drained to ask for clarification. He was too tired even to seize the stranger and eat him before he had a chance to run away. They followed his progress as he stumbled off into the distance, watching him with idle curiosity until he disappeared over the horizon.

"It's a funny old world," Runt remarked, reflecting on the events of the past 24 hours.

The Lord of the Trolls nodded his head sagaciously, in complete agreement with the philosophy behind this perceptive analysis.

"Too bloody right it is," he said, as the three of them took the first weary step on their way back home.